This book is dedicated to a long-suffering Earth Angel without whose patience, understanding and encouragement, this book would never have been written, and to all those gifted people who I have been lucky enough to have crossed my path.

E Attwood

One Foot in This World, One Foot in the Next

Austin Macauley Publishers™
London • Cambridge • New York • Sharjah

A CIP catalogue record for this title is available from the British Library.

ISBN 9781528919340 (Paperback)
ISBN 9781528962667 (ePub e-book)

www.austinmacauley.com

First Published (2019)
Austin Macauley Publishers Ltd
25 Canada Square
Canary Wharf
London
E14 5LQ

I would like to start by acknowledging what I feel are the three most important men who I see as having crafted me into the person I am today, there can't be many people who have been lucky enough to have had three such mentors who were kind enough to bestow their knowledge and wisdom on somebody so young and unworldly. As I look back now on the impact these three men had on my life, I shudder to think what would have become of me as a headstrong dyslexic if they had not been a part of my growing up.

The first is my father, Robert T Attwood, who was an old-fashioned gentleman and taught me old-fashioned values and courtesy that hold me in good stead to this day. My dad commanded respect from all those he met, not because he was academically clever or lorded it over people, but because he was the nicest kindest person I've ever known who taught me that you can get far more done with a smile and a kind word than with a frown and a caustic tongue.

I lost him in 1998 and miss and love him as much now as I did then. He also gave me the one thing I sought in my spiritual quest through a gifted medium, who was to become a dear friend, namely that he still lived on albeit in a different form, and that what we perceive as heaven existed through what was to become known as the 'Marrow Moment', which is covered in detail in the following texts.

The second is Mr Nixon, who I feel we lost in sad circumstances long before his allotted time because of a broken heart, he was a quiet but confident man who was a carpenter by trade, but taught other subjects in our local schools, and someone who I could have listened to for hours on end.

He had a gentle, melodic voice and a way of expressing things that made the most boring and mundane subjects sound so interesting, you always wanted to know more; his grasp on life and what was important and what was not, and his understanding of what you needed to do to be happy had a profound effect on the rest of my life.

The third is Reginald Tubby, who I first met by working for him and who was later to became a good friend, and with whom I was to spend many happy hours doing odd jobs around his house and tinkering about with cars, his one-line anecdotes that both censured and advised, accompanied by a wry smile, taught me far more than I realised at the time.

There are so many warm memories of our time spent together, I often use these anecdotes to this day as these few words convey as much as a chapter could in any other presupposition, and of course he taught me how to cut guttering straight with a paper bag amongst a myriad of other skills that have served me well ever since.

If I could spend an hour with each of these three men today with the questions that hindsight has raised, I'm sure I could put most of the world's problems to rights.

Chapter 1
A Glimmer of Light

Until September 2001, I had considered myself just an ordinary little person living an ordinary little life, but it was in early spring of that year that I made a decision that was to ultimately change my life forever. With two failed marriages behind me and a car wreck the year before that had cost me my beloved Citroen BX, and living in a damp, mouldy flat in the depths of despair I had seriously considered suicide. My mind could not think past this terrible event I was planning, and at the time I thought the world would be better off without me, and I thought I would be better off without a world that had treated me with such cold indifference.

So on the morning of the 18th of March 2001 I picked up the phone and rang one of the few friends I had at that time, my mother, and told her quite matter of factually that there was no point in me carrying on, and further because I had had enough, I was going to take my own life. In my mind this was not a cry for help, I had thought things through and was merely stating the facts as I saw them, my mother has always been stoic and resilient and is not given to hysterics or emotional fragility so I knew she would see the logic in my decision. At the time, I was fifty-two years old and my mother was eighty-two, but to my surprise for the next hour and a quarter, she would not let me off the phone until I promised her I would not do this terrible thing.

After she made me promise not to take my own life, I see now what has turned out to be a remarkable set of coincidences started to happen, "No, I hear you saying there are no such things as coincidences." Well, I know that now but as anyone knows who has been through similar events in their life, you cannot see the wood for the trees when you are at the lowest ebb in your life.

After that phone call, I started to go for short walks in my local area as walking has always been one of my life's passions, and I had always gained peace of mind in my solitary walks as it affords time for quiet contemplation within nature's calming embrace.

I also started to go to an Asda store in the area on a Sunday morning because I knew my daughter Amanda would be working there, and the sight of a radiant smile on her pretty face brought me enormous comfort and brightened up my day more than words can express. She had turned into what I had affectionately started to call her 'mini mum' and constantly fussed around to make sure I was alright.

It was on one of these sojourns when the first of my coincidences was to happen and it still seems remarkable to this day. It was the 10th of June 2001 and I was pottering around the store taking as much time as I could as I was in no hurry to return to my damp, mouldy flat. As I came around the end of one of the isles, I, so I thought, bumped straight into a trolley coming from the other direction. I dared not look up and just muttered an apology as the last thing I wanted right then was a confrontation with some big burly bloke, but when the trolley in front of me did not move, with mounting apprehension I was forced to look up.

When I did so I saw the gently smiling face of a dear friend and the son of one of the three men I had most loved and respected in this world. A long forgotten but much welcomed greeting issued from this young man that immediately transported me back to memories of wonderful summer days spent tinkering about with cars with his father, who sadly we had lost many years before and is still very much missed.

Time seemed to disappear into oblivion as we spent the next twenty minutes in delicious reminiscences of glorious days gone by. At the end of this trip down memory lane, he said, "Where are you living now as I heard you were on your own?" When I related my sad tale of the damp, mouldy flat he said, "That's a coincidence, I've sadly just lost my mother and moved into the family home, so I have an empty bungalow if you want to use it for a while."

When he told me where the bungalow was I immediately said no as I knew the location well and knew that I could not possibly afford the rent of a property in that area. "No, no," he said, "I know how much you did for my father and what high regard he held you in." I knew what was coming at this point and started to protest as I could not impose on his good nature on the strength of deeds done many years before, but he would not be budged and continued, "If you look after the gardens, keep the place decorated and look after the 'old girl' we'll call it quits." The 'old girl' referred to a 1957 Chevrolet Bel Air in pristine condition in the garage.

I again protested that this was far too generous and that I could not possibly presume on his goodwill for any length of time, but all my protesting fell on deaf ears and consequently within a couple of days I was to meet him at the property for a look around.

I knew the area well that I was going to but the sight of the bungalow and its gardens was truly jaw-dropping. With its sixty feet of front garden and a driveway leading to the back garden which was a staggering one hundred and eighty feet long, with a beautiful forty foot American blue spruce as its centrepiece who would not have fallen in love with it having just walked out of a damp, mouldy flat.

It was a few moments before I could gather myself together and say anything, but needless to say, I moved into the bungalow on Saturday the 23rd of June and was to spend a very happy two and a half years there. It was, without doubt, the start of my road back to wanting to live a full and happy life again.

Looking back on my time in this beautiful back garden reclining on a sun lounger drinking coffee and watching the myriad of wildlife, it was definitely where I slowly started to see everything in a different light and regained my zest for life.

Listening to the songs of the blackbirds that frequented the lawn and flowered borders from dawn till dusk and squirrels whose antics would keep me mesmerised for hours on end, all the time I spent in that idyllic setting was like a waking meditation that soothed and reawakened my spirit to the wonders that this world had to offer. I don't think you can underestimate the healing power of nature in all her dynamic as well as subtle facets.

That back garden was the gentlest of those facets as its visual and sound effects washed over me like a lullaby. Contrast this to the waves crashing onto a beach of pebbles and you have one of nature's most dynamic sights and sounds. I could sit on a beach like that for hours, allowing the power of nature to transport me to the distant shores that my mind sees these waves coming from.

From gardens to oceans, from dramatic to serene, nature offers us everything to calm, cleanse and re-energise the soul and lift us to a point where everything becomes clear and possible.

There is something wonderfully restless about a garden or a seashore as it never actually comes to a standstill in its march through time. This type of atmosphere always focuses me these days and reminds me that we should embrace and enjoy every moment as a gift, because if we allow time to slip through our fingers there will come a time when we will wish that we had spent our time in pursuit of these simple pleasures, rather than chasing after every last penny we can earn.

It was while sitting in that back garden reading the local paper one weekend that I spotted an advert that aroused my interest. The advert was for a national singles club that was not about dating or trying to pair you off but just for making friends and having some fun. So, of course, I called "mini mum" first and asked if she thought I was doing the right thing or just making a fool of myself.

"Not at all, Dad," she said comfortingly, "I think it's a good idea and it will get you out for a while." Confident now that I was not going to make a fool of myself I determined to call them Monday morning before my afternoon shift at a local warehouse.

I rang the local number and spoke to a very nice sounding chap who told me they met up every Wednesday in a venue not too far from where I lived. So I got myself ready that Wednesday and drove over to the venue for the half-past eight time he gave me. Sitting outside in the car park I almost talked myself out of it but told myself if I had come this far I might as well go in and if I didn't like it I could just have one drink and leave, no harm was done.

I walked up to the entrance that displayed a notice showing the direction to the room it was being held in. I stood in the doorway looking at a group of people talking in the middle area and a few standing at the bar. At that moment, my nerve deserted me and I turned to leave thinking, *what in heaven's name do you think you are doing here?* As I turned to leave a tall lady standing in the middle of the group shouted, "Are you Eddie?" I stopped dead like a rabbit caught in a car's headlights and felt like a naughty schoolboy.

The lady was called 'Big Jan' who sadly passed away from cancer a few years ago and is very sadly missed by all who knew her. When I turned to say I'd made a mistake and was leaving she was already halfway across from the group and held out a hand to shake mine. Obviously, this was a well-practised routine for cowards like myself because once you've walked out you're never likely to go back or go anywhere else like it for that matter.

She took me by the hand and led me right into the middle of the group and said, "This is Eddie, it's his first time here." I think I must have resembled a beetroot so they felt sorry for me and tried to make me feel welcome.

I stayed for the next hour and a half and left with five new friends, of which two were women which was a great surprise to me. I arranged to not only go back the next Wednesday but also to join some of them on a country walk that Sunday, which would be punctuated by a pub lunch.

That Sunday walk turned out to be a truly enjoyable event in which I had a chance to talk at length to some of the other members, which convinced me that I had made the right decision and the walks and other events planned would give me a bit of a social life. The pub lunch was also very welcome as I didn't have to cook or wash up after afterwards.

One of the men I worked with had a sideline of building computers, so now safely settled in the bungalow I asked him to build me one. Within a week I was the proud owner of a Windows 98 setup and contacted the phone company to arrange an internet connection. In the meantime, a newsletter arrived from the singles club and announced that their yearly holiday had been planned for September and invited members to apply for tickets.

My second coincidence was about to go into the planning stage although I would not be aware of it until we reached our destination, Cyprus. I had the money in the bank but was reluctant to spend it so once again I rang 'mini mum' and asked what I should do.

"For heaven's sake, Dad," came the curt reply, "don't you think you deserve a holiday?" With a friendly flee in my ear I once again determined to phone the lady who was organising the holiday to book a place. That evening after work I rang the number in the newsletter and asked if I could have a ticket. She said there would be about thirty people going from all over the country and for a deposit of one hundred pounds she would send me all the details.

Up until this time in my life I had never been out of the country, so was filled with a mixture of excitement and apprehension. I had also never flown on a commercial aeroplane before and the thought of being in a cigar tube at thirty-five thousand feet was scary. I put the thought of flying out of my mind for the present time and sent off my cheque, and a week later received the full itinerary for the holiday plus my confirmation of a ticket.

There were nearly six months until the holiday so I had plenty of time to plan for it, but never having travelled abroad before I was at a loss for what I needed so once again "mini mum" came to the rescue. She gave me a full list of clothing that I would need for a hot country and a list of pills and potions that looked as if it could cure anything from a gyppy tummy to the plague, but as a mother of two young boys she was used to dealing with anything that fate could throw at her.

I had never owned a passport either and this posed a few challenges I had never thought of before let alone had to deal with. The form for a first time passport looked daunting enough but when I had to get two specially-sized photographs of me, then had to make an appointment with my bank manager so he could say the photos were really of me, and confirm that all the details on the form were correct I was starting to wonder if it was all worth the effort, but as I had already paid my deposit I could not back out without losing my money so I soldiered on.

It took several shopping trips punctuated by coffee and cream cakes to kit me out with everything I needed, but by the end of the summer I had everything I needed including a suitcase which I had never owned before, and worryingly air sickness pills that didn't do my nerves any good when there were only a few short weeks to go.

I learnt in the weeks leading up to the holiday that there were three local people that were also going on the trip, and as they were all seasoned travellers one of them offered to drive the rest of us to Gatwick Airport and we would all chip in for the petrol. So at half past seven on the 15th of September 2001, I stood on the pavement outside the bungalow reciting the well-known mantra, money, passport, tickets — money, passport, tickets.

Chapter 2
Where It Began

When you see a place like Gatwick Airport for the first time the thing that hits you first is the sheer size of the place. It's like a whole town within itself and the car parks alone were like nothing I had ever seen before. Having parked the car we got on the shuttle bus that took us to the beating heart of this exciting metropolis, the terminal building, where we met the lady who was organising the holiday plus all the other members of the party who were as diverse and interesting a group of people as you could wish to meet.

Standing in the terminal building it was hard to take in the scale of the place with people hurriedly rushing in all directions dragging suitcases behind them. There was obviously an intricate and organised plan in operation but to me, it looked like a melee with somebody representing every part of the globe.

It was like a carnival atmosphere in our group as a lot of the people knew each other from previous trips and were in small groups excitedly talking and laughing. Being introduced to all the other holidaymakers and being fascinated by all the shops and restaurants I quite forgot about my nerves and flying until it was time to board the aircraft.

We all made our way to the departure lounge from where you could see the aircraft quite clearly through the windows with its umbilical walkway attached. All this time I had been distracted by chatting away to everyone about their experiences on foreign holidays but now my mouth dried up and my legs felt kind of wobbly as if I were drunk.

After showing our boarding passes, we all filed into the plane and I was surprised to see how big it looked on the inside. There were rows of seats on either side by the windows and another five rows of seats running down the middle. I was to find out in later years that normal short-haul planes were much smaller than this one and I was grateful I had one of the seats in the middle section so would not have to sit next to a window.

It seemed to take forever to taxi out to the end of the runway where we sat stationary prolonging the agony before hurtling down the tarmac and up into oblivion. When the plane did eventually launch itself down the runway I was staggered by the amount of raw power that pinned me back into my seat, and I was filled with a mixture of fear and excitement that this invention could generate such instant acceleration.

I wanted to shut my eyes but was afraid to in case something went wrong and we had to do something crazy like jump off the plane. Watching the ground disappear out of the corner of my eye was the worst bit as once I could not see it anymore I knew we could fall out of the sky if something went wrong.

I then watched horrified as we ascended through the clouds and emerged into clear blue skies and sunshine as the plane levelled out. I had felt some form of protection while we were in the clouds as there was something to see around us but now there was nothing. I then had a white-knuckle ride as I gripped the armrests for the next thirty-odd minutes as I glanced to my left and saw nothing but blue sky.

Then as the starboard wing dipped and we banked around to the right to make a turn an incredible thing happened, as the port wingtip intersected the sun high in the sky I heard my father's voice inside my head telling me I was safe and that he was looking after me and nothing bad was going to happen. It was as if the wingtip had touched his very soul and that he and God were telling me to just relax and enjoy the flight. At that moment I had a feeling that this was going to be an extraordinary holiday that I would never forget.

When the plane levelled out again I undid my seatbelt, went to sit in an empty seat next to the window and was amazed to see what looked like a map stretched out beneath me. I sat there transfixed for the rest of the flight as I watched every kind of terrain slip by and was particularly fascinated to see the Alps as they passed by far beneath us.

The others in the group were making friendly banter about me being like a kid in a trance as they were all seasoned flyers. When it came time to land at Paphos Airport I was so relaxed I just sat there smiling as some other passengers around me gripped their seats as evidently this was the worst bit, but I knew that my dad and God were looking after me and bringing us safely into land so what could possibly go wrong when you have that kind of protection.

After a perfect landing with hardly a bump, I was eager to get off the plane and have my first sights and sounds of a foreign country. When the plane's doors finally opened, warm dry air wafted in that smelt of herbs, and I don't think you ever forget your first smells of a different country and Cyprus could not have been more different from what I was used to in England.

It didn't take long for us to get through customs and I was shocked at how small the airport was compared to Gatwick. We then filed onto a coach that was to take us to the hotel complex in Coral Bay a few miles West of Paphos, and everything I saw out of the windows on both sides of the coach fascinated me on the way as there was nothing like this anywhere in the UK.

When we reached the Corallia Beach Hotel we could see it was quite a large complex as we left the coach and made our way to the checking in desk. We were starting to get a little hot by the time we were finished so we all went to change out of our English weather jeans and jumpers into something more appropriate for the gloriously hot weather. We then met in the bar for a much-needed drink to lay the dust before going our separate ways for the afternoon. We were told that all thirty-one of us were going out together for a meal at a local taverna that evening to celebrate our arrival, and it was at this taverna that my second so-called coincidence was to take place.

Most of us had a lazy time around the pool on sunbeds the first afternoon while the more adventurous of our party went exploring, apart from one lovely old chap who was retired, the rest of us had been working right up until the day before and just wanted to chill out. Eventually though the time came for us to leave the pool area and head off through the complex to our rooms to get showered and changed for our evening meal. There was a buzz of excitement around all of us when we met in the hotel foyer before we headed west along the Coral Bay road to where the taverna was situated looking out over the Mediterranean Sea.

I don't think I took in much of the casual chat as we strolled along the coastal road because it was still light and I was too busy looking at every new strange or exotic sight that came within my gaze. When we reached the taverna all the tables had been placed end to end to form a long line overlooking the deep blue sea that stretched out from the bay to the far horizon, with just a few tables at the far left-hand end forming an 'L' shape so as to accommodate all of us on the building's veranda.

I have tried many times to remember the menu that first evening but it was so overshadowed by the events that were to follow it has faded from my memory. I think there were half a dozen main meat and fish dishes accompanied by lots of side dishes of vegetables that I had never seen before. I was the only one who had not drunk local village wine before that was freely flowing which probably explains what happened towards the end of the meal. I can, however, remember liking most of the mixed meze dishes including to my great surprise squid, and being the only person seated at the table who had never drunk this local wine I was by then a little worse for wear and not my normal reserved self.

We must have been eating and drinking for a couple of hours when it happened and everyone was well oiled by this time and me more than most. I suddenly realised to my horror that I was talking to a chap sitting opposite me on the table about having done some healing a short while ago, and all this on the strength that a week before I had held a lady's hands for about a minute and she said her hands tingled for fifteen minutes afterwards. She had then told the group of ladies she was sitting with about the sensations that she had felt during this very brief event which I didn't think constituted healing.

I remember feeling embarrassed about talking to him as I had sworn to myself never to tell anyone about that incident as I had been unable to explain it to myself, and here I was blabbering on about wanting to be a healer to a complete stranger when I hadn't the foggiest idea how to be one.

But before I could extricate myself from this embarrassing situation a lady sitting to my left swished her hair to the left to expose her upper back and said, "I don't know if you can help me, I think I strained something playing tennis," and she circled an area with her finger indicating the affected area. Being as inebriated as I was and very much lacking inhibitions I put my left hand over the area she had pointed to and instinctively closed my eyes.

To my complete astonishment, my hand got so hot that she let out a long low moan as if she was getting relief from the pain, after I had finished and opened my eyes a few of the blokes were looking at me as if it was a clever way of getting my hands on a younger woman. I wanted to get up and walk away at this point but if I had it would only confirm their suspicions so I just kept quiet and waited for the meal to finish.

When the meal was over and people started to drift away, I got up to make my escape and hoped that if I didn't draw attention to myself no one would notice. But before I could leave the blond lady on my left who had been chatting to her friends said, "That was amazing what you did, the pain has almost gone, but I'm not the one you should be talking to."

A wave of panic washed over me as I wondered what I had got myself into as she pointed to another lady sitting at the far end of the line of tables to our left. At this point, she got up and said, "Come with me and I'll introduce you," so I plodded reluctantly after her wondering what trouble my big mouth had got me into now. When we got to the table the blond lady said something like, "This man's a healer. He might be able to help you," with that she left and a very sad face looked up at me, the expression on her face made it look as if she could burst into tears at any moment. Healer or not you would have to be a very hardhearted individual not to feel the compassion I felt right then at the look on this lady's face.

I asked her what the problem was and she just put her hands over her heart and said, "It's in here." By the gestures she made and the expression on her face, it seemed clear to me that this was not a physical problem. I looked down at her with as much compassion in my face as a drunk man could and said, "That's the easiest one to cure but the hardest one to deal with." She did not speak but just nodded a sad agreement and I said that I would talk to her in the morning when I was sober and a bit more awake.

With that, I wished her goodnight and joined a few people making their way back to the hotel as it was now dark and I hadn't a clue which way to go. When we reached the hotel I made my way to my room to get some much-needed sleep and I wondered where the words had come from that I had spoken to her. It sounded very profound and I could not have made it up because at that time I had no knowledge about such things so where had this profound statement come from. As tantalising as it was the origin of that comment and the implications surrounding it were going to have to remain a mystery for now as I was far too tired to figure it out.

In the morning, I felt a little delicate, to say the least as I was not used to drinking that much wine and came down late for breakfast. I was hoping that seeing as we were all three sheets to the wind the night before nobody would remember what happened and I would avoid any embarrassment. I could not have been more wrong as the lady with the long blond hair spotted me as soon as I walked into the dining room. She made a point of telling me that her back was much better, also said the other lady I had spoken to late last night with the heart problem wanted to meet with me and talk about it as soon as I was free.

I arranged to meet her in a quieter room after breakfast for a chat and I gave her a short healing by just holding her hands and letting the energy flow through me. I did not know at this time that you could use a massage couch for a much more relaxed healing session as I had never seen anyone else do any sort of healing.

I didn't do any prayers or ask for help from any angels or guides with the healing because I didn't know at that time I had any. Again when I spoke to her this second time there was an outpouring of such wisdom and deep caring from me that it astounded me as much as it did her. It was as if I had the ability to instantly turn into a counsellor and confidant and speak with such clarity about what she needed to do to remedy the situation she was in.

I went on to heal and talk with her another two or three times during the holiday and by the end of our stay there, she was quite bright and optimistic about the future. I also had time during the holiday to think rationally about what was happening every time I met with her, and it was clear that something or someone must have been working through me but that was as far as I could go at the time with my limited knowledge.

Another strange and unexplained thing happened when a group of us went on a trip around the extensive Roman ruins not far from Paphos harbour. Within a few minutes of entering the site, my head started to fill up with the voices of the people who must have built and lived in this ancient city, I walked around the site for over an hour in a kind of daze and every time I touched a wall or archway another voice would overlay the others. I didn't get sentences just a jumble of words as I walked around gazing at pots and rooms that although now deserted had once been a thriving bustling community.

It felt for all the world as if I was tapping into the memories of the people from a long distant past who had lived and worked there all those years ago. It wasn't scary at all as it felt more like I was just an observer listening to them all talk at once as I stood in the middle of the throng.

When it was time to return to England I thought long and hard about what had happened and decided not to tell anyone when I got home about the events that had happened here. Only two people came from my area and I was pretty sure they would not be interested in anything I had done or experienced, and I would probably never see any of the other people again so anything that happened on this holiday would just fade into history if I kept quiet about it.

So, on the 1st of October dressed once again in our English clothes, we said our goodbyes to the hotel staff and filed onto the coach once more for our return trip to the airport. I was sorry to be going home because I had enjoyed my first foreign holiday but was more than ready for what I had done there to become just a fading memory.

Despite my wish for certain memories to fade my head was full of questions that I could not answer on the flight back to England. The events that happened were so outside my life experience and understanding that I had no idea who I could talk to about it. And despite any good I might have done for this lady, I was very sure that I would never again repeat what I had done in Cyprus because a holiday is one thing but real life is quite another and besides, I couldn't think of one person I could tell who would believe me anyway.

I had heard it said that people do crazy things on foreign holidays and in my mind, they couldn't get much crazier than this. I wanted nothing else at this point than for someone to explain to me what had happened so I could make sense of it all and then just forget it ever happened.

Little did I know then that I had just taken my first doddery steps on a journey that would lead to me finding my true purpose for being here. A journey that would see me crossing paths with some amazing and gifted people who would guide and steer me on a life's mission that is still unfolding to this day.

Chapter 3
My Dream

Going back to work after my holiday in Cyprus was a welcome return to normality and routine where I didn't have to think about my attempts at healing, and there was no way I could talk about it with anybody where I worked as I had no idea how any of my workmate's felt about such things. I imagined there would be a stigma attached to it as with so many things that come under the heading of alternative therapy.

And there was another strange thing that occurred to me once I had returned to England and had some quiet time to think. As I was trying to heal this lady in Cyprus and make her feel better was somebody somewhere trying to heal me and make me feel better, because I hadn't felt this healthy or alive for a very long time. And I couldn't think of any other reason for me feeling this good, because nothing else had happened or changed in my life since I returned so there was no other explanation apart from the holiday and the things I experienced there.

This now added to the questions I had in my head on the flight home so rather than just resolving the original questions I now had, even more, to get to the bottom of. I thought I just had to find a few answers to what had happened on the holiday and then things would get easier, not harder and more complicated.

I also had another more pressing dilemma after enjoying such a lovely holiday with all the nice people I had met in Cyprus. The big national singles club that arranged the holiday was quite expensive and I couldn't afford to stay with them any longer, but I didn't want to lose the type of social life it had given me or the opportunity it offered to make new friendships.

Then one day at work around the middle of October a good friend who knew I had joined the singles club but couldn't afford to stay with them showed me an advert in a local *What's On* magazine. It was for a small independent singles club that met at a local golf club about five miles from where I lived. The time I had spent with the larger club had given me a bit more confidence so I rang the number the following day to see if this club ran on similar lines to the national one.

A man answered the phone who told me his nickname was Butch which didn't exactly fill me with a great deal of confidence, but I had already done this once before and had been pleasantly surprised so I figured I had everything to gain and nothing to lose. They also met every Wednesday around eight o'clock so after work I got showered, changed and for the second time prepared to throw myself into the not quite so unknown.

Once I arrived, I found the man who I had spoken to on the phone and luckily for me he was nothing like his nickname. He introduced me to the committee members who ran the club who all seemed like a nice and fun-loving bunch of people.

I then got myself a drink and started to circulate chatting to various people here and there trying to get a feel for the sort of people who went there. When the event's secretary announced the itinerary for the coming month I was pleased to learn it was run on very similar lines to the bigger club but at a fraction of the cost.

So I was not only able to carry on with my social life very much the same as before albeit with different people but I also after a few weeks made a number of suggestions as to possible future events and as a consequence was asked if I would like to join the event's organisers. Little did I know that this would lead to my next so-called coincidence and ultimately to an outcome that I had privately sworn to myself would never ever happen again.

I really enjoyed the next couple of months making lots of new friends and having fun with all the events we had planned leading up to the Christmas festivities. I particularly got to know the other members who made up the events team as we spent so much time together putting the bi-monthly program together. We were a diverse bunch from all walks of life, backgrounds and careers which lead to the program including something for everyone.

The pre-Christmas dinner which they said was always one of the year's highlights had been planned for a meal at a local Chinese restaurant, and there was one lady on the events team bringing up two teenage girls on her own who couldn't afford to go. This seemed a shame as the team did everything else together so I offered to pay for her meal as she would be the only one not going. When she questioned why I would want to do this I just said, "I can pay for a meal for a mate, can't I?" and after a bit of friendly banter, she reluctantly agreed to accept as she didn't like the idea of charity.

The Christmas meal had been arranged for the 22nd of December 2001 and it turned out to be one of the coldest nights of the year. I had arranged to meet this lady in a car park a short distance from the restaurant as she was babysitting for her sister-in-law until they got home. As I pulled into an empty space it was clear she was not there as I could see all the other cars from where I was and hers was not one of them. I switched off the engine and checked my watch that told me there were ten minutes until the start of the meal so we had plenty of time as it was only a three-minute walk to the restaurant.

After waiting for five minutes the car was starting to get decidedly cold with the engine and the heater switched off and I was starting to wonder if she had changed her mind. After another five minutes I was starting to shiver and decided that she was not coming so got out of the car and locked it accepting that we would be dining without her tonight, but as I started to walk away a car pulled into the car park that I recognised as belonging to the lady in question.

After her profuse apologies about her sister-in-law being late and the traffic being snarled up by the weather, we made our way out of the car park. As we stepped onto the high street pavement she slipped her arm through mine and smiled at me warmly, at which point I almost pulled my arm away but it felt rather comfortable so I left her arm there. And anyway I told myself she was probably just worried about slipping over on the icy pavement and looking silly so what harm could there be in it.

By the time we arrived at the restaurant, everyone else had arrived and were seated around a large round table that had been reserved for our group. We were treated to a few knowing looks and some cheeky but good-humoured remarks when we sat in the last two remaining seats because no one had been told we were arriving together. Once we had exchanged pleasantries with the others and the food had been ordered my companion and I started talking. We hadn't really talked much before because we were always at the club organising events and now it was as if we were long lost friends. I don't think either of us realised at the time how easy the conversation flowed between us and for the next two hours or so the rest of our group might as well not have been there.

When the meal was over, there were some more good-humoured remarks that we had been so absorbed in each other that we hadn't talked to anyone else all evening. With the few suggestive looks that passed around the table, I think we both went a bit red and apologised to the rest of the group for ignoring them all evening.

When we met at the club the following Wednesday which was the last meeting before Christmas I acted as if nothing had happened at the meal. I had only bought a friend a meal so she wouldn't feel left out and I had already talked myself out of there being any more to it than that, and anyway I had already promised myself I was not going to go down the relationship road again with anyone so that was going to be the end of that.

But luckily for me, the lady in question was not prepared to give up that easily and at the end of the evening asked what I was doing for Christmas. When I said I was having Christmas dinner with my mother and not much else she asked if I wanted to have Boxing Day dinner with her and her two daughters. It was the last thing I expected to hear and it must have shown in my face because she quickly added that it was nothing special just using up the Christmas turkey.

It had been quite a while since I had a family meal like this and felt a bit nervous at the prospect of meeting her daughters. But if I was honest with myself I didn't want to be on my own again if there was a chance of a good home cooked meal, and with that same easy conversation between us she made it sound very tempting and the company would be very welcome so I accepted her kind offer. With my acceptance, she planted a kiss right on my lips and gave me another of those warm smiles that didn't seem at all out of place.

When Boxing Day morning arrived I almost rang the lady to say I couldn't make it because once again I was talking myself out of it for all the wrong reasons, but told myself this was silly because I was probably only going to have dinner with them as a thank you for paying for her Christmas meal. With that thought in mind, there could be no good reason I could come up with for staying home with a frozen ready meal.

As it turned out it was a lovely meal because although I didn't know it then, she was a very accomplished professional cook, and her two daughters were polite and charming and nothing happened to make me feel like the odd one out which put me completely at ease and probably explains why I accepted what came next.

When the meal was over and I was thinking about leaving, she hit me with another option that really did give me something to think about. She said she and her daughters were going over to spend the afternoon with her brother and his family a few miles away and would I like to join them. I think I must have looked a bit nonplussed as it was the last thing I expected to hear because she quickly said I didn't have to but it would be nice if I said yes.

Things were starting to move a bit quicker than I would have liked if this was the direction I was heading in and I felt a bit uneasy, but a part of me seemed to be going in a different direction from the rest of me and before I knew it I had said yes. The girls had arranged to leave before us as one of their boyfriends was driving them over which gave us a chance to talk before we left.

My companion said her brother and family were very friendly and good company as I think she was sensing I felt a bit trapped. So reassured that I wasn't being put under any pressure and we were just going to have some Boxing Day fun we made our way over to join them. Her brother, wife and two sons were very welcoming and we had great fun talking and playing the usual Christmas games. We all seemed to get on like old friends and they all included me in everything that was going on so again I didn't feel at all like an outsider.

The evening was spent in fits of laughter as one after the other, the family recounted stories of things that had happened as they were growing up. Wine and nibbles relaxed me and made it very enjoyable as this sort of family fun had been missing in my life for quite a long while.

There were no club meetings until after the New Year celebrations but there was a glittering New Year's Eve party at a very popular venue that all the local clubs attended. Everyone looked forward to this event as it was one of the highlights of the festive season and a chance to get glammed up and let your hair down. So seeing as the pre-Christmas meal and Boxing Day had gone so well I wondered if I should suggest we go to this party together, but I didn't have to wonder very long as the lady in question rang me before I had plucked up the courage to ask her and suggested it would be a nice idea if we went together.

Nobody else at the club knew we had seen each other on Boxing Day so when Jan and I walked into the New Year's Eve party together a few eyebrows went up, and for the next hour or so Jan was cornered by all her lady friends one after the other to find out what had transpired since the Christmas dinner. I think that both Jan and I knew that after this glittering New Year's Eve party that this was not going to be just one of those casual friendships.

We started to see each other on quite a regular basis from then on to see if we had enough in common as neither of us wanted to rush into anything. We had a brilliant time at all the events we went to together but domesticity could be quite another thing, so we decided to take it slowly and just enjoy each other's company and see how we got on with the normal things in life.

When everything between us had gone well for a few weeks and we were starting to get serious I had to come clean about something I had been planning for quite some time. I had seen before how a revelation no matter how trivial had come between a couple if it was not bought out into the open at the beginning, so I wanted us to talk this particular thing through as it could affect the relationship we were building and could even threaten it.

It was a dream I had built up over the years I had lived on my own because I had come to accept I would be living alone for the rest of my life, but now Jan had unexpectedly come along and against all the odds I might have someone to share my future with. I thought my dream was a good one that two could share and I now hoped Jan would want to be a part of that dream.

So one day in early spring of 2002 when we were both off work and alone I sat Jan down and told her I had something important to talk to her about. When her face took on a look of fright I quickly assured her I was not breaking up with her but there was something we had to discuss before we went any further and got too serious. This was not an average thing that came up with a couple in the early stages of a relationship so I wanted to know how she felt about it.

I went on to explain that I had accepted I would always be on my own from now on and had planned to retire to France and buy a little property there. Now we were getting to like each other a lot so I wanted to see if it was something she would also like to do for a while and possibly permanently.

Jan was obviously relieved that it wasn't a breakup but was still taken aback as it wasn't what she had expected to hear, but she didn't dismiss it outright as a cranky idea which I hoped was a good sign and said she would think about it and let me know.

The rest of that day we spent together was a bit cooler and subdued than the preceding weeks as a lot was discussed that had far-reaching implications for us. When I got home I had to do some soul searching myself as to where I wanted to go with this relationship if she decided it was a bad idea and said no. I knew that Jan would be doing the same over the next few days so I left it to her to ring me with an answer when she had had a chance to let it all sink in.

I knew I had to be honest with Jan about my dreams but it did bother me as I was starting to like her a lot and I might have to make compromises. Before I met Jan I had always told myself that a woman would not come between me and my dreams but now I wasn't so sure. I didn't know if this was a step too far for her so I had no idea at that time if we would be seeing each other again or even just as friends.

Up until then, I hadn't told Jan about my spiritual experiences in Cyprus either and that was potentially as big a hurdle as this one as I had no idea how she felt about things like that either. So if I managed to get over this hurdle I knew there was going to be just as big a one waiting for me just around the corner.

The last few weeks had been such good fun for both of us in so many different ways and given us a possible bright future, but was I now about to blow my chances with a revelation that had only been conceived and planned out of loneliness for a single person.

But little did I know that the outcome of that revelation and the discussions that would follow it would not only shape the rest of my life, but also the development and course of my spiritual and psychic journey in ways I could never have imagined in my wildest dreams.

And Jan had her own revelations that would surprise me as much as mine had her and elevate her in my estimation through her bravery and tenacity. It would, in fact, lead to us having our own healing retreat years later in an exotic location in a part of the world I would never have considered.

Chapter 4
Angel Face

My three children had known for quite some time that I was planning to retire to France and had come to accept the idea. At the age of fifty-four I was not expecting to meet anyone to spend the rest of my life with so had been happily making all my plans for one, accepting I was going to spend the rest of my life on my own meant I hadn't had to worry about what anyone else thought about my plans.

I had chosen France because it wasn't far away from the South East of England where I lived and where all my children lived, which meant that although I was living in another country that offered all the newness and excitement moving abroad would offer, it was also close enough for me to drive back for birthdays and Christmas or just to see everyone if I got lonely.

And I expect the kids had secretly thought that if I had a house in France that would mean the odd free holiday with the old man, and as we are all very close. I, of course, secretly hoped they would also want to come and spend time with me, as this would mean I would get to spend a couple of weeks of quality time with them and of course, the grandchildren when they came along.

But now Jan had come along to share my life and hopefully my dreams before I got too old and crusty and set in my ways, and after many years of struggling to bring up a family on her own, she might like a change of scenery and a more relaxed lifestyle.

I didn't see Jan for a couple of days after telling her about France so I had no idea where my life was heading until I saw her again. When we did meet again I couldn't read anything in her face to give me a clue as to what her answer would be. But Jan has always had the ability to sit down with an inordinate amount of patience and rationally weigh up the pros and cons of any situation, and once she has made up her mind what the best option is she has the courage to tell you very directly what she has decided regardless of the outcome.

This is one of Jan's traits that I admire the most as I'm more likely to take the line of least resistance to try and keep everyone happy, but this can cause more problems than it cures and can leave you wishing you'd had the courage to speak up in the first place.

But my fears could not have been more wrong because she smiled at me and said she had given it a lot of thought, and if you care enough about someone you will follow them and their dreams. I can remember my eyes filling up and getting all choked up as she gave me her answer and saying that we would find a way to make it suit what we both wanted, but my future wife was going to bowl me over with a surprise of her own in a revelation I would hear about soon that would pale my suggestions into insignificance.

A few weeks after we had sorted out the little matter of our future we thought we would celebrate with a weekend in the New Forest but things didn't quite go as planned. I felt fine when we started the journey from Jan's home in Kent but halfway there I started to feel queasy and my stomach didn't feel quite right.

By the time we arrived and were shown to our room, I didn't feel well at all and headed straight for the bathroom. For the rest of the weekend, I was confined to our room with a very nasty tummy bug that meant Jan had to dine alone. This was quite an up-market establishment that served food that was equally up-market with silver service and I missed every single meal.

On the last day of our visit, the waiters felt so sorry for me they insisted on serving me toast and tea in our room, to say that it ruined what was supposed to be our first romantic weekend away and cement our relationship is the greatest of understatements.

After a couple of months or so, it had become a habit of ours to watch *'A Place in the Sun'* as we ate our evening meal on the weekends Jan stayed with me. Almost all the programs were of people moving to France to set up a new life there which was giving me lots of ideas about the best locations and what was possible with the properties there.

We didn't tell anyone what we were planning as I still had eleven years to work before I retired and an awful lot can happen in eleven years. So we carried on watching and getting ideas but put all our plans on the back burner until we got nearer to the time of retirement, in the meantime confident that if it was meant to be an opportunity would arise, we got on with enjoying our lives and building a future together.

Well, that was until one particular weekend when we sat down to watch *'A Place in the Sun'* and this particular episode was about Crete, after I made various positive comments throughout the program, Jan said, "Did you like what you saw in the programme?" I said that it reminded me of Cyprus but I thought it would be a lot more expensive than France.

"Oh, that's good," she said, "because I used to work and live just outside Athens and I'd rather go live in Crete than I would France, and I'm sure they must have just as many run down places out there as you've been looking at in the French programs." Now it was my turn to be nonplussed as I sat there with my mouth open trying to rationalise what I had just heard.

I had no idea Jan had been that adventurous and followed a dream of her own as it was a very brave thing to do in the seventies. But it was a lot further away than France which worried me so I said we would have to think carefully about it before we made a choice of which country would be best.

But this was another coincidence as the Greek and Cypriot cultures were very similar in many ways and we had both fallen in love with their way of life. And the Greek diet is recognised all over the world as one of the healthiest with all its fresh ingredients which would be a big plus as we got older.

About this time, we were walking past one of my favourite shops in our local town that sold crystals and dream catchers and all things spiritual. I couldn't help but stop and look in the window at all their crystals as I have always been drawn to them, ever since I can remember as a child I would pick up stones and pebbles and be fascinated by their different shapes and colours. I'm sure that even way back then something was drawing me to them that would eventually lead to me working with crystals.

Jan said that she was also drawn to these types of shops and she had books at home she had bought over the years on Astrology and Greek Mythology, so we went in to have a look around as we both seemed to be on the same wavelength. It occurred to me as we walked around the shop that it might be a good time to reveal my interest in healing and my attempts to heal the lady in Cyprus. It almost felt like we had come into this shop to give me an opportunity to talk to Jan about my experiences so I grabbed the moment.

After listening to my story intently, Jan said that she had always had an interest in that way of life but had never had the opportunity to pursue it further. Now, this was getting spooky what with both of us liking the Greek lifestyle and now both of us wanting to develop spiritually, and I was starting to wonder if some force somewhere had been working to draw us together because we both wanted to follow a spiritual path.

What surprised me the most, however, was that Jan said that I should concentrate on improving my healing abilities as it seemed I had a gift and it should be used. Like Jan people had only ever poked fun at me and said it was a load of mumbo-jumbo if I ventured to talk about anything remotely spiritual, but I was slowly learning that all the spiritual arts and mantic tools had been used for aeons and the people that had used them were considered special or gifted.

One word I would never have associated with myself was special because as a dyslexic I had always been told that I would never amount to anything, but maybe you didn't need to be academically clever to be a healer and that is why I had been chosen to follow this path. I say chosen because it had never been my intention to become a healer, in fact, I had been studying nutrition since my early twenties, and had decided to take it up as a career but now somebody somewhere seemed to have other ideas about which direction I was going to follow and was Jan a part of this.

But if I had to be honest it felt good to work with this lady in Cyprus and the thought of doing something meaningful with my life was exciting. But my vivid imagination has always raced ahead of itself and created obstacles and problems that will probably never happen, and it was already planting pictures in my mind of impending disaster and situations where I was messing up people's lives. Luckily, Jan was very good at calming my fears and worries and said to just take things one step at a time and that I always had a choice. So with the voice of reason pushing the doubts from my mind, I allowed whatever or whoever to guide me along the path that had been chosen for me.

Jan and I spent the next year enjoying each other's company as we grew closer and shared ever more of our time and lives together, and along with the clubs events as well as our own trips out and family gatherings we had a pretty full year. By the spring of 2002, Jan had started to spend a lot of weekends with me at the bungalow. We spent many happy hours talking and learning about each other's lives and aspirations in its beautiful back garden, and it was here amongst the tranquil greenery that we started to make plans for our future lives together having discovered that we had both been searching for very similar things.

And it was Jan, during this time, who encouraged me to find out more about healing through books and research and to try and find people who could help me. It was also through Jan's friends and work colleagues that I found a few more people who needed help that gave me the chance to practice, and with every new person I helped I gained more confidence and more knowledge and got to know the energy of the guides who were working with me.

By late spring of 2002, however, a phenomenon started to happen between Jan and myself that would seal our destiny and our future together. As I think back and remember how those remarkable events unfolded I get goosebumps all up my arms, and I wonder what incredible forces were at play that could have manifested such wonders for me to witness and if there was any limit to what they could do.

It started one day when I went to kiss Jan and as my face entered her aura her face changed completely into someone much younger and angelic looking. It didn't seem to register with me the first time because as a true romantic I was enjoying the moment, but as it started to happen every time I went to kiss Jan it became impossible to ignore and I couldn't figure out how or why I was being shown this beautiful face.

Jan has always looked young for her age but when this happened she looked as if her face had been airbrushed to flawless perfection. Also, the image I was seeing wasn't in perfect focus but almost misty looking as if being viewed through a thin veil. I have only ever seen this before when an artist has tried to soften an image in a fantasy film to give a look of innocence and I don't think I have ever seen anything so beautiful.

On more than one occasion, I would pop my face in and out of her aura while her eyes were closed to test it and see what would happen, and every single time I did this, no matter how many times, her face changed to this young angelic vision. I also became aware of a calm serenity that would wash over me as it happened so that no matter how bad my day had been it all melted away as we shared these precious moments.

After a while, the novelty turned into a deep and pressing need to find out why this was happening as I had a feeling it was going to be very important to both of us and our future. I had bought a few spiritual books by this time so I spent every spare moment trawling through the pages trying to find some clue as to what was going on. It became like an obsession as I spent hours at a time looking for just one word or sentence that would point me in the right direction.

I could find no parallel or reference in any of my books as to what could be causing this and, worse, no possible idea as to why it was being shown to me. However, a common theme running through all of my books was that if you needed answers to situations you couldn't explain then you should meditate. I had tried meditation several times before and it was not one of my strong points as I found it difficult to clear my mind of chatter so I could concentrate.

So I bought a new book that covered meditation and this one unlike all the rest I had read advised, "Not to try to clear your mind of the chatter, but instead acknowledge the thoughts that were running through your mind and just dismiss them and watch them disappear." Once again I must have been guided to this book at my favourite spiritual shop because it seemed to glow as my eyes scanned the shelves for the third time. I had got into the habit of scanning the shelves three times when I was looking for a new book and so far it had always led me to the book I needed for whatever I was searching for.

I found that I could do this new method of meditation quite easily and within a few weeks I was able to enter into a sort of dream-like state where I could concentrate on one particular subject. As I continued with this method my connection to spirit got stronger and stronger and I was eventually given the answer I had been so desperately searching for.

The face I was seeing as I entered Jan's aura was her spiritual self and not her physical self which astounded me because it was intensely angelic. Up until this point, I didn't know we had two different selves so this entered me into a whole new realm of discovery. It was becoming evident to me that the more I learnt about realms outside the physical one just how little I really knew.

I had read a few accounts by this time in books and magazines of people who had seen and been involved in amazing and unexplainable events, but most of these people were famous, world-renowned and respected mediums and psychics with years of experience from things they had encountered. So how and why was it possible for me with my very limited knowledge and experience to see something of this magnitude with such clarity on such a regular basis.

Now my search took on a whole new direction so that I could find out why I was seeing this angelic face as the obvious answer was too fantastic to even contemplate. But try as I might I could not come up with an alternative even after talking to the lady who owned the crystal shop who had years of experience in spiritual matters. So I had to accept after all my exhaustive searches and discussions that what I was seeing as I entered Jan's aura was, in fact, the face of an earth angel.

It is almost impossible to describe even now after all these years how I felt when I finally had to accept the truth of what I was seeing. A healer and an earth angel meeting and falling in love at this time when my gift was starting to show itself had to be more than just a coincidence. For both of us looking back on it now, we agree it had to be a convergence that was preordained long before we incarnated into our present lives. The implications of this meeting and the work we were meant to achieve together were profound and daunting but also incredibly exciting and empowering to both of us.

When I finally plucked up the courage and told Jan what I was seeing she didn't seem surprised as she had always felt an inner calmness that came from deep within. So after revealing what I was seeing Jan started buying books on all known angels as she also wanted to learn the meaning behind what I was seeing. It is difficult to describe what it feels like to sit with her and feel this calm serenity wash over you and soothe your entire being, and I'm not the only one who has noticed this about Jan as countless people have commented on how calm they feel when they sit beside her.

And if I were to be asked if I feel lucky! Well, I don't need to win the lottery or have the trappings of wealth because what I have with Jan cannot be bought, and as long as she is by my side sharing this life with me I'm the luckiest man alive. If I could bottle how I feel when Jan heals my tired body and soul I'm sure this world would be a much better place for everyone.

Jan's knowledge through the books and experience with angel cards expanded rapidly and meant she soon had people asking her for readings. And so started Jan's spiritual journey that would eventually see her became an angel therapist and teacher with one of the most prestigious schools in the United Kingdom.

Chapter 5
Rescue and Sweat Lodge

A short while after I revealed what I was seeing with Jan's face she was talking to a good friend about her new interest in angels and about the healing work I had done. In the conversation, Jan heard of a young mother having terrible trouble with her three-year-old daughter, who was waking up every night crying saying she didn't like this man who kept coming into her bedroom. This had been going on for weeks and the mother was at her wit's end unable to find a reason or cure for her daughter. So after a long chat, Jan's friend asked if I would be able to help find the reason why it was happening, and hopefully, find a cure for the little girl's disturbed nights.

We contacted the mother, made an appointment to go and see her and the little girl to try and find out more and see if we could help. It turned out that the little girl's father had tragically died of a heart attack just before she was born so she had never seen her father. The little girl and her mother had stayed in the family home and all had been well until her mother started seeing another man. Although he was a lovely, kind chap and adored the little girl and her mother this is when all the trouble with the nightly crying fits had started.

I had read in one of my books how an American couple regularly did rescues with earthbound spirits that had decided not to move on to the next world. So if this is what was happening I had a little knowledge of what I was supposed to do in order to release the father from his earthbound state. But there was a lot of difference between an experienced couple sending people home and me attempting it single-handed with no experience whatsoever. But I told myself this couple must have started somewhere and they didn't have a book to guide them through the meditations necessary to succeed as I now had.

After asking for help from my guides, I was told to spend a little time with the mother and her daughter to see if I could sense anything from the little girl. I went into granddad mode and picked up the little girl and talked and played with her for a few minutes but could detect nothing. Apparently, during the daytime when there was lots going on to distract the little girl she was delightful and as untroubled as any other three year old. When we had spent a little more time with them both, a family member took the little girl to the park so we could be on our own with the mother and I could try to solve the problem.

However, the little girl's bedroom furniture was crammed with things that had belonged to her dead father that were probably holding a strong connection to him. So with her mother's consent, we spent the next forty-five minutes clearing all the stuff out of her bedroom and putting it into the garden shed so it left the house clear of his belongings.

I then sat the mother down on her settee and pulled up a chair in front of her so I was able to hold both her hands in mine. I had never seen anyone conduct a formal treatment before so it was the only thing I could think of doing to connect with the mother.

I then talked her through a fifteen-minute meditation designed as a rescue for the father who I was now sure was stuck to the earth plane. It would have been quite natural for any father in those circumstances to want to stay and help his young family, and without any specialised knowledge on the subject, he couldn't possibly have known he would end up trapped between the two worlds needing to be rescued.

When I brought the mother out of the meditation, she started sobbing so I thought it best to let her have a cry to clear the pent-up feelings. After making a cup of tea and taking a short break so the mother could compose herself I asked if she had experienced anything during the meditation.

She said she saw their wedding day, them walking down the aisle and some other memorable times they had shared during their married life together. But the very last thing she saw was her husband slowly walking away from her towards a bright light, and every now and then he turned around with a big smile on his face and waved goodbye before disappearing into the light. This is exactly what the American couple described happening at the end of their meditations so I was confident that my attempts had succeeded.

After relaxing for a while and discussing the first meditation in detail I again held both the mother's hands and took her through another meditation. This one was designed to heal her emotionally and physically and give her the ability to move on with her life. After this treatment, she said she only saw colours and shapes but it was very calming and relaxing and she felt lighter as if something had been lifted from her.

We again discussed everything that happened in the second meditation as well as the whole treatment to make sure she was feeling alright and grounded. It was good to see that worry and anguish had disappeared from her face and her eyes looking bright and clear. Her conversation was now taking on a much more positive view of the future with the plans she had been making with the new man that had come into her life.

Jan watched both these treatments intently as she has watched all the treatments I have given over the years since that time and said that my face changed as I was giving both the treatments so my features were altered slightly. Jan also said that one of three ceramic angels we took with us started to glow while I was giving the treatments. I would have been totally unaware of anything had I been on my own as my eyes are always closed when I'm working, so her observations over the years have helped me understand my work better and added another dimension to the treatments that I give.

When we got back to Jan's house, I said that I didn't know where the instructions had come from to do these meditations, as this situation with the little girl was different to anything I had read in the book which dealt with far older occurrences. I seemed to have done a reasonable job but something was still telling me I needed to talk to professional people to progress properly, but who!

When we heard back from the mother about a week later, the little girl had not woken up again crying since the day of the treatment. So although everything had been a total success and the situation had been resolved I still had a feeling I was working in a field I didn't fully understand, and I ended up with more questions than I had before and I needed to be able to explain to people what was happening. It was becoming clear that I could follow instructions from whoever was giving them to me but I had to find someone to train me properly and explain to my logical Virgo mind that why what I would have considered impossible was now being presented to me as perfectly normal and possible.

Then in the summer of 2002, I had to go to my local hospital for a blood test as I have Type A Haemophilia. As I waited in the treatment room for the nurse to come in I noticed a picture on the wall of a unicorn standing in a woodland glade. Sunshine was pouring down on the creature and it seemed to be staring straight at me. It was as if the picture was drawing me into the scene and there was a message it was trying to convey to me.

When the nurse came in to take my blood, for some reason I told her that I was drawn to the picture as if it was talking to me. "Oh," she said as if it had happened many times before, "you need to talk to my friend, she's working in the other room, when I've done this I'll get her for you."

When her friend came in to see me, it turned out she was not just a nurse but was also a Shamanic healer and teacher who ran her own healing clinic. She did this in a bungalow about four miles from where I lived and after a short conversation, she gave me the telephone number and address, said I should come along and see how it was run and meet the two lady healers who practised in the clinic with her.

Looking back on it now, it seems incredible that in a hospital with hundreds of nurses I should walk into the one department that had a Shamanic healer working in it. To say that the heavens had conspired to make our paths cross and give me exactly the information I had been looking for is the biggest understatement ever.

I left the hospital on cloud nine as I had found someone who could explain what was going on in my life and what I should do next. I felt instantly sure that if I wanted to follow the path that had been placed before me, then the means had just been found to do so. It was as if the few words that passed between us in that brief meeting had opened up the doors to a whole new world, and possibly, my future as a healer.

When I told Jan what had happened at the hospital, she was delighted for me and said we should arrange to go there as soon as possible, so that evening I rang the number I had been given and made arrangements for us to go and see the Healing Clinic in operation.

When we arrived, we were shown into the waiting room where I again met the nurse I had seen at the hospital and introduced Jan. After a very interesting conversation with her, she suggested that when the two lady healers had finished with their clients we should go in and meet them. The waiting room was quite plain and uncluttered with a few magazines and brochures just like any other you would expect to see at a doctor's or dentist's. But when we went into the healing room I was mesmerised as there wasn't a spare bit of wall or ceiling not covered with crystals, Shamanic and Native American artefacts of every description. The two healers had been working in the room non-stop for over two hours and I could feel the energy in the room like a warm blanket wrapped around me.

After a very interesting chat with the two healers about how they worked, one of them said, "Would you like to jump on the couch and I'll give you some healing?" When I said that I didn't need any as I was a healer myself, she said that I might like the experience and that healers needed healing just as much as anyone else. After a blissful few minutes receiving healing from this remarkable lady, she said to the other healer, "I was getting as much energy back from him as I was giving."

The other lady healer replied, "That's what they told me when I first came here." This was brilliant news that an experienced healer could feel my energy but they went on to explain they were not qualified to train me.

The nurse I originally saw said that she couldn't train me either because she didn't do the sort of healing I wanted to practice. But I had seen healing done on couches now by these two gifted ladies and the crystals and artefacts in the healing room showed me the environment I needed to work in, so while we were there we picked up a booklet that listed all the therapists and healing centres in our area that could lead me to find the type of teacher I needed. We thanked everyone there especially the two healers as it felt like a door had been opened to my future, and made our way home feeling very positive.

She might not be able to train me to be a healer but as part of her shamanic skills, the nurse ran Celtic sweat lodges on sacred ground. She explained these were very similar to Native American sweat lodges that I was drawn to and very much wanted to experience. Like most people I had heard of sweat lodges through books and films but didn't really know what happened during the secret ceremonies. Something deep inside me was urging me to do this so my guides must have thought it would help in my development as a healer.

It transpired that I would be totally unprepared for the emotional experience and it was to increase my spiritual connection on so many different levels. Looking back on it now, I think it was one of those defining moments in one's life when it felt as if my mind had been unlocked and everything suddenly made sense. As if for the first time in your life the mists cleared and you can see your place in the universe, and what you are meant to be doing with the rest of your life.

It would be over two months before she held her next sweat lodge as they were only held on certain days. I booked my place as soon as I got the time off work as I felt it would help with what I wanted to become, but I had no idea at the time just how little I knew about myself. You have no concept of the baggage you carry around with you until you are confronted with a situation that makes you do so.

When the day finally came for my sweat lodge experience it turned out there was a lot more to it than I had expected. Around nine of us arrived at the special sacred site early in the morning and were taken into a large wooden shed that looked more like a fairy grotto. We were taken through several rituals like meditations and mantras to prepare us and get us in the right frame of mind. The one that stands out in my mind was us having to write everything we disliked about ourselves and our lives on paper and keep it to be ceremonially burnt on the red-hot stones inside the sweat lodge.

I had never had to confront myself or my shortcomings on this intimate level as I think you only think about what you like about yourself. You conveniently tuck the rest away in the back of your mind and smile at the world, but what we were writing was never going to be read by anyone and it's amazing how honest you can be when you are writing to yourself. The serious looks on people's faces around the room told me that I wasn't the only one having to face some unhappy truths.

Next, we helped build the fire that would heat the special rocks to nearly white hot that would turn water into steam that would purify us. After lunch the fire was lit, we all danced and sang sacred songs around it, playing the drums that would have looked and sounded very strange to anyone not involved in it. But incredibly, by the time we had done this for about ten minutes, we were all beating out the same tune and were all dancing the same steps in perfect harmony. There is something very primal about beating drums that connects us with long distant memories buried deep in our subconscious from our earliest days on this planet. By that point, we all felt a change within us and were getting into a frame of mind that saw the modern world and its trappings disappear into insignificance.

While the two fire-keepers kept the fire blazing we made our way to a wooden dome about four feet high at its middle made of special saplings, then lead by our shaman we covered the dome in a layer of old blankets until it was about two inches thick. Finally, we pulled an old tarpaulin over the entire structure so that although it was still sunny outside you couldn't see your hand in front of your face inside.

The boys were then led into the large shed and the girls into the house so we could all get changed into something more appropriate for the high temperatures of the lodge. The boys wore just swimming trunks and the girls underwear and sarongs with bath towels around our shoulders that would be folded to sit on. We all then filed past the blazing fire and ceremoniously entered the sweat lodge to take up our positions where we would stay for its duration.

We then sang sacred songs and prayed as our ancestors would have done to generate the right atmosphere and invoke the right spirits, then the first seven rocks were called for and were placed in the central fire pit and we could all feel their searing heat. The daylight was almost blinding as the rocks were passed through the flap before it was once again shut out and we sat in the red-hot glow of the rocks.

By the time we finished the sweat lodge, the temperatures would rise to around one hundred and twenty degrees and we were glad we were so scantily clad. And if anyone had asked me how long we were in there I would have said about an hour and a half as time seemed to lose its importance, in fact, by the time we all filed out of the sweat lodge it was night time and we had been in there for around five hours.

Although most sweat lodges follow the same basic pattern of four or five different elements, the groups will often have differing experiences. This is because all groups are made up of a different set of people as diverse as if you had plucked them off an average street. Of all ages and backgrounds and from all walks of life so that they will be totally different from the group that came before them, and totally different from the group that will follow them so that the combined energy of them all will take them on a journey, whereby every member gets exactly what they need in a way they will understand to continue their spiritual growth.

Out of respect for the shaman, I will not go into detail about what took place in the sweat lodge as I consider it sacred and intensely personal, but it was the most liberating and deeply emotional experience I have ever had and it had a profound effect on all who took part. While in the sweat lodge I felt completely cleansed of my troubles and free and unencumbered to the point where I thought I could fly with eagles. I have goosebumps up my arms as I write this so strong is the memory of it, and I would encourage anyone to take part in one who gets the opportunity.

When we emerged from the lodge at the end of the ceremony, the sky was inky black with the stars looking close enough to touch. The whole experience had a profound effect on me on so many different levels. I think it fair to say that it was to prove one of those pivotal moments in one's life when nothing would ever be the same again.

Things that had taken most of my attention before and that I thought was the sole purpose for my living and working, now seemed rather insignificant and shallow against my new found spiritual awareness and perception of what was important. I seemed to be looking through new eyes that saw the material world as transient and of little importance. My new connection to the ancestors had given me an insight into what the world was all about and shown me that our earthly life is just a small part of our existence.

At this point, I would like to talk about my so-called coincidences and that each one at the time just seemed like a stroke of luck, but looking back on it now they were definitely a guided sequence of events that ultimately led me to where I am today.

I know there are probably people out there reading this who are at the same point in their journey as I am, and there are people out there who are far more experienced and further along their path than I am. To these people, I would say that I have read many books by people like myself and have at least learnt something or confirmed a belief from these books. I wish that these people reading this book will gain the same benefits from my experiences laid out in these pages.

But it is not these people that I am talking to right now. It is the people who are sitting on the fence or just starting out on their journey and may not have recognised a coincidence that has happened to them and don't think that because you are of a certain age that you should be at a particular stage in your journey by now. Remember that although I might have been reading books and seeking something for many years before, my real journey of discovery didn't start until I was fifty-two years old. The only truth is that your personal journey will not start until the time it was destined to start for your particular life's purpose.

And don't be in a big hurry to finish your journey as it is not the end that counts but the journey itself. I sincerely hope that I never finish my journey because it is still unfolding for me, and if it ever stops unfolding, I would have lost the most interesting and rewarding part of my life that I have ever experienced.

So keep a watch out for something that may seem, at the time, like a stroke of good luck and search for the deeper meaning in what has just happened.

Chapter 6
Making a Commitment

Most of 2002 was taken up with Jan and me doing the things that courting couples do and getting to know each other well. It was becoming clear to both of us that although we had very different backgrounds, both our lives had followed a similar path towards being spiritual and trying to help people. I had met Jan from her workplace a number of times by now and met some of the people she worked with, and it was evident that people naturally gravitated to her. She had a bit of a reputation for being an agony aunt as people trusted her not to gossip about what they told her, and they felt very calm and reassured around her.

I, on the other hand, have always been a dreamer with my head in the clouds and constantly found it difficult to understand what Jan saw in me. It was while I was contemplating this that I heard the lyrics 'angel and the dreamer' from a song by David Soul on the radio and I instantly understood. Jan was my anchor to keep me grounded in the here and now while giving me just enough rope to float between the two worlds and interact fully with both. It is thanks to this that my connection to my guides in the spirit world grew stronger and stronger until I could recognise their energies as second nature.

It was during this time that Jan and I would make regular trips to our local spiritual shop and browse through the books, crystals, ornaments and mantic tools. We were on one such trip in 2002 when I spotted a set of stones in a glass cabinet that drew me to them like a magnet. As I entered a dream-like state while staring at them I knew I had to have them although at the time I didn't know why. When I finally returned to normal reality and asked what they were I was told they were Boji stones, that were dug out of the ground in matched pairs of male and female, and had to be kept in their original pairings to gain their combined energies. So I held three or four sets before finding the ones I connected with, and although they were rather expensive, I bought a pair as my intuition told me they were going to be very important to me one day.

It would be many years before this intuitive purchase would prove its worth but when it did it was in the most spectacular way that would give me and my clients access to other realms and dimensions. When these stones were incorporated into a special healing technique that my guides had taken three years to teach me, they would prove to be very powerful in transporting us into a deep meditation that facilitated extraordinary healing.

Jan and I spent many hours talking about all sorts of spiritual things in great detail and the part this had played in making us who we were and that had ultimately drawn us together. In all these talks it was amazing how similar our views and our opinions were considering we had never met before, although our paths had almost crossed several times. We both agreed that had we met on any of these other occasions it would not have worked out between us at that time and that this was the perfect time for our paths to cross.

It's amazing when you have the opportunity to look back over several decades and see a pattern emerging that puts you on a course where a predestined eventuality is almost unavoidable. Jan is also one of the most caring and compassionate people I have ever met and although I have physical and emotional issues arising from my childhood and teenage years she has an amazing ability to heal my past. It is true to say that I am not the person I used to be thanks to her and with this in mind, it had become clear it was time to put the past behind me and move on to a better place. It must be rare if not an impossibility that you have the opportunity to marry an earth angel. I have made enough mistakes in my life and wasn't about to let this one slip through my fingers, so by late 2002 I started to make plans as what better time could there be, and I'm sure this kind of opportunity would not come along twice in one lifetime. Besides who better to stand beside me on this journey than an earth angel, and if heaven was conspiring to pull us together they must have known what extraordinary work we could accomplish as a team.

Our second Christmas as an item was better than the first as I had got to know the family better and everyone had accepted that we were serious about each other. Once the festive season finished, all attention was concentrated on Valentine's Day and we spotted an advert in the paper that would suit us very well. It was for a weekend coach trip to Paris that we liked the look of, and being the city of romance, what better place for us to get engaged. We both felt nervous that people would think we were rushing things but also excited that we had been given a chance to make a new life together and share our common interests. Jan had been to Paris many years before with one of her friends so knew what was in store, but I had never been there so I wanted to see all the famous sites.

We arrived late afternoon at a hotel on the outskirts of the city and I must admit to feeling a bit like a schoolboy who was about to go in front of the headmaster. There was no way I could put this off until morning as I would be a gibbering idiot by then, so even before we unpacked I took Janis's hand in mine and tried to go down on one knee gracefully although if memory serves me well I nearly fell over. My hands were shaking and I'd forgotten everything I was going to say to this earth angel who was now looking down at me expectantly and now slightly bemused. I can't remember now exactly what I said to her although no doubt it was a little farcical but I do remember the answer and to my great relief it was, 'Yes'.

The rest of the weekend was glorious as we took in all the top attractions the city had to offer and standing on the banks of the Seine watching the ceaseless and timeless flow of the water I had the feeling that something special had just taken place. Almost as if a predestined and long-awaited convergence had finally come together to create a whole out of two separate and very different halves, and that what was to follow felt almost as if it had already been written down somewhere in anticipation of the actual event.

When I told Jan how I was feeling, she reminded me of a tape recording she had of a reading that was made in 1987 that we had listened to a few months before. By the description of the man being spoken about on this tape, it had to be me, and standing on the banks of this river in such a beautiful city we didn't need words to tell each other how we were feeling at that moment. As we stood there hand in hand daydreaming about the future we both knew that something miraculous could happen if we allowed ourselves to be guided in the right direction.

When we returned home, our families were delighted as Jan showed off her engagement ring but we kept quiet about our spiritual experience while standing on the banks of the Seine. We had only just accepted the implications of Jan's face changing when I kissed her, and although Paris was another confirmation of what we were feeling neither of us had the confidence to tell anyone about it at this stage. Although living on my own in the bungalow I was able to study and meditate freely and the magnificent back garden was a sanctuary where I could contemplate without interruption.

When Jan had taken time to think and make plans, she set the date of our wedding for the 24th of September 2003, and now that we were settled in our relationship I spent more time doing healing on friends and family whenever the need and opportunity presented itself to allow me to practice the disciplines needed. Although I was still aware I needed formal training of some sort, despite the fact that I was succeeding in the treatments I was doing I was conscious there were things I needed to know that only a qualified trainer could teach me. I had learnt a great deal from the two lady healers in the short time I had spent with them but that had only served to prove I was merely scratching the tip of an enormous iceberg.

Our wedding was on a lovely sunny day in a listed building that was once an arch bishop's palace overlooking the River Medway set in immaculate gardens. I suppose like most men the day was a bit of a blur for me, punctuated with 'I do' and the photographs were taken in a beautiful herb garden with family and friends dressed to the nines and smiling happily. But the thing that stands out in my mind in full technicolour is Jan arriving in the classic 1957 Chevrolet Bel Air with the tyres crunching on the gravel as it glided to a halt outside the main entrance of this beautiful old building. When I looked inside the back of the car I hardly recognised Jan as she had flowers in her hair and dressed in a gorgeous ivory lace dress that dropped away on one side. She looked an absolute vision as she smiled at me sweetly and to me, she looked exactly the way an angel would look if she had dropped out of the sky. She looked radiant in the sunshine almost glowing as if some unseen energy was creating a dazzling aura around her to show everyone what only I had been able to see up until then.

We honeymooned on the lovely island of Zante and the deep blue Mediterranean Sea literally lapped within a few feet of our hotel steps. Every night we stood in the moonlight listening to the waves gently caressing the sandy beach. The first night we went out for a meal we were treated to typical Greek hospitality as the waiters learnt that we had been married only the day before, and at the end of the meal, we were given special cocktails that were reserved for couples who had just got married. But Jan had planned something special that would reduce me to tears when we returned to our room that night.

As I opened the bedroom door, there were rose petals scattered over the bed that Jan had placed there before we went out. If I didn't know it before I certainly knew that night that I had married a very special lady indeed and without being too sentimental I think she was a gift from heaven. All I had to do now was to endeavour to deserve her and there was no doubt in my mind that the way I would do that was to follow this path that had been set before me with all my heart and soul.

Once Jan and I had moved in together, it gave us lots more time to talk about the things we really cared about and we spent every spare moment in spiritual shops looking for new books to help us on our journey. I already had two mentors in the form of writers who shared their journeys through the books they had written. These two writers had taught me that you didn't have to be a special or clever person to follow a spiritual path and that it is more likely you will be chosen by spirit because they have seen something in you that you are not yet able to see yourself.

The first of these books were bought at least three decades ago when I was in my mid-thirties and since then I had been actively looking for my right path. I'm sure the second series of books that I found in the middle of the nineties was destined to cross my path at a time when I could best understand and make use of the information they contained. So I am a great believer that you should not try to find a specific path to follow but instead browse these amazing shops frequently and just see what you are drawn to. Because as with myself, the path that I ended up following with my guides' influence was so far removed from what I was trying to achieve before. It was like chalk and cheese.

Jan as a single mum had been unable to buy many books or mantic tools to follow her path so I was very keen that now that we had a joint income, she should indulge the passion that had lain dormant in her since her twenties when she had bought two books on Astrology and Greek Mythology.

The Christmas of 2003 was also special as for the first time we gave each other gifts of a spiritual nature that would not raise too many eyebrows and that only Jan and myself would know their true meaning.

Jan and I also agreed that once Christmas and New Year was out of the way we would start seriously looking for someone who could teach me what I needed to learn if I was to become a professional healer. Now I had the backing and encouragement of an earth angel I was eager to see just what I was capable of with the energies that could be directed through me into those who needed its healing powers.

Chapter 7
Divine Intervention

As we promised ourselves, when the festivities were over we started looking for a teacher who could show me how to use my gifts properly and professionally. We bought all the local papers we could find and searched all the ads for anything that resembled a healing centre or spiritual church but with no luck. Then while sorting through some old papers I had brought with me from the bungalow, which had been a New Year's resolution because it was one of those jobs you keep putting off, I found the booklet we picked up while visiting the shamanic healer and her lady healers. There were quite a few in the North Kent area so we picked two from the list that were nearest to where we were living as frequent visits to them for training wouldn't cost too much.

As it was getting late by then, I decided to ring the first one 'The Sanctuary of Healing' the following evening when I got home from work and make an appointment to see them. They were open on Wednesdays and the next available date would be the 14th of January 2004 so I rang the number given in the booklet but there was no answer. We decided that because we'd had the booklet for a while they might have changed the telephone number so we would just go there the next evening and introduce ourselves. But when we went there the doors were locked and the place was in darkness, but the telephone number on the notice board outside was the same one I had rung a couple of nights before and the opening night was still Wednesday. Again, we said anything could have happened like sickness to prevent them from opening so no matter I would ring the following evening and speak to them about a visit.

The following evening I rang the number that was now confirmed on the notice board outside the building as the right one but again there was no answer although I let it ring for quite some time. We thought there might be something wrong with the phone line so we would go there on the following Wednesday which was the 21st and introduce ourselves as it wouldn't be closed two weeks running. Again, we drove over on the appointed evening at the right time but again the doors were locked and the building was in darkness. Not one to give up easily we went home and rang the number just in case there was a problem that prevented them from opening but again there was no answer.

Having no luck with our first attempt, we turned our attention to our second choice 'The Temple of Light' and as I was passing it one day I stopped and checked the opening times and the telephone number on the notice board outside. I wasn't going to get caught a second time and the opening times and telephone number was correct so that evening I rang the number, but although I let it ring for quite some time in case someone had trouble getting to the phone there was no answer. No matter, we thought, I really needed a teacher so we will persist and go there on the next evening they were open which was Thursday the 19th of February and introduce ourselves.

We duly arrived on the right day at the right time but again the doors were locked and again the building was in darkness. This was getting tiresome and we were getting disheartened but we were not ones to give up easily so the following evening I again rang the number but there was no answer. I started to wonder if someone somewhere was trying to tell me something and I said to Jan that we would go there the following Thursday, and if the doors were locked I would not try any more options from the booklet and just see what Providence would send to me. Well, the following Thursday evening came and yes, you've guessed it correctly. All locked up and in darkness so now I've got the raging hump despite Jan's calming words.

Well, unless I was being taught an important lesson which I had not yet been able to fathom, my search for a healing centre and a teacher wasn't going to be as easy as I thought. A few weeks later we were visiting my son, his wife and grandson and when they asked why I was looking a bit out of salts I relayed the story of our four failed attempts to find me a teacher. My daughter-in-law said, "You should try the place I go to, I'm sure they could help you there."

This was another of those jaw-dropping moments, as I hadn't the slightest suspicion she was interested in spiritual things, let alone went to a spiritual centre. So I made a note of the name and address she gave me and arranged to meet her there so she could introduce me to the lady who ran it. The following Sunday the

28th of March we made our way to Wainscot village hall that was converted into a spiritual and healing centre for the evening.

When Jan and I walked into the main room the place was buzzing with lots of people greeting each other and groups of people excitedly talking and the atmosphere was very upbeat and friendly. I had expected it to be rather sombre and formal and church like so this was a pleasant and unexpected surprise and exactly what I was looking for. Although the end of the hall had tables draped in satin cloths with candles, flowers and spiritual ornaments it didn't look or feel like a church.

The first half of the evening was very enjoyable as it went through its various stages of opening prayer and surprisingly followed by a song that had been in the charts a few years before. I found out later that any song could be used even a pop song providing it had words of a spiritual or positive nature that would encourage and empower people.

This was followed by a medium standing in front of the assembled gathering and giving messages to anyone who's dearly departed had passed to the spirit world. I had never seen anybody do this before and to have it done right in front of me and hear the gasps from people when the information was so accurate was fascinating and extraordinary to watch. After a closing prayer, there was a half hour tea break while the room was darkened by lighting candles and switching the lights off and couches set up for anyone who needed healing from qualified practitioners. It was during this tea break that I was introduced me to Sandra the lady who ran the centre about the healing I had done and the training I was hoping to get.

Sandra would turn out to be a very gifted healer, medium and teacher who said she would asses my abilities the following week, she looked quite stern and obviously old school and a little intimidating but I was to learn that she had a heart of gold for those who didn't mess around or waste her time.

I must admit to being a little daunted at the prospect of being assessed because although I had done quite a lot of healing by this stage nobody had ever monitored my work, come to that, no one had ever watched any healing I had done apart from Jan and the drunken people in Cyprus so it was a bit scary.

So had divine intervention played its part in preventing me from going to the other two centres to make sure I came to this one to find Sandra and had my daughter-in-law found this place first in order to guide me to the destination that best suited my gifts and what it would take to develop them? I have very definite opinions on the subject but what do you think, dear reader? Because we have been to the Sanctuary of Healing many times since those first two attempts for services and training sessions and met all the people who run it, and it does serve to show us that even if we come up against an apparent brick wall it doesn't mean there isn't another avenue for us to explore providing we don't stop looking for it!

Although I had to go to work the week following the first meeting with Sandra my upcoming assessment was never far from my mind, and also the crushing thoughts were crowding in on me of what I would do if she said I was not good enough to be accepted for training. But it was now spring of 2004 and surely I had done enough healing by now to know that I wanted to pursue this path and be the best at it that I possibly could. And I had no doubt the only way to do that was find a professional body of people who would say I was good enough to practice what was rapidly becoming a passion for me. So I was just going to have to do my very best and show that I was worthy of the training I was asking for and the commitment from somebody to spend the time with me that was needed.

So by the time we went back to the centre the following Sunday, I was feeling decidedly nervous as I had no idea what Sandra was going to ask me to do. The only healing I had done up until then was for family and friends in the privacy of their homes and only after being invited to do so, but this was going to be on somebody I didn't know in an environment that would feel strange and with people scrutinising my every move.

When my turn finally came after the tea break, I was led into the darkened main room where other healers had already started working with their clients. I was taken to a couch in the corner of the room on which a friend of Sandra's was already lying who it turned out was also a qualified healer, 'no pressure then!'

My future teacher just said to me, 'This lady has a number of things wrong with her and I want you to find out what they are.' When she saw the look on my face, she said encouragingly, 'Just run your hands over her body and see what you feel, I know you can do it.' Well, she had a bit more confidence in me at that stage than I did because I hadn't done anything like this before, but she said it with such conviction that I thought she must be able to see something in me that I can't and it inspired me.

When I put my hand over the lady's abdomen because that's what I was nearest to, Sandra said, "Just start from her head and work your way down her body." So I went to her head and put my hands on either side about two inches from her ears and closed my eyes and asked for help from my guides or anyone else in the spirit world who might be listening. The thoughts were then put into my mind to hold my hands over the clients head. This had a remarkable effect as I didn't actually see anything but the thoughts were given to me that she was getting very bad pains in her head, so I asked her, "Are you suffering from migraines?" to which she answered, "Yes."

Feeling a bit more confident now, I carried on down until I had covered her entire body and correctly identified two other areas where she was getting problems. When I was finished, my teacher asked me to sit down while she conferred with her friend on the couch. When they had finished talking, Sandra came back to me and said, "I can't teach you this stuff as you already have it in you, but I will teach you the protocol, the techniques and finer points of healing. If you accept you will have to do a nine-month course under my guidance and demonstrate forty hours of healing on people that come to the centre."

After the week I'd just had, worrying about how things were going to turn out and if I was good enough, my feet lifted off the floor as I had found what we had been searching for. And so when all the paperwork had come through on the 12th of May 2004, my journey started along the path of discovery that would stretch my abilities, and interact with my spirit helpers in ways that I could never have imagined in my wildest dreams.

I was given a training manual to study that covered everything from meditation to psychology and from physiology to the different forms of healing. I was also given a code of conduct that set out what I could and could not do and reading its content it looked like it had been inspired by a government department somewhere.

It had only been a few weeks since I had spoken to my daughter-in-law to the point where I had been accepted as a trainee under the wings of this amazing lady. For a few weeks, my clients at the centre were restricted to those my teacher had chosen for me in what had now become my corner, so I was a little daunted but excited when I was told one Sunday that I would be joining the other healers treating whoever came to the centre that week needing healing.

After the service and mediumship demonstration had taken place, we all went into the lobby area for a cup of tea while the people needing healing gradually drifted into the main room. I was a little worried that no one would come to my couch as up until then everything I had done was organised by Sandra, so when the healers made their way into the room I followed them and stood by my couch indicating I was ready if anyone wanted healing from me. To my great relief, a lady who was sitting close by came over to me and asked if I could help her, so after making her comfortable on the couch I asked her what I could do to help. Patient confidentiality means I can't relay any details about what she needed or the treatment given for it but suffice to say she gained relief from it through my healing.

While I was healing this lady in nothing else but candlelight, my teacher was in the lobby area behind a glass partition having a cup of tea and chatting to her friends, although I was in this darkened room with gentle music playing while I was giving healing I was to get a surprise when I finished my client.

I only had the one client that evening so I went to join the others in the lobby and when Sandra finished talking she asked me to sit opposite her at the table. She then proceeded to tell me in infinite detail everything that I had done to my client throughout the whole of the healing session. I was gobsmacked as it had never been my intention to cheat or cut corners as I am passionate and dedicated in all my healing work, but it did teach me there are people so gifted that they are aware of what you are doing although they are talking to other people in another room.

This was one of those defining moments in one's life that you can look back at and realise something remarkable happened so that nothing will ever be the same again. It gave me a new understanding of what is possible and a real incentive to become as good as I could be and it fostered in me a memory that is impossible to forget. In reality, I'm still trying to be as good as Sandra but the experience taught me to look at things from a different perspective that has enabled me to become the healer I am today.

So when I had recovered and closed my mouth I said to Sandra, "I couldn't bull shit you if I wanted to, could I?" She just said, "No, you can't so don't even try." I'm sure she already knew I wasn't that sort of person as she would never have accepted me for training, but was just letting me know spirit is always watching and conveying what you are doing to those who are training you.

The second week at the centre we met a lady called Heather who helped run the meetings and is also a very experienced medium and healer. Jan and I had a long chat with her in the tea break about what we had done so far and towards the end of our chat she said, “You are making plans to go somewhere abroad, aren’t you?” We said yes and told her about our plans for opening a healing retreat somewhere on the island of Crete, to which she replied, “You will know the place when you find it because you will walk through a stone arch to happiness and never look back.” This was the first time we had spoken to anyone about our plans because we thought it was just a pipe dream with no chance at all of coming true, but Heather was so precise with the details she told us that we believed her and for the first time thought it might actually be possible.

The third week we went was the 11th of April and I got a real surprise as the medium who came to the centre bought my dad through to talk to me. It was another gobsmacking moment as it was the last thing I expected but as he died in 1998 he had obviously waited a long time to connect with me.

He said through the medium that he knew we had got married and was very pleased for us both as he liked Jan very much. To identify himself he said he had been a grocery boy when he first started work and delivered things on a bicycle which I can remember him telling me. He said he could see us going on a trip and mentioned a man called Donald who I think was a friend of his. He also said that he saw me with a paintbrush in my hand which was no surprise as I’m a bit of a D.I.Y nut and am always doing something. The last thing he said to the both of us as he faded away was that Jan and myself should “look, listen and learn”, which we took to mean we had now found the place we had been looking for and we should both concentrate on learning all we could from the gifted people who ran the centre.

By the end of June, I was making good progress, learning how to conduct a proper healing session and developing my own unique style of hands-on healing. Jan and I had decided by then that we wanted to be more involved with the centre so we asked Sandra if we could help out before and after the Sunday meetings. She agreed so on the 4th of July 2004 we started going to the centre early to help set the hall up for the meetings and staying late to help put everything away afterwards.

We got to know Sandra better by spending more time with her while helping out at the centre and were constantly asking her all sorts of questions about spiritual things. We let our desire to learn more in no doubt, so she told us that she ran development circles at her home in the evenings for people like us, and was starting a new one on Monday the 13th of August if we would like to join it. When she explained all the things she did at these circle meetings to help you identify your spiritual gifts and how to use them we both jumped at the chance. So on the appointed evening, we arrived at Sandra's home to join three other people who also wanted to learn and we started one of the most interesting periods on our path to enlightenment.

The experience in the circle with Sandra would serve me well when several years later I would find myself running my own circle meetings with people as eager as me to learn all the ways that spirit could help us to help others who needed healing and direction in their lives.

I will cover in detail in a later chapter all the things you experience and learn in these circles and how I opened new dimensions by introducing mantic tools, and by extending its scope by writing my own psychic development program that became an A to Z guide to identifying and developing your spiritual gifts.

Chapter 8
The Right Place at the Right Time

Things were going well for Jan and myself and as our first wedding anniversary approached we decided to celebrate and have our first holiday as a married couple in the warm sunshine. We would fly to Crete for the first time on the 21st of September and were both excited at the prospect of seeing this beautiful island for the first time. There are several holiday destinations that still hold a strong mystique that fires the imagination because of their remarkable achievements and legacies. And it is certainly true that Greece and its islands come under that category as the foundation it laid down for architecture, medicine, democracy and civilisation and helped to make the world what it is today.

We bought a map of the island at our local Waterstones bookshop and spent many hours searching through the place names hoping that one would jump out at us and show us where our retreat should be. But when this didn't happen we decided to take the logical approach and start at the western end of the island and work our way east on successive holidays until we found the stone archway Heather had told us about.

The furthest west we could go was a place called Kissamos but the nearest airport was Hania which was quite some distance away, so we decided to stay in the popular resort of Agia Marina and hire a car to explore from there up to Kissamos. We had seen some stunning countryside and a number of potential properties by the end of the first week but we hadn't found anywhere suitable and we hadn't found our stone arch. So we decided to take a break from what was starting to feel like a fruitless search and take a boat trip to Gramvousa Bay and its legendary white sandy beach.

The day we picked turned out to be lovely and sunny with deep blue skies and clear views in every direction and the only choppy water was as we rounded the headland of the peninsula. Once we came into calmer waters again, the boat headed for a small island about a mile from the mainland with a ruined

Venetian fort that covered its entire surface. When the boat moored at a little jetty I was eager to go up and explore as I've always been a bit of an amateur archaeologist but Jan wasn't so keen.

I said to Jan that we should do the touristy bit while we were here as it doesn't look as if there are many steps and the view from the top will be amazing. But I couldn't have been more wrong because when we had climbed the steps visible from the boat, three times as many snaked off around the corner.

I had comfortable sandals on and found the going quite easy but Jan only had flip-flops on as she hadn't expected to go mountaineering as she put it. The view was incredible from the top but Jan's legs were aching by then so I left her sitting on a large stone slab while I explored the ruins. As you can imagine by the time Jan had climbed back down all those steps she was in considerable discomfort so I found her a comfortable seat and made sure I pampered her for the rest of the day.

When we reached the white sands of Gramvousa Bay, the boat moored just offshore and the crew gave us a most welcome barbecue cooked on gas stoves mounted on the stern. Suitably refreshed, we were supplied with beach mats and umbrellas and ferried in a small dingy to the beach where we made ourselves comfortable. We spent several hours there taking in the vistas and chatting to other holidaymakers which gave Jan much-needed time to recover from her ordeal. I did some snorkelling while Jan relaxed under the umbrella and was amazed at how colourful the fish were and how close they let you get to them. It was a truly magical place and we were told that Charles and Diana moored in this very bay while on their honeymoon so we were sharing it with some very special people. By the time we had to return to the boat Jan had spent a blissful time reading and enjoying the sunshine and I was almost out of the doghouse. The return journey to Kissamos harbour was relaxing and enjoyable and once back in our apartment Jan had a hot shower and a much-needed nap on the bed.

We normally walked to a taverna for our evening meal but this time Jan quite rightly refused and I drove us so that Jan had the minimum amount of walking possible. Jan now suitably dined and laced with a stiff drink. We got an early night so Jan could have as much rest as possible before we continued our search the following day.

Unfortunately, Jan had a restless night and only slept in the end because she was totally exhausted and by early morning, her left hip had seized up and she was in agony. I tried to make her comfortable but she was crying by then, as the pain was unbearable and said through her sobs, "You're going to have to do something as I can't stand the pain and I can't move my leg."

What happened next I can only call divine intervention as my guides instructed me to lay Jan on her right side and elevate her left leg on a pillow, I was so desperate to relieve Jan's suffering I didn't think about what I was doing and just blindly followed the instructions that were being put into my mind.

The sequence of events that followed was another one of those defining moments when on reflection nothing can ever be the same again because the ramifications would change the way I worked forever. Using my left index finger, I made a six-inch incision on either side of Jan's hip joint and inserting a hand into each cut removed the ball joint from its cup socket, having cleaned both ball and cup surfaces to remove calcification and old tissue, a substance was injected into the socket to form a new cartilage before replacing the ball joint back into its socket.

I can remember sealing both cuts at the end but I had no concept of what had just happened or how it was possible so I couldn't have told anyone if they had asked me. Jan said the pain stopped about halfway through and I was just grateful she was no longer in pain and was now resting peacefully beside me. Satisfied that Jan was now comfortable, I laid down beside her and we both slipped into the deepest and most refreshing slumber I have ever had. That's a potted version of what I can remember of the healing process as the whole thing took about thirty-five minutes and ended with my hand over the joint pouring energy into the entire hip.

When we woke up sometime later in a bit of a daze, I was half afraid to ask Jan how she was as all this had been my fault and I wouldn't blame her if she was still mad at me. But she said that the pain had gone completely and she could move her leg, so she tried to walk and everything seemed normal and we were convinced a miracle had taken place. Although that was over ten years ago Jan has never had the slightest problem with that hip, and it set me on a course that would see me doing some amazing healing that would not only amaze me but defy all rational explanation.

Jan and I spent another couple of days looking for somewhere to set up our healing centre and when we still couldn't find anything suitable we spent the last three days of our holiday just enjoying ourselves. We had picked up a brochure for a secluded chapel on the peninsula of Akrotiri founded by a monk in the 17th century that we wanted to see, having first visited a working monastery on the way that made and sold its own olive oil and honey products, we found the car park at the top of the steps that led to the chapel. The steps went around an outcrop of rocks for about a hundred yards and then disappeared in a downwards direction so I was dispatched to see where they went. When I returned to tell Jan that the steps descended down what looked like a cliff face and out of sight, she said I could go on my own after her experience at the Venetian fort.

Jan had only just got over that ordeal so there was no way I was going to risk upsetting her again so wearing my trusty straw hat I set off to find and explore the chapel. The steps went on for about half a mile and very steep in places so I was now very glad I left Jan in the car. About halfway down, I passed a group of people going in the same direction who looked as if they were tired already and suffering from the heat, but they were speaking a language I didn't understand so I just smiled politely as I passed them and carried on with my solo descent.

Having reached the chapel I was amazed that it was built into a natural cave that could not be seen from the shoreline but with views over the Mediterranean Sea. After taking photos for Jan to look at later and taking a short break, I started the long climb back up to where Jan was waiting in the car park.

On the third flight of steps up from the chapel, I found a large stone in the middle of a step that seemed to sparkle, and I was certain it wasn't there on the way down as I'm sure I would have noticed it because it was quite unusual. Something in my head told me I needed to take this stone with me although because of where I was and what I was doing I couldn't think of any reason for this.

Then three-quarters of the way back up I caught up with the group I had passed on the way down and one of the men had passed out on the path and was barely breathing. The man who seemed to be the leader was crouched over him trying to bring him around so with hand gestures I asked if I could give him healing. The pleading look on the leaders face told me everything I needed to know so I placed my hand over the man's chest and asked for some serious help from upstairs.

As I continued placing my hands in various places on the stricken man and letting the energies flow into him, I noticed the leader and some of the other members on their knees praying so I was sure they knew what I was trying to do. After a few minutes, his breathing had improved but he was still not conscious so the leader put him over his shoulder and carried him which was no mean feat in the blistering midday sun. Then as the man regained consciousness the leader sat him on a low wall at the side of the path and I again put my hands on his chest and gave him healing.

It was then that I noticed the man's right hand was tightly clenched as if he was holding something precious and didn't want to lose it. When I carefully unfurled his hand, he was holding a tiny piece of grey stone he had obviously picked up before he became unconscious. I gently removed his small stone and replaced it with the large sparkling stone I had found on the way up and closed his hand around it to show him it was now his.

He was obviously pleased with this new stone by the look on his face and when our eyes met I have no doubt he could see the divinity that was flowing through me into him. Our eyes remained locked for what seemed ages as this man, myself and the divine healing presence shared this moment in time that I find difficult to put into words.

When I had finished giving him healing, I signalled my goodbyes and left them there as I made my way back to the car park at the top of the steps. I was telling Jan what had happened when the group came to the top of the steps and it was heartwarming to see the man who had been stricken a short while ago walking normally. It shows clearly that we should all follow our inner promptings as it was only when I saw the look on that man's face that I realised the significance of that sparkling stone. And that it must have been put on that step by unseen hands for me to find because I'm very observant and wouldn't have missed something of that size and sparkly right in the middle of a step.

It has been nearly ten years since that day on holiday in Crete and I often wonder what happened to the man and if he remembers that day and if he kept the sparkly stone. And just as important to me who put that stone on the step in a place that I wouldn't miss it that seemed to play such an important part in his recovery. But although I will probably never know the answers to these questions, isn't it comforting to know that there are angels and loved ones in the spirit world looking after and guiding us in times of need.

Although we hadn't found anywhere to set up our retreat we returned home in good spirits to settle into the routine of work and me continuing my training to become a qualified healer. Then towards the end of 2004 when I had gained more confidence in having worked with so many different people who came to the centre with a wide variety of problems. It came as a total shock when one Sunday we were about to start the evening's healing session Sandra walked into the darkened room and said, 'Right, tonight you can work on me as you know I have a problem with my legs.'

I must have looked terrified as the thought ran through my mind, *Oh hellfire, this is going to be like working on God*, and it didn't help when she said, "Just pretend I'm one of those people who have come here for help." Although I tried to push all the panic from my mind and be calm, my concentration evaporated and my connection to my guides disappeared. It took every ounce of mental effort I could muster to tell myself I was here to be trained as a professional and if I wanted to succeed I just had to get on with it.

The trouble was I had already done Jan's hip which I now wished I hadn't told Sandra about because it was probably what led to her asking me to treat her legs. All I could do was the same as I did in Crete and ask the spirit to show me what they wanted me to do and what followed turned out to be quite amazing.

After making Sandra comfortable on the couch, I was directed to her right knee where I replaced the cartilage between the upper and lower leg bones and under the kneecap. When that was finished, I was directed to her foot where I carried out the same type of work on some of the many bones as well as the ankle. I then did exactly the same on the left leg and after explaining to Sandra what I had done she carefully got off the couch and I gave a big sigh of relief and I think I can remember shaking a little.

Sandra's legs had a tendency to collapse under her without warning and she would end up in a heap on the floor unable to move. So when the following Sunday she said she had once again collapsed my heart sank as it would seem all the work that I had done was to no avail. But when she explained that before the healing I had given her she would have been unable to get up for at least half an hour. This time Sandra told me she got up straight after the fall and walked away to get on with whatever she was doing so I was relieved, and she was obviously delighted.

I think Sandra knew that if she didn't give me this sort of challenge there might be situations in the future that I might not be able to handle, and she was right, because there have been several times working alone in Crete without her backup that have tested my mettle, where I'm sure I could have failed if it wasn't for Sandra putting me in these sorts of situations and making me explore my capabilities.

By the time the Christmas and New Year festivities of 2004 were over, Jan and I had become permanent fixtures at the Wainscott Centre. All my training under Sandra's guidance had gone very well and my final test to qualify as a member of the Corinthians was fast approaching, so it was a very proud day for me and the result of many years searching when on the 14th of February 2005 I became a fully qualified healer practitioner.

I had given up many material things over the years in the search for my true path in life and had often wondered if the sacrifice was worth it, but standing there with my certificate in my hand and seeing all the smiles on people's faces who had done it all before me I was reminded of words I had read many years before:

It goes to prove that wealth, possessions and notoriety are only brief distractions from the tedium of life. The only path to true happiness is pure unconditional love of self, and then others.

I am sure that the healing energies I had been working with from the spirit were love in its purest form and I couldn't have been happier with myself at that moment.

It had taken me until my mid-fifties to reach where I now found myself, but because of things that had happened to me when I was younger, I thought I knew what life was about. I thought I had life sussed back then, but through the experiences of my spiritual journey from that fateful day in 2001 I now see things much clearer and appreciate the saying 'wisdom comes with age'.

Chapter 9
A Soul's Transition

Jan had got to know two ladies very well from where she worked and after working together for nearly ten years all three had become really close and confided in each other about most things. One of these ladies we will call Miss L had suffered from back problems for a number of years and over that time had tried everything to relieve the pain but with no lasting success.

During a conversation in late spring of 2005, Jan told her about the deep tissue healing I had done on her hip in Crete and the same kind of treatment I had done on Sandra's legs. After hearing this, Miss L asked if I would be able to do the same for her back.

So an appointment was made for Jan and me to meet her and we would take our therapy couch with us if it proved possible for me to help. When the three of us met on the appointed day, I conducted a consultation with her which is something I had got into the habit of doing with people I hadn't seen before. Although it caused her some discomfort I then asked her to lay face down on the couch and made her as comfortable as possible considering her condition.

After scanning her lower spinal area, my guides told me it would be possible to help her using the deep tissue healing they had taught me. I then relayed to Miss L the procedure I had been shown in my mind and asked her consent to continue although I could promise nothing at that stage. She said she had been in almost constant pain for many years now and was willing to try anything regardless of how bizarre or how unlikely it may appear to succeed.

Using the same techniques I had used before, I made an eight-inch cut over the lower spine that allowed me to detect what was causing the pain. I then removed three complete discs that had become damaged and cleaned all the surfaces of the vertebra that were exposed using the same procedure I had used on Jan's hip.

Then the same material I had used on Jan's hip and Sandra's legs was injected between the vertebrae to form three new discs. When this was done, I pulled back into place two vertebrae above and below this area that were out of alignment before wrapping the entire repaired spine in a sheath to hold it in place while everything set. I then sealed the cut I had made and held my hand over the lower spine so my angels and helpers could pour their healing energies into the repaired area.

This again is a potted version of what happened as the whole healing session was quite complex and lasted around forty minutes. When Miss L came around from her deep meditative state, she said the pain had completely gone and said she felt rejuvenated although I told her to take it easy for a few days.

I asked Jan to check on her from time to time to see how things were going but the pain never returned and she was able to continue a normal life which was brilliant as she had a young family to look after.

I would go on to treat Miss L on two more occasions and the last time just a few days before she emigrated to Australia. It was incredibly emotional as she sat in her car at the end of our road shouting, "I love you both, I'm going to miss you both so much." With tears streaming down all our faces, I had to shout out, "Go on, clear off, you have a plane to catch," and with that, she disappeared out of sight and with none of us knowing if we would ever see each other again.

When you conduct this type of healings on people, it can generate such intense spiritual bonds that it can transcend whatever time and distance that may separate you. And on several occasions over the years that followed, I have felt that something had changed and on emailing Miss L she confirmed that something had taken place and although she was on the other side of the world it made us all feel closer.

I know how all this must sound to people not familiar with the healing process and I wince sometimes when I hear myself talking about it, and when I look back at some of the things I have done it can appear like something out of a science fiction movie. But it would be an injustice and an insult to my spirit friends if I didn't record what happened accurately and diligently, and I know I'm not the only person doing this kind of work.

Humankind have and continue to screw up in the most spectacular way while on their brief stay on this beautiful and abundant planet we call home. I can only postulate that to do the kind of work I am doing is a signal to us all that there is something innately good available to us if we care to tap into it. I know from the very depth of my being that as long as there is breath in my body, I will never stop tapping into the spirit world in order to help those who seek it.

People have gazed at the heavens and written about unfathomable mysteries throughout the ages, and I think there are some things we are not meant to understand but just accept on faith, and spiritual healing in all its facets has to be one of these things.

The second of Jan's close friends who was mentioned at the beginning of the chapter we will call Miss N, she was having pains in her abdomen and thought she had pulled a muscle lifting a heavy box. After hearing about their mutual friend, she asked Jan if we could meet up to see if I would be able to do the same for her. After making her comfortable on the couch, I scanned her abdomen and felt something was not quite right but could not determine exactly what.

I had never healed a pulled muscle before so assumed that was the difference I was detecting and carried on with a normal healing session as I had been trained to do. I was not aware of anything unusual as I went through the various stages of the healing treatment and felt nothing other than the energies being given by my angels and guides.

But when I was finished and bought her out of her deep meditative state she said her grandmother had appeared to her in a vision holding a baby boy while I was working on her abdomen. She said her grandmother had been in the spirit world for a number of years and initially, we were unable to understand why she had shown her the child.

All the pain in her abdomen had now gone and she was feeling very calm and serene and said she felt as if something had been lifted from her which I assumed was her pain from the pulled muscle.

It was only when Miss N confided in Jan a while later that her normal monthly cycle had returned after a short absence that we come up with a possible answer, this along with the location of the pain it could have been an ectopic pregnancy which was a shock to her as she had no idea she could have been pregnant. And if this had been the case it would explain why her grandmother had appeared holding a baby as she would have then taken it back to the spirit world.

If I'd had any inkling of what the real problem was I would not have conducted any form of healing on her which is probably why it was hidden from me. We still cannot be certain that this is what happened but Miss N has a strong spiritual connection and sees things that I am not able to. So I am happy to accept her conclusion of what happened. I am happy to report that a few years later Miss N had a beautiful healthy baby boy who is now nearly six years old.

There is no way I can explain how it is possible for me to do this healing other than to say I seem to be in the right place at the right time when it is needed. And the ability to do so which is way past my understanding is given to me for the benefit of whoever needs it. If you were to ask me if I have faith then the answer is a definite yes. I have absolute faith in whoever is giving me this ability and it must be the highest form of benevolence I have ever or am ever likely to witness.

In July 2005, a man had asked to see me who was suffering from advanced terminal cancer and was very poorly indeed. This disease is always distressing for the whole family and I don't think there's a healer, spiritual or otherwise, in the land who would not like to conquer this debilitating condition.

When I met him, it was clear there was nothing I could do for his condition other than making him as comfortable as possible with whatever energies the angels could give me. When we are faced with this kind of situation, no matter how difficult, we have to rise above our empathy and impending grief of the family and consider what help we can give. I knew I could not help his poor tired body that had battled this disease with the sort of courage one rarely has the opportunity to witness.

So I turned my attention instead to his soul that would already have started to prepare itself to leave his body and make its way back to the spirit world. I put on a CD with lilting angelic music and lit my favourite nag champa incense. I then cupped his head in my hands and guided him into the deepest meditation I could summon from my guides and helpers. I then called in all the angels that might be listening to open his mind and help me lift it to where it could see heaven and the outstretched arms of his forebears waiting to receive him back into his spiritual family.

I could feel his body relax as his mind connected with this beautiful vision of where his soul was going when it departed from its earthly life. I left him as long as I could connect to this vision as I knew it would take away any fears he might have about what would happen when his time came. When I eventually brought him out of the meditation, he had the most serene smile on his face and thanked me for what I had been able to do for him.

I was pleased to hear him say this but how inadequate and feeble I felt at being able to offer him nothing more than this. But when I received a letter from his wife saying he had died two days after my treatment and how peacefully he had slipped away, and read how she thanked me for giving him such a worry-free send-off on his journey I realised I had done a lot more than I thought.

It also demonstrated that healing is not just about trying to mend a sick body of whatever it might be suffering from at any given time but extends into other areas where we can offer support and advice on spiritual matters people might not have come into contact with in the normal course of their lives.

I also received a large cheque from his widow shortly after his funeral which she thought I deserved for the help I had given to her husband and the family. I wrote back thanking her for her generosity but explaining that the cheque would never be cashed as it was a privilege to be invited to spend those brief moments with them all. I think he was the bravest and most humble person I have ever met in the way he faced the inevitable with such dignity and fortitude.

In the autumn of 2005, a lady came to the Wainscott Centre on walking sticks who had heard about the work I had done on Sandra's legs. She explained her knee had been troubling her for a while. It was very sore and painful and slowly getting worse, so I said I would see her after the first part of the service. When the tea break was finished I went into the darkened healing room where the lady and her daughter were waiting for me by my couch.

I explained that I was going to put her into a deep meditation where she would feel no pain while I carried out a ligament replacement. After making her comfortable on the couch I put a cushion under her leg so the pain in her knee would be at a minimum and she could relax. I thought everything was as it should be as I made preparations and put my hands around her head to guiding her into a deep meditation.

I used my deep tissue therapy in the same way I had done before and found some calcification on the lower leg bone that made up the knee joint. Having cleaned all the surfaces, the same material was given to form new ligaments after which I put the knee back together and sealed the cuts I had made, cupping the knee joint in my hands I felt the energies from the angels pour into the knee to complete the healing process.

When I bought her out of what I thought had been a deep meditation she gave a long sigh as if from relief so I asked if she was alright. "No," she said, "it was a bit painful when you were working on my knee." I was mystified, as no one had ever felt the slightest pain or discomfort through my healing treatments.

After hearing a message in my head, I said to her, "You didn't go into a meditation as I asked you to and you were monitoring what I was doing."

Her daughter was standing by the couch at this time and when her mother looked at me sheepishly, she said, "That sounds like Mother."

I scolded the lady playfully and said, "Well, at least that proves something has been done to your knee," and advised them to sit for a while before going home.

When you do this sort of work there are no physical signs after to show what has been done, and it's a matter of faith that what you intended to do has been carried out. But this lady said that she had experienced some pain throughout my treatment which would be the last thing I wanted to happen as spiritual healing is non-invasive. So although I never want this to happen again it did prove beyond doubt in this instance that what I intended to happen did actually take place, which would stop me from doubting in the future.

After this incident, I started asking my angels to make sure no pain could be experienced before I started any deep tissue healing in the future, and thankfully, there has never been a repetition of any kind of pain or discomfort being experienced in any healing treatments I have carried out up to this day.

I was overjoyed the following week when this lady walked into the healing centre almost normally and without the aid of walking sticks. She and her daughter were staggered at how quickly the knee had mended and I don't think she or I will ever forget the day of the treatment. Thanks was unnecessary as seeing her pain free and walking normally was all the reward I needed, and isn't it good to see the results of the work we do no matter what part you play in caring for others.

Unfortunately, too many times when you do this sort of work in an impromptu situation as with the young man in Crete you never get to see the results. But this will not deter me from helping in any future situation I find myself in because I know when I have done my part these people are left in the loving care of the angels when I leave them.

Jan and I had arranged our holiday for that year from the 20th of September to the 4th of October in a place called Platanias from where we would explore the next section of the island of Crete. From pictures we had seen on the internet, this area looked flatter and not so mountainous and more suitable for our healing retreat. On arrival after settling into our hotel and picking up our hire car, we started to plan our search starting at Maleme and working our way east. Jan said we would have two days searching and one day on the beach as we did last year otherwise it wouldn't feel like we'd had a holiday.

We had again printed a few renovation projects off the internet from estate agents in the area but when we saw them they were almost inaccessible by car or so dilapidated you would have to pull them down and start again. We were shown one house by an enthusiastic agent that was built into a hillside and only had windows at the front and was very dark inside. As there was no bedroom in the main house, they had built a small single room on the roof only accessible by an outside staircase that was suggested could be where we sleep. Needless to say, we made polite comments about the sea view and made our way back to the hotel to sunbathe and wonder what on earth we would be shown next.

Although we enjoyed the beaches and coastal areas around our hotel, the rest of our searches proved just as disappointing and unsuitable. We had chosen renovation projects because we didn't have hundreds of thousands of pounds at our disposal like some people and thought it was our best option. But after this holiday our optimism was beginning to wear thin and we started to wonder if this was such a good idea.

But once we got back home and settled back into the routine of work and social life again, we comforted ourselves that we had many more years left to search before I retired. I had nearly seven years working life to go before I could retire so something was bound to come up for us by that time.

What we didn't know was that our spirit friends were planning to drop a bombshell in our laps a few months later that would turn our lives upside down. I had bought Jan a new set of angel cards in the summer and she had bought me a set of runes for my birthday that I had always wanted. So we read the accompanying books and practised on each other blissfully unaware of what was about to happen.

What was about to transpire in the early months of 2006 I would have considered impossible and even considering where this information was to come from it was going to take some digesting and even believe that it could be possible.

Chapter 10
The Marrow Moment

There was a shop close to where Jan worked that sold all manner of spiritual things and as it was the largest shop of its kind in our area we were frequent visitors. Because of these numerous visits buying books, CDs, crystals for me and angel cards for Jan and of course, spending ages staring at things we couldn't possibly afford, we had got to know the girls who worked there very well and they knew I was a healer through the many in-depth conversations we had over the years we had been visiting the shop.

We were on one of these shopping trips in early 2006 when the senior lady named Gursel, who by then had become a good friend said that her young colleague kept bursting into tears and was there anything I could do to help her.

After a brief chat with the young girl, we went into a back room where it was quieter and I did a healing session for her while she sat on a chair and I stood behind her. When we came back into the shop with the young girl looking bright-eyed and much refreshed. Another girl said she could do with some of whatever I had given her friend so could I do the same for her. So once again we went into the back room and I performed a similar healing session for the second girl who also came back into the shop looking bright-eyed and refreshed.

Gursel having seen the two girls come back happy and refreshed said that as I was there would I mind giving her the same treatment as it was doing wonders for morale in the shop. So for a third time, we went into the back room and I performed the healing treatment on Gursel who was like a spiritual counsellor and helped customers with their purchases.

When we came back into the shop, Gursel said there was a book they had on the shelf she thought would be of great benefit to me, and could help me become the healer I wanted to develop into. When she handed me the book I thought it was a Bible as it looked like the one my mother gave me when I was a child.

The book was written by two eminent and highly respected American professors of medical psychology and were also physicians who were by their own admission "anything but spiritual". It was first published in 1975 and is called *'A Course in Miracles'* but its price tag of thirty pounds was more than I could afford at that time. A brief flick through its pages was enough to tell me it was definitely something I could benefit from, so I said I would come back at the end of the month when I got paid if they would put it by for me.

As promised we returned to the shop at the end of the month to collect the book but there was a surprise waiting for me that I could never have dreamt of. The book was brought from the storeroom for me and the three girls stood behind the counter smiling mischievously as I got the money out to pay. When I handed the money to Gursel, she said, "There's no charge. The three of us have put in equal shares to buy the book for you as a thank you for the healing you gave us."

It's not often I'm speechless as Jan will testify but I just stood there and welled up in front of the whole shop as it was impossible to stop the tears from running down my cheeks.

After countless hugs and promises that we would all meet at a later date for coffee, we dragged ourselves away from the shop and made our way home. This book is full of simple but extraordinary truths that are so thought-provoking that they always lead to a clarity of mind that results in the right path being chosen. *'A Course in Miracles'* is designed as a teaching aid to bring the very best out of you, and for those on a spiritual journey intending to do good in the world, I cannot recommend it too highly. That book has been treasured ever since and the fact that it is now falling apart is a testament to how well used it is and has without a doubt led to miracles. Jan and I have stayed very good friends with Gursel who went on to become an important teacher and guide in my life, and I hope that one day in the future will see us working together and sharing our collective gifts for the benefit of humankind.

By early spring of 2006, Jan and I had become permanent fixtures at the Wainscott Centre and helped Sandra with the Sunday meetings. On the 16th of April, a medium came to the centre called Lorraine Knight who we hadn't seen before and was reported to be very good. When it was time for Lorraine to give her demonstration, she got up and pointed straight at me and said, "I've got to come to you first because I've had this man from the spirit world with me for ages now and he's driving me crackers. His energy feels like a father figure but what he's asking me to tell you now makes no sense to me at all. He's telling me to ask if you remember the story about the marrow."

Well, how could I ever forget such a funny story that I had heard so many times as I was growing up from members of our family that have now sadly passed on. This is a true story about my dad and it goes like this; my dad was with the Eighth Army (Desert Rats) in North Africa during the Second World War and when he was demobbed and returned home to England there was widespread food rationing, so everyone who had a back garden like my dad grew whatever they could to supplement the meagre amounts they could buy in the shops.

My dad was a good gardener and grew all the staple crops like potatoes, onions, carrots, beans, etc., but one particular year he felt a bit adventurous and bought five marrow plants from a local nursery which he planted in a small strip of ground at the top of the garden close to the fence.

Unfortunately for some reason four of the marrow plants died within a month but Dad was not one to give up easily. Despite watering and feeding his one remaining plant all through the summer, it only bore him one tiny little marrow. In the autumn, he ripped it out of the ground in total disgust to throw it on the compost heap, what he hadn't noticed was a tendril running just under the surface of the ground that disappeared through the fence.

When after a couple of tugs he couldn't move it as the other side of the fence was full of brambles and nettles he donned his wellingtons and hacked away following the tendril. What he found nestled in the undergrowth a few feet from the fence was the biggest marrow he had ever seen in his life. Having several brothers who were all growing the same staple crops, it very quickly became a family joke that Dad got teased about every year after the event.

I don't think there's a medium in the land who could dream up a story about a marrow so it had to be my dear old dad who was putting those memories into Lorraine's mind. He was not a particularly religious or spiritual man and said he found it very strange to be standing there talking to me, but with all I'd learnt up until then it wasn't strange to me at all and the main part of his message for me was in two parts.

The second part of this message was going to leave us wondering what an earth spirit had in mind for us in order for it to come true. The first part, however, was very tearful and emotional as my dad thanked me for looking after Mum so well since he had left us through a heart and renal failure in 1998.

My dad was a real English gentleman, a true romantic and the sweetest man I have ever known. I've always said if I can be half the man he was I would be very happy indeed. He also said not to waste any part of my life and to make the very best of every moment that I have, which I'm sure was a reference to my healing work wherever that would take me.

In the second part of his message, Dad said he knew what we were planning to do and that something was going to happen that would mean this plan was going to come about a lot sooner than we thought. I don't think the full implications of Dad's message hit us till a few days later when we read the notes Jan had made after the reading.

I was fully expecting to work until I retired which would be just over five years and how could we possibly have the money it would take before that time. Jan and I had read in our spiritual books about divine timing and that all would be found to make something possible at the allotted time, but considering our finances at the time, we couldn't see how this would work in our situation.

Dad hadn't given us any details on how this was going to happen or any future date we could put on a calendar, which was probably for the best as it would have scared me to death to keep thinking about it. So with advice and comforting words from Sandra and Heather, we would just get on with our lives and wait for signs that would lead us in the right direction. As it turned out we wouldn't have to wait too long for the first of those signs to make itself known and there was no way we could have dreamt up its location.

Through trying to choke back tears one moment and howling with laughter the next, it became one of the most memorable events of my life. And in all the teaching we did after Dad's message, whenever anybody in our development circle had a similar experience with a loved one it became known as 'The Marrow Moment'. So through his message, my dear old dad will go down in history even if it was through an embarrassing moment and being teased by his family.

A local Asda store where we did our weekly shopping and where I bumped into my old friend who loaned me the bungalow had become a spiritual hotspot for us. When we parked the car on this trip, however, Jan opened the glove compartment and started feverishly rummaging before pulling out a map of Crete we had bought back from our last holiday. When I asked what she was doing Jan said that she didn't know for sure but had to look at the map to see where our next holiday might be.

Jan had a glazed look in her eyes as if she was in a trance so I kept quiet and waited to see what would happen when she was finished. Jan opened the map that was given to us by the car hire company and scanned it as if she was looking for somewhere she already knew. It was only a few moments before Jan pointed at a name and said, "There, we have to go there for our next holiday." She hadn't poured over the map for ages waiting for something to jump out at her but appeared to know what she was looking for.

We had read about these sorts of cognizant moments in our books where people are given information from a higher source but now it was happening to us, I looked at the name.

"Georg…i…oup…olis," but it didn't have a wistful or romantic sounding name as I had been expecting and it was stuck in the corner of a headland. "Are you sure?" I said, "It looks a bit out of the way, stuck in a corner."

But Jan just stared at me with a knowing look and repeated, "We have to go here next," and I realised it was another one of those coincidences that seemed to be stacking up in my life, so I figured it must be divine intervention and accepted it without another thought.

This had to be the sign we were waiting for so we would google it when we got home to see if we could find any pictures of the place and sort out a holiday there. But the spirits were not going to make it smooth sailing for us and it was going to take another leap of faith before we could set foot in what looked like a picturesque little fishing village.

We searched through all the websites of the tour operators we had dealt with before and then all the ones we hadn't and could find no one who did a holiday in Georgioupolis. I was talking to a work colleague about our difficulty finding a holiday and he said, "Why don't you do what the wife and I do and book it yourself?" which left me staring at him questioningly.

"What do you mean?" I asked.

He said, "Look at where you want to go on the internet, find a hotel and book it, when you've done that book a flight, it's easy we've done it loads of times." I think the look on my face told him the very thought worried me because if something went wrong you'd lose all your money, but reassured by his knowledgeable advice I said I'd talk to Jan when I got home.

Fortunately for me, Jan had already done this several times before when she was in her twenties and worked on the outskirts of Athens, and so would start another scary chapter and a steep learning curve for me who before 2001 hadn't left the shores of the British Isles.

Over the following few days, Jan searched the internet for hotels in Georgioupolis looking for somewhere in the village we could afford that had a telephone number on the website. Of course, I came up with lots of possible problems like what if they can't speak English, we could get all the dates wrong and end up with nowhere to stay. But my calm unflappable little angel dismissed all of my possible problems and said we would deal with anything as and when it happened and wait to see if everything would turn out right.

And of course, she was right, there was a little hotel right in the middle of Georgioupolis called 'Sofia's Apartments' that looked lovely and was reasonably priced that had an international telephone number. I normally make the important phone calls because I'd had a few jobs where using the phone had been an integral part of the work, but this call was making me decidedly nervous, not least of all because I couldn't speak the language.

When a man answered my call and heard me speaking English, he said, "Wait Sofia speak English," and put the phone down. When no one came to the phone after a couple of minutes, I just looked at Jan, shrugged my shoulders and said, "This is a waste of time," but she told me to hang on because if it was a small family concern she could be anywhere in the hotel.

And of course, Jan was right again, when after about five minutes a lady answered the phone introducing herself as Sofia and how could she help me. When I said we would like to book a room for our holiday, she sounded very pleased and asked for the dates so she could put them in her diary. She confirmed there was a room available for the dates we wanted and she didn't need a deposit, just turn up on the day which is typically trusting of the Greek people, so we would arrive on the 5th of September and leave on the 19th.

We tried to book flights into Hania Airport as this is where we had flown to on our previous holidays, but none of the airlines had space on their flights for the dates we wanted. We found out later all space was taken up by package holidays, customer services at

Gatwick said we would have to fly into Heraklion Airport and hire a car if we wanted to book it ourselves, which is the other end of the island, so with no other options open to us that is what we did.

Jan found a car hire company called Mike's opposite the airport so we would collect a car there and drive the two hours it took to get to Georgioupolis. And that way we would get to see more of the island so we sat back quite pleased with ourselves, as we now had a hotel, a flight and a hire car booked for the dates we required so we were all set.

But typical of me I started to worry over the following days that because Sofia didn't speak perfect English and I was a bit flustered when I made the call the dates might be wrong. There was a Greek Cypriot shop not far from where we lived that we visited most weeks as their produce reminded us of our holidays. We had got to know the lady owner very well so I suggested that if we paid for the call would she ring Sofia's Apartments for us and confirm our booking.

Jan gave me a bit of an old-fashioned look but said if it would put my mind at rest (or shut me up) it wouldn't do any harm, that is of course if the lady was willing to do it for us as it was a bit of a cheek. So on our next trip to the shop to get more goodies I explained the situation and asked if she added five pounds to the bill would she ring the hotel for us.

I had written all the details down before going to the shop and again in typical Greek kindness she rang the place, then confirmed our booking and wouldn't accept a penny for the call. It was springtime when that call was put through so I could now relax and look forward to our holiday and whatever spirit was planning for us when we got there.

I had been a healer for around five years by this time and although I had gained a lot of confidence in what I was doing, all my clients were friends of mine or Jan's so knew and understood how I worked, but I was starting to wonder how it would work in a foreign country with people I had never met before and didn't know what healing was or understand how it worked.

Jan was by then a fully qualified aromatherapy masseur and it was very evident to the client what was happening throughout their treatment because of the physical aspects of it, but unless a client could perceive the energies being used in healing it could appear to be a non-affective treatment where nothing has actually been done.

It was while having these thoughts that I hit on a brilliant idea that could give my healing sessions as much credibility as Jan's massage by introducing visual aspects to it. I have been fascinated by stones from early childhood and always had my eyes cast downwards scanning the ground for the next unusual pebble that would send my mind into another dimension.

These flights of fancy could last for hours or days as my mind conjured up stories of where the stone had come from and who had last handled it and for what purpose. My mind's eye could see everything from primitive cavemen gazing at its unusual colour and shape to wizards and witches using its magical properties to cast spells.

I had always been drawn to the myriad of crystals in the spiritual shops we visited and thought if I incorporated them into my healing it would give a physical aspect that people could relate to. That was the only reason I was going to use crystals and I had no concept at that time of just how potent or the level of cognition they contained.

Their strength and power were to be demonstrated to me one day in a very dramatic way that I have never forgotten and led me to gain a level of respect and awe that has only grown stronger over the years I've been using them. I was holding a newly acquired crystal one day that looked impressive and musing about how useful it could be for my idea for my healing sessions.

At that moment, it was as if someone had lit a match in the palm of my hand and the pain was that intense it made me throw the crystal across the room. There was a red mark in the palm of my hand where the crystal had been as if to confirm exactly what had caused the pain and it left an indelible mark in my consciousness.

I then purchased *The Crystal Bible* by Judy Hall and started to study what the crystals were that I already owned and what their healing properties were. I then started to use them in my healing sessions matching them to my client's requirements and was amazed at how the results improved dramatically. I was taught an invaluable lesson that day not to underestimate any mantic tool you might use in conjunction with your natural abilities.

A few years later took take a full diploma course with a respected college in crystal healing and because I had already been using them, I passed with a ninety-eight percent distinction. I would not now consider conducting any healing session without the appropriate crystals to help my clients, as they are a gift from mother earth infused with celestial energies that we can use to bring health and balance to everything and everyone on the planet.

Chapter 11
Proof in a Picture

Jan and I have been very fortunate to have become good friends with a gifted healer and teacher called Sheila Appleton who was later to play a very important role in my training. Sheila regularly held training sessions and ceremonies in outdoor locations and we were lucky enough to have two of a limited number of tickets to a full moon ceremony with her in a walled garden in Staplehurst.

When we arrived in the car park next to a gift shop, although it was starting to get dark it looked like a country estate. Once we had all arrived and assembled, it was twilight and Sheila led us along a path lined with shrubs and flowers towards a high wall. We then walked through a wooden gate into an enormous enclosed garden that looked typical of the style used on all the larger country mansions and in the fading light looked very well tended.

As instructed, we had all bought folding chairs and tea lights with us, Sheila arranged us in a large semicircle and as darkness stole the daylight away, we all lit our tea lights. As stars started to appear in the night sky, we were illuminated by these small candles, it looked and felt magical as if we were in a secret fairy grotto.

Over the next hour and a half, bathed in the light of the full moon we sang sacred songs and Sheila took us through guided meditations that honoured the lunar feminine aspects. I can remember being deeply affected by the energies that were generated in that wonderful garden and it was almost as if the rest of the world had melted away. We were all wrapped in jumpers and coats against the cold early spring night air. When we finished, our breath billowed foggy mists as we spoke of how we all felt like we had been transported to another realm or dimension, and I personally was very sorry when it ended.

We only spoke in whispers as we left the garden in reverence and respect for what we had just experienced and I think we all felt we had been joined by our friends from the higher realms. We made our way back to the gift shop that stayed open for these late night events for a very welcome hot cup of tea and to warm ourselves up in their heated cabin.

I was drawn to buy an ornament there, of two upright forearms with cupped hands that held a tea light that I still have that reminds me of that wonderful night. I consider myself fortunate to have had such inspirational teachers over the years, and each of them has influenced me in different ways and left impressions on my consciousness that have guided me to become who I am today.

I think we can all look back and see how certain people have impacted on and shaped our lives, but when that past is influenced by the spiritual realms everything becomes more intense and personal. When we are working spiritually, we can be dealing with people's hopes and fears, sometimes the challenges and tragedies they have had to deal with in their lives. I know my angels and guides are constantly by my side in all the work I do with people that cross my path. That also includes writing this book and I couldn't do any of it without their constant help and guidance.

We had bought a beautiful wooden massage couch in 2004 when Jan started her training to become a professional masseur. But it was very heavy and as I was doing more and more healing sessions, some of which were in friends' homes, we needed something lighter that I could lift in and out of the car. Jan had heard from a lady who she met on her massage course that there was a beauty exhibition at London's Excel Centre on the 6th of March where we could buy a lightweight couch at a discounted rate.

Although it was going to cost about a hundred pounds it would make life a lot easier for us, and if we were going to Crete earlier than expected it made sense to buy it now as it would probably cost more there. I had never been to an exhibition before and as all the therapies would be represented I was eager to go, and now I was a qualified healer I could go as a professional.

The Wainscott Centre also said if we could get a good price they would order two new couches to replace ones that had seen better days and were looking a bit tatty. I hate driving anywhere in London because of the volume of traffic and everyone knows where they're going except me. I had to go through the dreaded Blackwall Tunnel, but with calming words from Jan who knew the way and considerable help from upstairs we got there without too much trouble.

Although Jan was studying aromatherapy at the time, she had already qualified in Swedish massage so it felt good for us both to show our professional cards as we walked in. We met and talked to a lot of people as we walked around and it was good to see healing represented which gave me the opportunity to discuss how I worked.

We did find a lovely lightweight couch that I could lift easily and with a discount for buying at the exhibition, it cost less than we thought. We had no idea at that time how much use that couch was going to get, especially in Crete, between Jan's massage and my healing. We still have that trusty couch today, and as I am now seventy-one years of age I am very grateful we bought it with its lightweight aluminium frame.

A memory returned to me a short while ago of a wonderful lady who was introduced to me by another practitioner who thought I might be able to help. I can't remember exactly which year this took place but Miss J was already receiving treatment from my colleague and the medical profession for advanced spinal cancer and was very poorly indeed. She was a gifted artist and a talented potter but despite her many accomplishments and achievements, she had surrendered to this horrible disease.

Although I had enormous respect and admiration for this wonderful lady she thought that when you died that was the end so she had little faith in anything but the physical world. I wanted her to immerse herself in the help that the spirit world could give her both for the time she had left in this world, and for the ascension of her soul when the time came, and the knowledge that she would see family and friends again that had departed before her.

So if I was to stand any chance of helping her I had to change her mindset from that of a victim to a fighter. And due to the advanced nature of her condition I didn't have time for subtlety or a long protracted debate about the workings of the spiritual world, so I had to get her acceptance of my beliefs as quickly as possible.

My spiritual friends then gave me some challenging words to speak to her that I couldn't have the slightest inkling of the reaction they would generate. So on our first meeting when she had finished telling me about all her achievements in life, I said, "If you've accomplished all these things in life why did you allow yourself to get cancer?", She looked at me with daggers in her eyes and blustered something about there being many different types of cancer, but spirits were right because it certainly gave me her undivided attention which is exactly what I needed to expound my knowledge of what was to come.

For the next twenty minutes or so, my spirit friends spoke directly to her through me giving her lots of evidence of theirs and the heavenly realms existence in a manner that would make sense to her. At the end of this attestation, Miss J who was quite advanced in years was calm and relaxed enough for me to give her hands-on healing that gave her a little respite from the pain.

I saw this lovely lady around six times in all and each time we would talk in more depth about the spiritual realms, what it was like, and how you pass from this world to the next. As her acceptance of the reality of the spiritual realms grew so did the healing, it got stronger and more intense, which led to her pain and anguish easing reciprocally.

With all the other treatments Miss J was receiving, my contribution was little more than palliative care with hands-on healing, but I hope it went some way to ameliorate her condition for what little time she had left. She had a painting of an Easter Island statue in her kitchen and I was totally humbled when she said it reminded her of me because it looked so powerful.

I can't remember the last words she spoke to me after my final healing session, but I do remember the mischievous look she had in her eyes, and they must have indicated she was starting to accept there might be somewhere beautiful and glorious we go to when we depart this earthly life.

However, I do remember my reply as I looked at her saucily and said, "Careful what you say, you might prove me right." We then shared the most heartfelt hug as I wished her well, I never saw her again but as I said before I hope my small contribution made what time she had left on this earth a little more bearable.

I'm not sure of her exact age when I treated her but that was over ten years ago so I imagine Miss J is in the spiritual realms now. I know it's a fanciful thought on my part, but wouldn't it be wonderful if it was this remarkable lady herself who bought the memory back to me. I will find out one day when I return to the spiritual realms myself, but I sincerely hope that won't be for a good long while yet.

Through reading books and watching documentaries on television, there were two things that had captured my imagination and I long dreamt of taking part in. I had already realised one of these by participating in a Sacred Sweat Lodge, and now the second was soon going to become a reality as I had become friends with a Wiccan. Stonehenge sitting proudly on Salisbury Plain had been beckoning me for many years, but I wanted to experience it at the solstices attended by the Druid priests and priestesses, as it would have been by our ancestors in prehistory.

May is a Wiccan high priestess and had become a good friend through me attending some of her classes that are part of her Hedgewitch College course for people who want to learn her craft. I had told May about my dream to experience the summer solstice and as she attends the ceremonies every year she said that she would get me a ticket. It is difficult to express my elation and excitement when she handed me the ticket and realised, at last, it was actually going to happen. I still have the ticket in my memory box and looking at it now and again evokes wonderful memories of a magical day.

There were nearly two months to go but as I was doing shift work at the time I had already booked the day off work as I didn't want anything going wrong. We were taking my car as a thank you to May so it was booked in for a service as I wasn't going to leave anything to chance. The car would be filled up with petrol the day before because sunrise was around ten to five, so we would be on the road very early that morning in case there were any hold-ups on the way.

I know everyone reading this would have had a similar experience at some time in their lives where something that had so captivated their imagination was finally going to become a reality. I have always been interested in archaeology and it is incredible to think this monument was built around 5,000 years ago. It was erected in the Neolithic and Bronze Ages. Until a few years ago, the people who built this incredible structure were thought to be quite rudimentary and primitive.

I have always maintained, however, that people in all ages were just as intelligent and capable as we are now, and the only thing that has changed over that expanse of time is technology. Certain people think that because we have sophisticated machines and electronic gadgetry these days, we are somehow smarter than they were, but forgetting that all we have today is thanks to a progression of inventions and discoveries from the earliest of those times until the present day.

The day finally arrived, leaving Jan sleeping peacefully, I tip-toed out of the house to pick up my passengers, and then in total darkness, we set off for Stonehenge. May had been to a roadside café many times just a few miles from the monument where we could stop for a hot breakfast and a strong coffee before driving the last few miles.

As we arrived at Stonehenge's car park where everyone congregated before processing in for the ceremony, there were people everywhere as they greeted friends from all over the country. There were campervans and assorted vehicles where people had driven long distances and parked on roadsides along the way, so they could arrive there that morning and the costumes and robes some people had on were very impressive indeed.

We all got out of the car and May produced a long green cloak from her bag that she swung around her shoulders. This was just as impressive as the others in the light of lanterns some people carried. I was introduced to the leaders of the Druid Association who would be performing the ceremonies inside the stone circle.

I was having trouble containing my excitement, knowing this amazing monument that is known all over the world was just across the road from where we were standing. For me, it was an agonising wait while everyone arrived and got themselves organised ready to follow the druids under the road and onto the plain of dreams as I have heard it being called.

The head of the Druid Order was a very impressive looking figure in his white robes belted at the waist with a sash, and with an ornate torc on his head and carrying a staff I felt that he would have fitted in when the monument was new. I felt decidedly underdressed in my jeans and overcoat and stayed in the background, although I did have a forester hat which was similar to what others were wearing. The time finally came when the gates were unlocked and we started processing through the tunnel that runs under the road and up onto Salisbury Plain. Some of the leaders were approaching the monument by the time I stepped onto the path and the stones looked dark and forbidding as their lanterns picked them out in the cold eerie early morning stillness.

As I got closer to the Stone Circle, however, it lost its cold eerie look as the centre was now illuminated by countless lanterns and it took on a soft candlelit appearance that now looked warm and inviting. As I stepped off the path and onto the grass just a short distance now from the monument, I noticed that people were stopping between the huge sarsen stones to honour them and some were also touching them. My heart jumped as I saw this because I was going to get a chance to touch these two megaliths myself as I entered, which was something I thought I would never be allowed to do.

When my turn came, I stepped between the sarsens and placed my hands on them hoping that as a healer I would be able to detect the energy running under this sacred monument. It is said to be positioned at the juncture of fourteen Ley lines making it an energy portal and one of the strongest alignments in the country.

These energy lines were well known to the ancients and it is incredible how they were able to detect them over 5,000 years ago, and would explain why they built their sacred spiritual centre here. I was not disappointed because as I touched the sarsens I felt their energy run up my arms. And as I was starting to learn about and work with crystals, I was hoping that it might help me attune to the megaliths.

I followed May into the Stone Circle and we stood against the outer ring of stones waiting for everyone to file in and take their places before the ceremonies started. As the last ones came in and took their places the whole of the interior of the circle was illuminated, and I got a feel of how it must have looked and felt to our ancestors as they stood on the very same spot I was standing on now.

It was an incredibly awesome feeling to think of how many hundreds of different feet had stood on this very spot over the centuries this monument had been here. I can't remember all the different rituals that were performed before, during and after sunrise, but I can remember being impressed with the sincerity with which the ceremonies were performed, and how heartfelt the words were that everyone spoke.

I felt that all the speakers understood and comprehended the significance of what they were saying, and that combined with where we were standing resonated with something deep within my soul. I could now understand why people flock here every year as something very personal, as well as collective, happens at these gatherings of likeminded people carrying on a consummation that transcends time itself.

As the ceremonies were coming to a close, I leant back against a huge upright stone of the outer circle and it was as if I could feel the people who built and used this sacred site. I can't remember how long I stood there in a trance-like state, but I became aware that people were starting to leave and I joined May and her friends as we walked around the outside of the Stone Circle taking photos.

Finally, we joined everyone else as they made their way to the underground tunnel and out to where the café offered a very welcome cup of steaming hot tea and a bite to eat. Before we returned to the car park, we crossed the road to take photos of the monument in full glorious sunshine, and the stones seemed to stand out from the landscape as if proudly showing themselves off.

I will be forever grateful to May for giving me the opportunity to take part in this time honoured ceremony as spaces and tickets are strictly limited. But I had one last surprise coming that would clearly show the significance of this monument and its location, if that is, I really needed it after being so moved by the whole experience.

The next time I saw May we had all had our photos of Stonehenge developed and I had a lovely long distance shot of the monument. But when May showed me her photo of Stonehenge taken right next to where I had stood at the fence with one of the new digital cameras, there were two bright colourful energy crescents one above the other over the entire structure. If this doesn't show clearly the power of the conjunction of Ley lines converging under Stonehenge then I don't think anything else could sway sceptical minds.

Jan and I said we would just get on with our lives after Lorrain's reading and leave the arrangements and details to Dad and our helpers in the spirit realms, but this was proving more difficult for me as the weeks passed. All sorts of questions were popping into my head and each one made it appear more unlikely it could happen earlier than planned, and what were we going to tell our five children if it did happen. It hadn't seemed so important earlier in the year but now that we had booked our holiday from the 5th to the 19th of September I was getting more jittery as our holiday approached.

We couldn't go on like this as I was getting a bit paranoid and thinking of calling the whole thing off, so we went to see Heather who as well as being a friend and a medium had now become a trusted confidant. Over a relaxing cup of tea, we explained my worries and how I was feeling and the fact that I was thinking of calling the whole thing off because I was getting to the point where I couldn't cope.

Heather had been there when I received the reading from Lorraine and had also picked up some of the message intuitively herself so we thought she would be the best person to talk to. She explained that our spirit friends would never give us anything we couldn't cope with and never put us in a situation that was detrimental or damaging to us.

It sounded the way Heather explained it as if we couldn't go wrong and that it was all planned out for us, so all we had to do was go through the motions. The trouble was we didn't yet know what those motions were and we would be 2,000 miles away on our own when we found out, but obviously, Jan was a lot more relaxed about it than I was.

The trouble was, as I said before, I hadn't been abroad until I was fifty-three and saw all sorts of problems whereas Jan had done all this before, and encountered and sorted all the problems out on her own so how lucky was I to have such a woman walking by my side.

So reassured by Heather I tried to keep calm and just go with the flow and see how it all panned out. I think secretly Jan thought it was a bit like going home as she had loved her time while working in Greece, and I had fallen in love with a similar culture in Cyprus.

It sounded like we were going to have an adventure, and come what may we would not be doing it on our own as we had our spirit friends walking by our side all the way. If I had known then all the wonderful things that were going to happen to us, and all the wonderful people we were going to meet and work with on this adventure, I think I would have wanted to go even earlier.

Chapter 12
Taking the First Step

Our holiday this year wouldn't be like any other holiday we'd had before on the island of Crete, or anywhere else for that matter, and would prove to be life-changing. We were flying into an airport and an area we had never been to before that was a two-hour drive away from where we wanted to stay.

Heraklion Airport was much larger than Hania and after clearing customs and collecting our luggage Jan and I made our way out of the arrivals lounge. As there would be no transfer coach for us on this trip, luckily, Mike's Car Hire could be seen easily from our side of the main road as a big sign marked its entrance. So all we had to do now was run the gauntlet of crossing the busy main road carrying shoulder bags and dragging our heavy cases.

There were lots of people trying to do the same thing as us and once there was a gap in the traffic a small army would make a dash for the other side. A few people like us were caught out because they drive on the right-hand side of the road in Crete, and to us, everyone was coming from the wrong direction and we weren't spring chickens anymore.

Eventually, there was a break in the traffic big enough for us to make our way to the safety of the opposite pavement and the entrance to the car hire company. Getting the car was relatively easy as we'd booked it online so passports proved who we were, but we had to drive a mile into the city to fill it up with petrol before we could get onto the highway.

Once we eventually drove onto the highway, we just had to stay on it until we got to Georgioupolis, but it was nothing like an English motorway. With its twists and turns, it was more like an A road but the view of the Mediterranean Sea on our right-hand side were stunning, as were the flower-festooned hedges on the way.

But the mountain about a third of the way there reduced our poor little hire car to second gear on the way up, and I think I must have melted the brakes on the steep two-mile run down the other side with the ninety degree bends making the descent even more dramatic.

I lost count of how many villages and fruit stalls we passed on the way as you don't bypass these as the English motorways do. We were both very pleased to see the sign for Georgioupolis when it finally came into sight, and all we had to do now was find the hotel as I couldn't wait to get out of the car and stretch my legs.

The resort didn't look very big on the map so we decided to park the car and walk around till we found Sofia's Apartments. We had gone less than a hundred yards when we came to a fork in the road and looking back along the road that branched off we saw their sign just a short distance from where we stood. As the hotel was so close and the car safely parked we wheeled the cases the short distance.

Sofia and her husband ran a small hotel and were very welcoming when we arrived. Sofia showed us to our room on the second floor where we could see the deep blue Mediterranean Sea, looking in the other direction we could see a café on the opposite side of the road from the hotel, whose delicious-looking cakes had not gone unnoticed as we walked into the hotel.

Having changed into something more suitable for the mid-thirties temperature, now in our holiday clothes we headed for the café for a much-needed coffee and a sandwich as we hadn't eaten since we left Gatwick Airport that morning.

The young lady spoke very good English and made me a coffee just the way I like it, and the toasted cheese sandwich was devoured with much gusto, while Jan, being a lady, sipped her orange juice and ate her cake in small polite pieces as we relaxed and watched the world go by.

Suitably refreshed and rested, Jan and I were keen to explore the village to find somewhere nice to have our evening meal, and locate the shops for our supplies as we had formed a habit on our Greek holidays of buying all the fresh fruit we could find and then I would cut it up for breakfast with fresh bread and butter.

This was a luxury we never had time for with our busy working lives at home, and besides most of the fruit had been harvested just a few days before from surrounding farms. Walking into Georgioupolis village square we both just stood and stared as it was so beautiful and we both said at the same time, "I want to live somewhere around here."

The village was busy with tourists and obviously very popular with people of all ages and with many different languages from

European countries and beyond, it must be well known. Whoever put that thought into Jan's mind in Asda's car park knew exactly what they were doing because this is what we had been dreaming of, and it would be a lovely place for our families to visit if we moved here.

There were three estate agents in the village and looking in their windows there wasn't much in our price range but time was getting on so we would talk to them tomorrow. There was a small but well-stocked shop in the square where we bought water and snacky bits if we got hungry between meals, and all the fresh fruit I could carry back to the hotel.

We had picked a nice little taverna for dinner that evening so laden with our goodies we made our way back to the hotel to get showered and while away some time on the balcony. Jan to read and me to dose and dream of things that might be if it was our destiny to move to this pretty little village.

I liked to have locally made moussaka on my first night in Crete because that confirmed to my inner being that I was really in Greece. Jan had a similar thing with gyros and as we shared a carafe of local white wine we allowed the atmosphere to wash over us and immerse us in the Greek culture.

After a delicious breakfast of chopped fruit in the morning, Jan and I decided to check out the three estate agents before heading off in the car to explore the area. The first two were very polite and sympathetic to our dream of a healing retreat but said they had nothing on their books for the funds we had available.

We walked past the smallest of the three estate agents on our way back to the hotel but it was shut but as the other two were open we thought this one might have closed down. So after collecting what we needed from our room, we set off in the car to explore the local countryside to see if there was anywhere we liked the look of and maybe find another estate agent.

Driving through Georgioupolis square we made our way down a short hill and turned left over a bridge on which we stopped to take photos of the fishing harbour. We then drove out through olive groves and after a steady climb and three hairpin bends, we stopped at the side of the road, because stretched out before us was the five miles of curving beach that ran from Georgioupolis to Kavros. It was a stunning view and we were to find out later that all the coach trips stopped at this very spot so tourists could take photos of the number one beach in Crete.

We were mesmerised by the sheer beauty of the vista before us that took in Mount Ida the highest mountain on the island whose summit was still shrouded in early morning clouds. After taking our own photos to show friends back home, we carried on driving through more olive groves with houses dotted here and there along the way, and people working in isolated fields tending their crops.

We then drove through two villages with names we couldn't pronounce and little did we know at the time that one of them was where we would find our traditional Greek stone house and ultimately, our healing retreat.

As we drove past the second village climbing steadily, we came around a corner on a road that was cut into the hillside and stretched out before us was a long lush valley. It looked as if a giant had scooped it out with a huge spoon and again we stopped the car and feasted our eyes on what was a dramatic awe-inspiring landscape.

We both instantly fell in love with this panorama laid out before us and although we had seen the White Mountains before, from our current vantage point they looked beautiful and almost close enough to reach out and touch. We found a lovely little café on our travels where we had a Greek salad which had become a favourite of ours for a midday break, and for the first time on all our holidays in different locations on the island of Crete, we felt we had now found what we were looking for.

We both felt joyous that day as we made our way back to the hotel along the highway that stretches almost the entire length of the island. So all we had to do now was find an estate agent with the right property at the right price in the right location, but we weren't going to let a little thing like that worry us on such a wonderful day as this. We felt all the predictions we had been given were starting to manifest themselves so we felt confident everything would be taken care of.

We also felt for the first time on our Cretan trips that our guides and angels and my dad were with us as the air was full of promise and possibilities. As we relaxed with refreshments back in Georgioupolis square we talked about what Heather and all the other mediums had told us. And if this was all being planned out for us and was meant to be, then someone not a million miles from where we were sitting right now had to have all the answers we were looking for.

We had a wonderful meal that evening in the most expensive taverna in the village and I think I got a little squiffy, as Jan had to help me up the stairs to our room while trying to stop me from giggling like an irrepressible child. We would start anew tomorrow checking out all the estate agents in the villages in the area until we found one who had the right property that we could afford.

After our customary breakfast of fruit and fresh bread, we had to walk into the village to get some money from the bank and stock up on supplies. We passed the small estate agent on the way and once again it was shut so as we thought it must have closed despite displaying properties for sale. We had picked out five places from our map to try and would gradually widen our search until we found what we wanted.

But despite all the agents being sympathetic to our dream none could help us and one man in a posh-looking shop actually laughed at us and told us we should forget the idea and go home. Looking at his establishment I suppose we should have known better but I was working on the premise of leaving no stone unturned and not prejudging.

I was bought up on the philosophy that if you believe in what you are doing then you shouldn't give up just because the going gets tough. So we would cross him off our Christmas card list and keep looking because we had been told through countless mediums over the last eighteen months that what we wanted to do wasn't just possible but almost preordained.

So after one more visit to an agent a few doors down on the same street, we wrapped it up for the day and made our way back to the Sweet House in Georgioupolis square, which had become a favourite watering hole for our afternoon refreshments, mainly because it sold the most amazing cakes. For me with a confirmed sweet tooth, this place was heaven with its sticky gooey creations washed down with a Greek beer. It was about as good as it gets and guaranteed to lift me out of any mood I'd got myself into.

After a nice meal that evening and a good night's sleep, we would head off in the other direction tomorrow and start at a place called Kournas where they have the only freshwater lake on the island. After trying several places in the area with the same results as the day before we ended up at the lake itself.

Sitting at the base of an enormous hill, it was stunning with all manner of waterfowl and with families in pedalos enjoying themselves it was a lovely place to have lunch. Towards the middle of the afternoon, we made our way back to the comfort of the Sweet House to watch the world go by, and once again passing the small estate agents it was shut as it had been every day since we arrived.

On the fourth day after a leisurely breakfast, we wandered into the village with some goodies in a bag as there was no searching for us today. We were going to the beach for a lazy day but as we passed the little estate agents low and behold it was open, with a man and a woman sitting at a desk looking at some papers.

Jan said, "Oh good, I've had a good feeling about this place all along." But I pulled a face and said, "No, I've got the hump now. They've been shut all week. I'm going to the beach, it can wait." But Jan insisted and headed for the door so I reluctantly plodded into the shop behind her with a look on my face that said I wanted to be anywhere but here.

Despite my grumpiness, we were given a warm welcome by the man who was obviously Greek but spoke very good English and explained he had spent twenty-six years in America doing construction work. After the formalities, we trotted out our story once again expecting the same kind of polite rejection we had received from everybody else.

But we were surprised when far from rejecting our idea he started asking questions about what we had done up until then and what we hoped to achieve in Crete. He seemed impressed with what we wanted to create in his homeland and told us he was also spiritual and had built a monastic cell in his back garden, where he regularly spent time praying and meditating and said it helped him in his everyday life as well as his work.

Once again Jan's intuition had been proved right so I launched into my story about all the healing work we had done in England and how we had been guided to Crete by our friends and my father in the spirit world.

I was very upfront with him about how little money we had compared to most people who had moved here, but he said although he had nothing suitable at that time he would endeavour to find us something in the coming months.

I think he was impressed that unlike some who just want a lazy lifestyle in the sun, we were on a mission to do good work through our healing skills. So with many heartfelt thanks, we exchanged details and he promised to email us in England when he had found somewhere that would suit our needs at a price we could afford.

The rest of that day was the best we had experienced on all our visits to Crete because the predictions seemed as if they might have started to come true. On our trips thus far, we had seen many nice houses that we couldn't afford as well as many ruins that were well past our budget to turn into a liveable dwelling. So naturally we started to wonder just exactly what we would get for the small amount of money we had, but as we had always done we handed the whole thing over to our friends upstairs and waited to see what would transpire.

As it would turn out it wasn't going to be very long before we found out but for now we would enjoy the rest of our holiday sightseeing and sunbathing, sure in the knowledge that at last something was happening and that the last two years of searching hadn't been a total waste of time as it had led us to this beautiful fishing village.

The man and the lady, who we found out later was his wife, were in the shop two more times as we passed by before we had to return to England. And each time we were invited in for a coffee and a chat and each time we talked in more depth about our healing work and the people we had worked with. There was no mistaking how spiritual this man was and he seemed to have a genuine desire to learn more about how we worked and how people could be helped.

On our return to England, we excitedly told Heather and the others at the centre what had happened with the small estate agent in Georgioupolis promising to find somewhere for us. Jan and I also had long serious conversations about our future at this time because I had been given a course of injections through my Haemophilia treatment that had made me seriously ill. I hadn't felt quite right ever since and it was making my job more difficult as time went on and I was starting to worry about the future.

Jan was also suffering in her job from continual changes that were eroding her responsibilities, running a staff canteen that was making it more difficult and stressful. We were both feeling exhausted and added to this was the growing forecast that there was going to be a major financial collapse of the banking industry that would affect everything from investments to property.

I had a private pension that was held in stocks and shares and Jan had a shared ownership agreement for the house we were living in so we could be seriously affected by a collapse. Consequently, we had many in-depth conversations about the growing situation and realised we could be a lot worse off if we worked for another five years until our official retirement age.

My dad had been a very shrewd man in his earthly life when it came to financial matters, so now from his position in the spirit world could he see future events that might adversely affect us. If so, is this why he said we would be moving to Crete earlier than we thought to avoid any detrimental impact on our finances? It would not be until the summer of 2008 that we would know the full implications of Dad's prediction and why he urged us to move earlier than planned.

As it transpired, my pension would have been decimated had I left it where it was and been of no practical help to us in our retirement, and Jan's house would only be worth around half the value she sold it for after the crash. So how lucky were we to have such good advice from the spirit world that allowed us to retain the integrity of our finances and live on a beautiful island like Crete.

The final piece of information that sealed our intent came in early November when the estate agent emailed us to say they had found us a suitable property that didn't need much doing to it and was within our budget. They wanted us to go out as soon as possible and view the property to make a decision. So now all we had to do was tell our families what we had been planning, and the way things were shaping up we could be going as early as next year which was not how either of us wanted to handle it.

At this point, it would have been nice if we could have told everyone earlier but everything had been down to personal interpretation and nothing had been set in stone. We didn't get Dad's final message until the summer of 2006 and neither of us expected things to happen this quick, but now things had overtaken us so to speak and it would be very unfair to leave it any longer before telling everyone.

I will not go into detail about us telling our families as it is private and personal, and suffice to say, it all turned out right in the end. Jan and I are both blessed with families that gained an understanding of why we made the choices we did, so we could fulfil a mission close to our hearts that would eventually help so many people.

At this stage, we still couldn't be sure things would work out so Jan and I were both respectful of our employers and enquired when we would be able to take a holiday. Luckily, nobody wanted time off early in the year so we both booked a week off in the middle of April 2007, which meant we would have to wait nearly six months before we would get to see the property, and after everything had happened so fast up until then it would feel like we were in limbo.

Until then we would just carry on as normal as if nothing had changed which was not going to be easy considering everything that had happened in the last few months. But needless to say, within a few weeks we had settled back into our routine of working and Sundays at the Wainscott Centre, and although things were back to normal in our everyday lives, Crete was never far from our thoughts.

Our friends at the centre had witnessed all the messages we had received in the two years up until then, and some like Heather had given them to us directly. There was lots of excited talk about who would come out and visit us once we were up and running, and I know there were some who believed it would happen even more than we did.

It's always interesting when you reach a certain age to reflect on what you have achieved in your life and then approaching my sixtieth birthday, I found myself thinking about what opportunities I hadn't been brave enough to attempt. There was a lot riding on our proposed move to Crete, and a lot we could accomplish if all the messages we had received through the various mediums were correct.

But still from somewhere deep inside me was a nagging doubt that somehow I had got it all wrong and that I was risking everything, even my new found happiness with Jan on a fool's errand. I didn't discuss these deep-seated concerns at the time with her because she had enough on her plate with equal shares of the planning, but without a doubt, she was the steadying influence at my side that gave me the confidence to carry on.

It's only at times like these if you have the right partner beside you that you realise how wonderfully supportive and reassuring it is to have such a person walking with you in this challenging existence we call life. So I tried to suppress all these feelings of doubt and just let events unfold as they were meant to sure in the knowledge that this capable intelligent woman would tell me if she ever thought this dream could not become a reality.

We emailed the estate agent in Georgioupolis with the dates of our trip in April and asked them to hold the property until we had a chance to view it which they agreed to do. We were in for a surprise, however, because when we finally announced our plans to the family both Jan's mother and mine wanted to come out with us to see the property. We told ourselves that they were just doing their motherly thing and looking out for us, and as they had both lost their husbands it was a chance for a holiday before they got too old.

As Christmas approached, Jan and I thought we would like to have as much of the family together as possible, so we invited our children and their families to Christmas dinner. It's not often in this busy life we have the chance to get everyone together and it would give them the opportunity to talk about our April trip.

Although our plans seemed to be in an advanced stage there was no way we could predict the final outcome because nothing had happened to give us an indication it might be possible. So for the time being everyone assumed it would not happen until we retired in five years time, and nobody knew how heavily involved I was in healing and how passionate we were about helping people, although everyone knew how good Jan was at massage.

I had received some friendly ribbing for thinking I had healing hands but we had never discussed the extent of the work we had done up till then, partly because I have never been one to blow my own trumpet and partly because the treatments can be about personal matters and I have to consider client confidentiality.

Hindsight is a wonderful thing and if we had known then what we know now we would have been more open about what we were planning. But from our perspective, at the time it looked almost impossible and it could have upset everyone for nothing if it all fell through in the end. Not to mention egg on face for me.

But we reckoned without what must have been a miracle that shifted heaven and earth to make it possible for us both to retire early, which would see our little Greek stone house turn into a healing centre, where we would teach psychic development courses that I would spend three years writing, and without the restraints of working for a living would see us study and grow and develop as healers and teachers at a rate impossible if we had stayed in the UK.

So without knowing it at the time that Christmas dinner with the family would be the last one for a long time as our spirit friends had only told us about going one way. Nothing had ever been mentioned in any of the messages about us coming back, so at the time we thought we would grow old and die and be buried there, but of course, spirit only ever tell you what you need to know at that time in your life.

I've always been impatient and wanted to know everything all at once, but if all the information about our Greek odyssey had been given to me at the beginning would it have turned into the success it eventually became. I think my dad and the rest of my guides knew exactly what they were doing drip feeding me only what I needed to know to complete each stage of the journey.

Chapter 13
Finding Our Stone Arch

It had been a long anxious wait for Jan and myself, but now the time was fast approaching when we would be flying out to see the property we were told about in the email last November. We had spoken about it a few times since our return from Crete and although we had spoken to the family about it, I don't think anyone thought we would really go through with it so it wasn't expected to happen, and certainly not yet.

I must admit that as the months had passed my jubilation was starting to fade and I was having second thoughts as to how practical this venture was. But as if on cue we got another message at the Wainscott Centre from my dad saying, "Just keep going. Everything will turn out alright," which was backed up by Heather, so with a deep breath Jan and I swung into action and organised the flights for ourselves and our mums.

As neither of our mums could walk very far, we had to arrange for them to be transported to the departure lounge by one of those little electric trucks that always beep behind you in the corridors. Then while we joined the other passengers in the departure lounge they were elevated up to the plane with a scissor lift that made them both feel quite special.

Jan's mum had travelled extensively by plane throughout Europe so was used to air travel, but this was my mum's first trip ever on a plane so at eighty-nine years old she was understandably a little nervous. And as she was the oldest person travelling on that flight she got a mention from the pilot that made her day and made her forget her nerves. Like myself a few years before, Mum found the airport a wondrous place with all the shops and restaurants and people from every corner of the globe coming and going to and from exotic sounding places.

I don't know what Mum was expecting but once seated in the aircraft she was surprised how small and compact it was and how it could possibly take off and fly with all these people in it. To take her mind off this and any nerves she might have left, I tried to explain the workings of the jet engines, their enormous power and reliability, and having worked in factories during the war building bomber aircraft with piston engines she grasped the idea surprisingly quickly.

Her face, however, showed that she wasn't expecting to get pinned to the back of her seat when the plane accelerated down the runway at a ferocious speed that seemed to defy the laws of physics. Mum had the window seat and leaving terra firma for the first time was scary, but once we had climbed above the clouds, she was fascinated that it looked as if you could get out and walk on them.

When later the clouds cleared and the Alps could be seen in all their glory, it was the most excited I think I have ever seen her. Like myself, Mum had seen the Alps many times in books and on television, but to look down and see them stretched out beneath you from thirty-five thousand feet is an unrivalled experience you never forget.

Although Jan's mum and dad had travelled throughout Europe before his illness and subsequent passing, they had never been to Greece or its islands so this was a new experience for her as well as my mum. It was clear to see the excitement on Mum's face as the island of Crete came into view as the plane banked around and prepared to land. I think she was relieved to see land again and the thought of stepping onto foreign soil for the first time gave her childlike excitement.

Because they were lifted into the plane we were all sitting right at the front and when the door was opened, warm herb-scented air wafted in to greet us. Mum had never seen sunlight as bright as it is in Crete and it was a few moments before her reactor light glasses darkened enough for her to have a look around without squinting. There is nothing in the English landscape to compare with the Mediterranean countries, and she was fascinated with the stark beauty that had enchanted me years before when I visited Cyprus.

As with our previous trip, we had to pick our hire car up from Mike's opposite the airport, but because of the busy road, we left our mums sitting by the pavement outside the airport while we collected the car. Having got our mums and all of the luggage in a much larger car than before, we once again headed into Heraklion to fill it with petrol before our two-hour trip to Georgioupolis. Sofia had been quite excited when we rang her a few months before to book two rooms for us and our mums as the Greek people are very family orientated and love to see everyone together.

We stopped a couple of times on the way at places we spotted on our previous trip so they could have a break and an orange juice and take in the views. Subsequently, it was a little later than planned when we pulled into the forecourt of Sofia's Apartments to be greeted with profuse handshakes and hugs. We had also bought both mums' three-wheeled walkers with us so after getting freshened up and changed, we took a slow walk into the village for something to eat and show them the square.

The lady in the Sweet House remembered us and made a big fuss of our mums and sat them in the shade where they could observe the entire square. It was at the start of their tourist season and not as busy as it had been in September, but there were enough people and things going on to keep them interested in the local life around us.

The delectable little cakes were a big hit with both mums and we had two each, washed down with a coffee for me and Jan's mum and freshly squeezed orange juice for Mum and Jan. We had already decided to take the two mums to the best taverna where we had celebrated finding the estate agent who could help make our dreams come true.

I can't remember what we all had to eat that night but it was a wonderful evening with delicious food, and we all got a little tipsy on local wine while exchanging stories of previous holidays. Both mums fell in love with the square and could see how it had captivated us the year before, and at night, the lights in the square made it twinkle like a fairyland making a lovely end to the evening.

We had arranged to meet the builder at ten o'clock at his office the following morning, so after breakfast at the café across the road from Sofia's, we made our way into the village. True to his word, the builder was waiting in his office and made us all a drink as he chatted to our mums. We hadn't told him they were coming to see the house with us and he took a little time to tell them about the village.

After the pleasantries, we followed him in our hire car on the same route we had taken in September and were surprised when he turned left into the first village we had driven past. We laughed at the time at not being able to pronounce its name and now we were fascinated to be driving through its narrow streets.

We had only gone a short distance when he pulled up in a driveway opposite a small church and graveyard which made Jan and I look at each other a bit dubiously. He got out of his car and pointed to the wall beside the driveway that must have stood at least twelve feet tall and said, "This is the wall around the garden." As the wall was so high we couldn't see anything and wondered where the house was because this looked more like a prison.

But the builder explained they don't do anything to a house in Crete until someone says they want to buy it so it had been left untouched since it was last occupied. We were going to have to use our imagination to picture what it would look like when it had been restored to its former glory, which made us apprehensive as to what was coming next.

He led us along the side of the wall which after a short distance lowered to about eight feet with large overgrown trees hanging over it. He stopped outside a pair of old rusty gates and said, "This leads into the courtyard and garden," but all I could see through the gates was what looked like a jungle and no sign of a house.

We said to our mums, "You'd best stay here for the moment." The builder pushed open the gates and we followed him up a narrow path as he made his way through the undergrowth. Eventually, we arrived at the wall of the house which was dingy and dirty with bits of plaster broken off here and there.

As we stood outside an old rusty door, he explained that he hadn't been able to open it but we could look in through the window if we pushed open the rusty shutters. Having fought with the hinges for a few minutes Jan and I could see the ceiling had fallen down exposing what looked like tree trunks holding up wooden slats that presumably held up the roof. There were brown water stains all down the plastered walls showing that the roof leaked badly so we were not impressed at this stage but kept that to ourselves.

Pushing on through the waist-high weeds we made our way to the end of the building where there were no windows that we could see from where we stood. Only old, battered, unpainted double wooden doors with metal hinges that looked as if they had long since given up any hope of supporting them.

With considerable effort, the builder pushed open the left-hand door with his shoulder to reveal a murky blackness that was dark and eerie looking, and a smell that was comparable to a damp cave that something unsavoury had been living in that you wouldn't want to come face to face with.

As Jan and I peered cautiously over his shoulder, the builder shone a torch into the darkness. At that very moment, a bat chose to escape the intrusion into its private domain and flew out so close to Jan's head its wings tussled her hair. With a flailing of hands and a high-pitched voice, Jan shouted, "I'm not living here," and beat a hasty retreat to the two mums who were waiting outside the gate.

To say the builder had a dejected look on his face would be the understatement of the century, but whatever he was about to say it was too late, Jan had already gone. "Well, I might as well show you the rest of it while you're here," he said trying to recover what was left of what for him might turn out to be a wasted day.

He pushed open the second door to let in more light and as our eyes adjusted to the gloom and aided by his torch we were able to make out the features in the room. Over in the far right-hand corner was a large walk-in fireplace with an old-fashioned, honey-combed bread oven, as the builder removed the metal screen door we could see it was still intact from the day it last baked bread.

To the left was a low-walled structure that took up at least a third of the room that he explained was a huge bath like construction, where large amounts of grapes were put to be trodden by the family to extract the juice for winemaking.

The rest of the room was filled with old rickety tables and chairs and although the house had been empty and abandoned for over twenty-five years, there were several bottles of wine that had been left on shelves that had presumably come from the last batch made here.

There was an overall feeling in the place that some tragedy had happened here that had caused everyone to just walk out leaving everything behind without a second thought. There were even articles of clothing on what was now a filthy dust laden bed with slippers tucked under it as if someone had kicked them off and walked out never to return. As a psychic, I could feel the sadness in the room and we later found a grave in the cemetery opposite of the man who lived there and tragically died at quite a young age.

We can only postulate that he had no family who wanted to take over his business so it closed down with his passing and had lain abandoned ever since. That bread oven is now painted white and sits proudly as one of the main features of the house and everyone who visits falls in love with it.

Closing the doors on this sad scene, we made our way to the other end of the building where I was shown a self-contained annexe, as the builder pushed open the old aluminium door it revealed a small kitchen with a sink now full of undesirable matter and all manner of dead bugs.

On the far wall was a plastic covered worktop on which were assorted pots and pans and a sort of camping gas stove still connected to a gas bottle that was supporting it and preventing its total collapse. But the most poignant thing we saw on a shelf above the worktop was a picture frame displaying a faded photo of the owner that kept us both in deep thought for a while.

Seeing this, it must have been the part of the house in which he lived while the rest of the building was for producing wine. To the left through a small doorway was a small bathroom and toilet, and to the right was a modest-sized room with a bed and an assortment of furniture that was his main living area.

After showing me what could be seen of the garden that extended around the side of the annexe we joined the two mums. We found Jan telling them of her experiences with the local wildlife. Although Jan said she could never live in a place like this, the builder explained that the bat would leave as soon as they started working on the house, and a good-sized window would let in enough light to illuminate what would become our kitchen. The room had always been a working facility that explained its drab appearance, but once the room had been plastered and painted to cover up the bare soot-stained walls, it would look bright and cheerful.

As the builder was explaining all this I looked back through the old rusty gates and my eyes were drawn to something above them that made me draw in a breath of amazement. There sitting proudly above the stone pillars that supported the gates was an old but beautifully carved stone arch looking regal bathed in the bright midday sun.

As I stood there staring at this old stone arch sitting majestically above the old metal gates, a melancholy warmth permeated throughout my body that I knew well. It was my dad's energy and at the same time, Heather's words flooded back into my mind and I couldn't have had a clearer sign if I had been hit over the head with a mallet. Without thinking, I just blurted out, "We'll have it," and both the builder and Jan turned to face me with astonished looks on their faces. The builder in total surprise after what had been said by the wooden doors, and Jan in total horror at the prospect of living here and both presumably relating to the incident with the bat.

As Jan stared at me incomprehensibly I just pointed to the arch and although it was a few moments before the penny dropped, the look of horror was slowly replaced with a knowing grin that told me all I needed to know. As far as I know, those gates still hang there to this day as we felt their part green paint and part rust have that classic Greek charm about them which is so typical of the country.

We didn't tell the builder about Heather's prediction until the sale was completed because if he knew it was preordained he might have increased the price. When we did tell him what Heather had said, he was fascinated and wanted to know more which led to us becoming good friends with him and his family.

The old house had stood empty and unloved for so long and was so overgrown that it now resembled one of those old temples that are stumbled upon in faraway jungles. But as with everything else that had happened in my life since that fateful day in the damp mouldy flat I knew this old house could be turned into our home and eventually our healing centre.

Although if I'd have known then how much physical work I would have to do to achieve that dream I might have changed my mind and searched for somewhere already restored. Although I have to admit now that I enjoyed all the work I put into creating a raised ornamental garden and clearing the side garden to make a growing area.

After we agreed the house would be suitable for our needs, the rest of the day was a bit of a blur as we were whisked off to the nearby city of Hania. First to the tax office to get tax numbers as you can't buy anything like a house or car until you have the right papers from the appropriate authorities.

Then to the lawyer's office to arrange checks of ownership on the property and draw up the necessary papers in our names once all the background checks had been done. On the way back from Hania, the builder showed us some places of interest that we might like to visit and chatted to our mums about what they thought of the island.

All the checks could take a few months and no money would change hands until everything had been thoroughly investigated just in case somebody objected to the sale. Back in the builder's office, we finalised our business for the time being and he would let us know by email when all the checks had been completed and we could go ahead with the purchase.

Sitting relaxing over our evening meal we all reflected on the events of the day and how Jan's mum had insisted despite her age on going into the garden to take photos for posterity. But the most amazing part of that day for Jan and myself was when I had looked back through the gates and spotted the stone arch sitting there almost glowing in the sun as if to say, "Look at me, look at me."

I think my heart skipped a beat when I realised Heather's prediction had come true and I couldn't wait to go back home and tell her. Nobody outside the Wainscott Centre knew about this prediction so Jan and I had to be content to keep it to ourselves until we got home to share it with them. I also wondered how long it would have taken us to find a house there if it hadn't been for Jan being inspired to pick Georgioupolis from the map in Asda's car park.

It had all come together very neatly over the past few years with messages from spirit, but it's thought-provoking to think who organised all this and how far into the future could they see to plan this incredible finality.

The following day we took our two mums through our sister village of Kalamitsi Alexandrou on our way to the small town of Vrisses, where we were to have our lunch alongside a torrent of meltwater from the White Mountains. Driving through Alexandrou, Jan's mum suddenly asked me to stop next to an old stone house that had sadly tumbled down into nothing more than a pile of rubble.

When she got out of the car and took several photos of the pile of rubble, we thought she had spotted something quaint and charming about it and wanted to keep it as a memory of her holiday.

It wasn't until some weeks later we found out that she had shown the pictures to Jan's brother and convinced him that this was what we had invested our life's savings on. Naturally, he was upset and somewhat perplexed and rang Jan to ask what on earth we'd wasted our money on as it would cost a small fortune to turn that pile of rubble back into a house. When Jan said that she didn't know what he was talking about her mum came clean and admitted it was a hoax and nowhere near the house that we had bought.

As you can gather, Mummsy, as I affectionately called her, was quite a character and it was the saddest of days to the entire family when we lost her on the 1st of November 2009. She recounted a story a couple of years before at a family gathering of how while sitting thinking one evening she realised she had never been drunk in her entire life. So at the grand old age of seventy-nine, she locked herself in her house to stop herself from doing anything silly and drank the entire contents of a bottle of apricot brandy.

She had a stair lift fitted some months before because she was finding it increasingly difficult to get upstairs, so imagine her surprise when she woke up the following morning fully dressed lying on top of her bed. She had no recollection of how she got up the stairs as when she checked the stair lift was still at the bottom of the stairs by the front door, so it was a good thing that she had a remote control on the landing. We all miss her terribly and the stories she used to tell of her very accomplished and colourful life, and I'm sure she's looking down and having a giggle at me telling this story.

We all had a lovely lunch that day listening to the ice-cold water cascading through the culvert on its way from the White Mountains to the Mediterranean Sea. For the rest of our weeks holiday, we took our two mums to as many places as we could including a waterside café in Hania Harbour, where we all had cocktails whilst watching the glass-bottomed boats coming and going filled each time with eager tourists exploring the crystal clear waters.

I have an enduring memory of my mother sauntering down the harbour footpath a little tipsy and oblivious to all that was going on around her. She was eighty-nine years old at the time and I would like to think her first holiday in a foreign country left her with lovely memories for the rest of her life.

On our last day, we said goodbye to Sofia who made a real fuss of our mums and made our way back to Heraklion Airport for the start of our homeward journey, flying back to England.

I was thinking we might have found our stone arch and started to fulfil what we had both felt was our destiny given to us by our spirit friends. But I wondered if I had set in motion something I couldn't live up to or control or even have the slightest inkling of how it would evolve into what had become our dream.

Another thing that occurred to me on that flight home was that I was only a healer and once I no longer had the backup of my teachers in England I was on my own. My original teacher Sandra Andrews had now retired and moved to the West Country, so I had to find someone else in my area who could give me the instructions I needed to move up to the next level, which was to become a trainer and able to work on my own.

Jan was already an accomplished aromatherapy masseur but wanted to become a healer as well so she could incorporate the two disciplines and give an all-encompassing experience to her clients. Jan could start her training in England, but because of the length of the course, I would have to finish it after we had settled in Crete, also, although I could still ring for advice I would be able to work autonomously once we had opened our retreat.

Asking some of the more experienced members at the Wainscott Centre we were told of a remarkable lady called Sheila Appleton, and listening to the way they spoke about her she sounded similar to my original teacher. She was going to be at the Sanctuary of Healing that very weekend, so we let our centre know we were going to meet her and see when she was holding her next course.

Jan and I felt it was another coincidence as when we met Sheila she was in the process of taking names for a healing course due to start in a few weeks. We had already heard how popular her tutelage was so we felt to be included in the next available course was meant to be the next step in our journey. Jan was to be trained as a healer, and I would sit next to Sheila, observe and take notes that would be a foundation to me putting together my own teaching course for anyone who wanted to learn in Crete.

However, before I could start my course to become a trainer I had to take a course in listening skills due to be held at the Sanctuary of Healing. That course was a total revelation to me as I thought of myself as a good listener, and even more so since I had become a healer. There are ways of listening to people impassively with patience and respect without injecting any preconceived ideas and holding your own thoughts of a possible answer until the other person has finished talking.

I think most of us are guilty of thinking of a reply while the other person is still talking and that's like reading a book while trying to drive a car. This means your attention is divided, so I was taught to sit still and look the other person in the eyes, which helped me focus on what they were saying before I started to assemble a reply. Jan did the listening skills course with me and towards the end of it, we were split up into pairs to practice what we had been taught, and then tell the other person what we had heard them say.

We were all a little embarrassed to start with because as children we are taught not to stare, but all agreed at the end that our perception was enhanced by doing so. If you want to be a good therapist you have to be aware of your clients' needs so that the treatment can be tailored to their requirements, and that can only be achieved by listening to them.

About this time we received an email from the builder in Crete to say all the investigations had been carried out and we could now proceed with the purchase. I had been so caught up in everything else that we were doing it took me by surprise. Jan and I had agreed we would not liquidate any money until we knew for certain we could have the house, because unlike UK sales the Greek houses could have multiple owners. In the case of our house, there were nine owners and they had managed to trace all of them and get their written consent for the sale, so we were now thrust into the next stage of the sale.

It would take us a few weeks to get the money together and wire it to the builders' Greek bank account to secure the sale and pay the lawyer and notary for their work so far. Now we had to make the decision of when we would actually be moving to Crete, so we hurriedly put the UK house up for sale and made enquiries with a shipping company about moving our home to our new country in a container.

We were suddenly propelled into motion with so many things to do at once to make sure every aspect of what we had to do came together at exactly the same time, but we still couldn't decide when to move until we had answers from all the people we had to deal with.

We had also written to our private pension providers for final settlement figures to see if we could afford it. I had done rough calculations but wanted to see the final figures to see how accurate I had been, so it would be a couple of weeks before we had all the information we needed to make a final decision, which led to quite a few sleepless nights.

It felt like I was driving a juggernaut with no brakes and we were rapidly approaching the point of no return. It had been a grand adventure in the planning stages but now reality had kicked in and the enormity of what we were trying to do was almost overwhelming.

But prepared or not, and like it or not, it looked like we were going to leave England and set up a new life in a foreign land. This was definitely a leap of faith and probably the biggest one we were ever likely to take, so I hoped and prayed our spirit friends had sorted out all the fine details for us. If this worked out right my faith would be unshakable.

Chapter 14
Destiny Awaits

The next nine days were an agonising wait for our pension forecasts to come through, and luckily, they all arrived within three days of each other. We had both sent off for our state pension forecasts a few months earlier and were both entitled to full state pensions. I would receive mine at normal retirement age of sixty-five, although Jan thanks to the chancellor and his benevolence was going to have to wait until she was sixty-two and four months before she received hers.

But for now, adding up our cash lump sums from our pensions and selling Jan's house it looked as if we would have just enough money to buy the property in Kalamitsi and have it repaired. All the forecasts stated that there would be bonuses and dividends added to the final amounts but we knew this wouldn't be a fortune, but hopefully, it would make enough difference to the final total for us to buy a car when we were settled.

So now the serious stuff began and we arranged to liquidate the money for the deposit and instructed our bank to send it to the builder's Greek bank account. We knew this would take a couple of weeks because we didn't have that sort of money sitting in an account as neither of us has ever been that well off.

It seemed that now that we'd made the decision to go, the spirit voices in my head increased and intensified as if they knew I needed reassurance and encouragement like never before. All of my messages and those at the centre were on the same theme, just keep going, it's all under control and it will all turn out all right.

Jan and I burnt the midnight oil several times and decided we would move permanently to Crete at the end of July 2007, but as we approached that date it would prove to be impossible for everything to be done in order to move by that time. We had agonised on exactly when to give our notices to our employers because when we did we would cease to have an income and that was scary enough. We had calculated we could live in Crete for about half the cost of the UK, but now we would have to go even longer without earning any money but while continuing to pay all the bills.

Luckily, we had a happy distraction once a week as Jan started her healing course at the end of April, and I would sit in on the lessons to learn how to be a trainer. There were over twenty of us on that course which took place in an enchanting old barn that looked like a fairy grotto inside, and sitting in the middle of beautiful countryside within a beautiful wooded park you wouldn't know it was so close to a major conurbation.

Jan's course like mine had to run for nine months, and whenever we were finally able to move to Crete we knew it would be before her course had finished, so it was agreed with Sheila and the principals of the Corinthians that I would finish Jan's course when we were settled in Kalamitsi.

It was amazing watching Sheila work because she had been teaching for more years than she cared to remember and was very experienced and professional. I watched in total admiration as she walked around her students correcting their interpretation of the messages they were receiving from the spirit world. I remembered feeling the same way watching Sandra work and wondering if I would ever be as good as these two remarkable ladies who had obviously been sent to cross my path.

It is very easy to feel inadequate when you're still learning while in the presence of such amazing gifted people, and to forget they probably started off just the same as you. And it's very easy to be a shrinking violet at the back of the class and not ask any questions fearing you will be perceived as naïve or foolish.

But I quickly learnt that teachers such as these would never think that way, because that is how the corporate world and most education systems have taught us to think, and these gifted teachers are about as far removed from that domain as it's possible to be.

Rather than admonish you for incorrect thoughts or perceptions, they will gently lead you to the truth with love and respect as an equal, regardless of your age or experience. Sheila also told me I could ring her from Crete with any problems I encountered, so I wasn't losing my teacher, and she taught me as Sandra had that she didn't need to be there to read a situation I might be trying to interpret.

Jan and I decided that I should resign my job first because there were a number of things we needed to do to the house before sale. We worked out that my last day of working would be the 1st of June 2007, and my private pension would start one month after that date. Once I officially took early retirement, my tax payments would be significantly reduced and I might even be entitled to a rebate for the rest of the tax year.

We were given two pieces of good news towards the end of May. We received an email from the builder to say our deposit had been paid into his bank so he could finalise the purchase, and the estate agent had written to us saying a young lady liked our house here in England and wanted to go ahead with the purchase, subject to all the current building checks taking place.

Unfortunately, it would turn out to be nearly six weeks before her surveyor conducted his inspection and us getting the necessary work done to his satisfaction. Although we finally got certificates to prove all the work had been carried out to current specifications, it meant we would not be able to meet our end of July moving date.

A shock for us was the surveyor finding a luckily abandoned wasps' nest in the loft that measured almost fifteen inches across close to the eaves. The window to Jan's daughter's bedroom was practically underneath where the wasps had made a large hole so it was a miracle she had never been stung. We had to get the pest control in to break up the nest and make sure no insects were left inside and spray chemicals all around the area, especially the eaves to deter them from ever returning.

We finally had all the paperwork we needed to hand over the house to its new owners when we received a letter from the young lady's solicitor to say she had pulled out of the sale. We had no idea why she pulled out and obviously, this plunged our plans into total disarray and us into an understandable panic mode.

All we could do was ring around the estate agents to put the house back on the market and contact the shipping company to let them know there would be a delay, and pray for a miracle.

At the time it seemed as if our plans were unravelling, as I had just handed my notice in at work. So in four weeks for the first time in my life, I would be without an income, but the monthly bills would still keep coming in for as long as it took to sell the house. But Dad must have been watching us because he came through at the Wainscott Centre again, and although he again said everything would be alright, it was hard to accept because things didn't seem to be going according to plan.

And of course, he was right because one week after my last pay packet from work our tax-free lump sums from our private pensions started to arrive. I had never seen so much money in a bank account with my name on it as it went up in leaps and bounds that would certainly keep the wolf from the door. Of course, every penny that came into the account was already spoken for but that didn't stop Jan and me dreaming of what we could do with that amount of money.

We also had an eight-year-old black tom cat that originally belonged to the girls so we had started investigating what would be involved if we took him to Crete. I must admit it was an extra complication we could do without, but he was too nervous to be re-homed and neither of us could bear to put him down. Up until then all he had done was eat, sleep and wander in and out of his cat flap as and when he felt like it, so I guess life was going to get a lot more involved and possibly stressful for him.

We had done some research on the internet and there was a lot of information on how animals readily adapted to new countries and climates so we had to trust nature to take care of him. As it turned out, it would prove more challenging to get him chipped and fit to fly so he could get a passport than it would to actually get him there. If we had all the correct paperwork there was one airline that flew to Crete that would allow him to fly on the same aircraft as us so he wouldn't be quarantined, and quite reasonable.

So it now looked like we had more time to get everything sorted out which was a blessing as his rabies injection had an incubation time to see if it had taken effect. What with the house sale falling through and now the chance of the rabies injection failing, the pressures were starting to mount, and it was becoming easier to count the sleepless nights than it was the good ones.

Some of our good nights were either sheer exhaustion or alcohol-induced and it was at these times it seemed easier to just throw the towel in and forget the whole idea. But Jan and I both seemed to have an inner force that was guiding and driving us on to our ultimate goal. As if it was more of a compulsion than just a mere flight of fancy, and we both knew where our driving force was coming from, and the constant stream of encouragement we were getting from the spirit world left us in no doubt that our destiny had already been planned out for us.

My last day at work was a mixed bag of emotions because it wasn't a normal retirement at sixty-five where you get to put your feet up after fifty odd years of work and relax in front of the telly.

But because I was taking early retirement at the age of sixty with an uncertain future in a foreign country, and lots of hard work for us both to turn our derelict Cretan house into what we wanted it to be.

The only people who I had seen taking early retirement before were the ones who had been forced to do so by redundancies and sadly normally left in tears, or those suffering from ill health and no longer able to work. So there would be no pipe and slippers for me for the foreseeable future and although a leaving do had been arranged for me in the office block it somehow didn't feel quite right.

I did, however, get a terrible shock after my presentation as I chatted to the office staff about our plans for moving to Crete that had been common knowledge for a while. I hadn't seen Miss S for a few weeks and assumed she had changed jobs and moved to another company.

We only had limited contact with office staff in the warehouse where I worked so when I said it was a pity Miss S wasn't there as I would have liked to say goodbye to her. The lady I was talking to just looked at me gravely and said, "Haven't you heard?" I could tell by the look on her face it was serious so I just said, "Heard what?"

She looked at me, astonished that I didn't know and said, "Miss S is on long-term sick leave with pancreatic cancer." I think the stunned look on my face told her that I really didn't know and although I was choked with emotions my spirit friends broke into my thoughts and urged me to tell her what I did.

It was my last day with the company so it didn't matter who knew now so I explained that I was a spiritual healer and asked if it would be possible for me to see her. She looked at me in total surprise and said, "Why didn't you tell me you were a healer?" and didn't seem at all fazed by my revelation, but I explained there is a lot of stigma attached to what I do so you tend to keep it quiet unless you know you are talking to sympathetic ears.

I said that Miss S was a lovely lady who everyone had the highest regard for and my legs nearly buckled under me with empathy as I said I would like to try and help. That conversation set in motion a course of healing for Miss S that started a few days later and lasted until we moved to Crete at the beginning of October.

Jan and I went to see Miss S at her home and she was very open to alternative therapies and was keen to get started with whatever we suggested might help. Both Miss S and her husband were aware of the restrictions governing what healers are allowed to do and both gave their unconditional consent for us to help.

After a long chat with her about her condition and my apologies for not knowing what had happened to her, I told Miss S what help I would like to offer her. I was under no illusions as to whether I could cure her but if I could help make her remaining time with us more comfortable then I would be happy with that.

I then put Miss S on our couch for the first time and she was surprised when she said I put my hand right over the tumour and felt the energy penetrating her body. At the end of the treatment, she felt very calm and peaceful and said she would like further treatment if we could manage it.

As we left, we said we would arrange another visit and I would bring a crystal bracelet she could wear plus some relaxing music similar to what I had played throughout her treatment. I would also bring a meditation CD she could listen to on those days when she had to attend hospital for chemotherapy and needed something uplifting when she didn't feel so good. We kept this routine up for a few visits and were surprised and pleased to hear she felt well enough to return to work on a part-time basis. By this time, the young lady had come back to us and said she had changed her mind and wanted to buy our house after all, so we recalculated our leaving date to Crete as the 2nd of October. This now gave me less than two months with Miss S and although she was doing incredibly well I wondered how she would fare when I had to terminate her treatments. But I had to ignore these apprehensions and just carry on as if nothing was going to change, and see her in my mind's eye as living a long and happy life.

I can't or possibly don't want to remember the last time I saw Miss S before we moved to Crete as it was a very emotional time and hard to say goodbye to her and her family. She had a very loving husband and was very close to her children who were an enormous support and comfort to her so she wanted for nothing. We had no idea at that time when it would be possible for us to return to the UK for a visit but Miss S promised to carry on reading the books and listening to the CDs and mediations.

It would not be until the end of May 2008 that we were able to return to the UK for a visit and sadly by that time Miss S was in a hospice with just a little time left to her. When Jan and I arrived at the hospice, her husband and family were there to greet us and after spending a little time with them, we were taken into the room where she was waiting to see us both for possibly the last time.

She was sitting up in bed with her hair pinned up when we walked in and my first words were to tell her she looked elegant which she most certainly did. The hospice staff were wonderful and allowed me to take as much time as I wanted to talk to her and give her what would turn out to be her last healing session.

Miss S got tired after a while so after exchanging the most heartfelt hug with her I went out into the garden where the family were waiting to talk to us. I felt incredibly close to the family and told them it was a privilege to have spent so much time with them and expressed our sorrow at their impending loss.

We were flying back to Crete two days after that last visit and I knew I would not see Miss S again, and was certain our spirit friends had arranged for our visit to coincide with seeing her that last time. I don't have to tell you how I felt on the plane flying back to Crete, suffice to say my heart was breaking.

We were out for an evening meal a short time after when I received a phone call from one of the office staff to say Miss S had passed away. I spoke to one of our teachers a few days later and mentioned the sad loss and was surprised to hear that Miss S had given him a message for me.

He told me her full name so it couldn't have been anyone else giving him the message, and said she was now fine in the spirit world and said to mention flip-flops to me. This totally blew me away because Jan had been trying to get me to wear flip-flops as they would keep my feet cool in the heat of summer, but it had become a bit of a joke between us because I couldn't keep them on and they kept flying off my feet.

No one outside of Crete knew about this so the only way Miss S could have known about it is if she had seen it happen from the spirit world. This totally amazed us and although it was terribly sad to lose her it made me feel better to think she could see this from the spirit world and appreciate the joke.

Because our original leaving date was the 3rd of July our friends and colleagues at the Wainscott Centre had arranged a leaving dinner for us at a lovely old pub we all liked. Although it was now clear we wouldn't be moving to Crete as early as we thought it was decided to keep this dinner date as it was difficult to get us all together at the same time. It was a fantastic evening with some tears but lots of laughter as we all recounted the many stories of our time together, and the shenanigans we got up to on our yearly weekend retreats. A lot of the work we do can be quite emotional so the retreats are an excuse to let our hair down and have some fun.

It was hard to believe looking back that Jan and I had been at the Wainscott Centre for four and a half years from the moment we first stepped through the doors. Although we all kept it going as best we could it was never quite the same when Sandra retired and moved to the West Country. She was a hard taskmaster and woe betide anyone who tried to cut corners, and although I was now a fully qualified healer I missed her presence and her energy.

Despite the fact she was strict, she allowed me to develop my skills in my own way rather than force some doctrine on me that would have altered the way spirit wanted me to work. She was so in tune with our spirit friends that she probably knew before I did the path I would be guided to take in order to bring out the best I could be.

I think without her by my side is what frightened me the most regardless of the fact that she had told me on numerous occasions that I didn't need her anymore and was quite capable of going it alone. It had been over a year since Sandra moved away and I had indeed not only survived without her presence but also continued to grow and learn. I think because we had established such a strong bond over the years, and she had taken me under her wing a little of her energy would always stay with me.

Jan and I did, however, have a big surprise at that evening meal that showed us how much our input into the centre had been appreciated. We were presented with a beautiful eleven-inch tall Amethyst Geode that sits next to me as I write this. It is truly spectacular and everyone who visits admires it and wants to know where it came from, and of course, it gives us great pleasure to tell how we acquired it. I think it showed the strength of the bonds between us all that evening that would transcend the nearly 3,000 miles that would soon separate us.

The 22nd of June 2007 was Jan's last day at work and I drove up to Bluewater to meet her for her leaving do at TGI Fridays, consisting of mainly women this was very loud and very flamboyant and so much fun. They all made sure Jan would not forget it for a long time. As Jan's birthday is on the 30th of June this was also combined and they had a tradition of making you stand on a chair eating your dessert while they sang happy birthday. I had been to some of Jan's other works' dos but this was something special as everyone made such a fuss over her and wished her well on her Greek adventure.

When the dust had settled the following morning and we were having breakfast, Jan and I discussed our plan of action for our move to Crete. Neither of us had an income now so we had to settle on a new leaving date and get everything organised as we couldn't sustain ourselves for long with no money coming in.

The sale of the house was now back on track so we had a projected completion date to organise the container that would ship our home to our new Greek house. After some number crunching, we settled on the 2nd of October 2007 as our new date for moving to Crete and the start of our new life.

We didn't speak to each other about the leaving date for a while and just got busy with all the preparations as we both knew there was no turning back now. It was now a little over fourteen weeks until we would fly out of the UK for the start of our adventure, and we knew the time would pass by quickly so we had to make the most of what time we had left.

Every week leading up to our departure, there was a party or a get together with friends or family so that we made sure we didn't leave anyone out. One thing was certain, we would leave with some wonderful memories and if we didn't know how many friends we had before we certainly did now, and it would be these links to friends and family that would sustain us in our first months in our new country and our leap into the unknown.

Chapter 15
The Adventure Begins

As the weeks passed, it was almost as if we had settled back into our normal routine because there were still lots of things that could go wrong, and in those circumstances, it's better for your mental wellbeing that you carry on as normal a life as possible until you know for certain everything is going to work out. The work I was doing in the house was progressing well and we could see an end to it, plus with all the visits to family and friends, we were kept very busy almost every day.

You have no idea how much stuff you accumulate over the years until you have to sort it all out and there was no way we could take everything to our new home in Kalamitsi. There was a constant stream of questions between Jan and myself like, "Do you still want this?" or, "Will we have a use for this over there?" or, "There is no way this is going to fit into the Greek house."

We were moving from a three-bedroom terraced house with a living room, a dining room with a separate kitchen and bathroom and all the furniture that fits into it. Plus whatever we wanted to take in the way of clothes, televisions and white goods all had to fit into a twenty-foot container, and trying to visualise everything fitting into a smaller space. It looked as if we had twice as much as we could possibly fit into it.

Everywhere in the house, there were lists pinned up that were gradually having items crossed off, as we slowly worked our way through the seemingly endless mission to separate what we were able to take from that which we couldn't. Jan was the organising force behind most of this as she was so methodical and diligent, whereas my dyslexia would leave me with a headache after a few hours.

It only needs one to manage an operation like that and I was quite happy to be the muscle and be given a list and told where to go and what to do. I have noticed in airport queues that most of the women are holding and sorting out the paperwork while the men follow on pulling the cases. I don't think we give our women folk enough credit for the organisational skills they possess, and therefore, the mental strain they alleviate from our shoulders.

Jan was definitely my anchor through this period, as it's amazing how the strongest and most determined resolve can be dented by a relatively minor event that under any other circumstances would go almost unnoticed and rapidly fade from memory.

But when so much is at stake that minor event can turn into a monster that can haunt your every waking hour and disturb the most deprived sleep. And the things that would normally give you a boost and kick those events into touch lose their potency and can even develop into a negative aspect leaving you in a worse mental position than before.

The thing for me that eventually turns these negatives back into a positive is divine in its nature and manifests itself in an angelic form. For me, this happens to be my little angel who I'm blessed to have as a wife, but I think most of us if we care to admit it have been visited by such entities in times of desperate need.

I pull Jan's leg by saying she has a hotline to heaven because whatever she asks for she seems to get, whereas I always have to do things the hard way. Jan is always calm, rational and works things out in an unflappable manner. While I, on the other hand, tend to panic getting nowhere, so maybe there's a lesson for us all in her approach.

You don't have to move abroad to have had to make a life-changing judgement, and I don't think there are many people who have not had to make a decisive decision that could ultimately change their lives or the lives of those around them.

But if we trust our gut instincts and little inner urges that pull us this way or that, things will normally turn out as we would have hoped they would. I have read many times that we create our destiny through our thoughts, so if we can keep focused on what we desire throughout those times when things seem impossible, then things should turn out the way we wish them to as those promptings are mostly from our guardian angel.

Jan had this confirmed twice within a month. The first being on the 19th of July 2007 while we were sitting in a circle with a very gifted husband and wife team who were teaching a group of us psychometry.

Towards the end of the evening, Mr L said, "I have a message for Jan and I'm being told there will be a big celebration for you coming up very soon." We both hoped this meant everything would fall into place with the house sale and our cat so that we wouldn't have to put everything on hold because that would mean we would have to start all over again.

The second was through a friend and medium on the 18th of August who told Jan, "With regards to all your hopes and plans, you will rejoice and prevail." We have known Mr B for quite a few years now and the accuracy of his readings has made him very popular at psychic fares and private readings.

Mr B has continued to give us updates and encouragement from our spirit friends over the years and bought through a very poignant message from Jan's mum just after we lost her in 2009. Readings like these throughout those uncertain times in our lives kept our hopes and dreams alive, and reconfirm our belief that our loved ones in spirit are watching over us and will always guide us in the right direction.

The first piece of good news came on the 31st of August when the vet confirmed Nefi's microchip had not been rejected, and the rabies injection had successfully taken and he was now 'fit to fly'. This was a massive relief as we were due to fly to Crete in just under five weeks.

A failure of the injection would have meant a delay of eight weeks or leaving Nefi behind. Either of these scenarios would have been devastating to us. So with the cat's passport now in our hands and a vet's bill we never wanted to mention again, we took a disgruntled Nefi home so he could go out and sulk in one of his favourite spots.

We had to wait until the 25th of September for the second piece of good news stating that after many hold-ups and endless phone calls, the sale of our house was now complete and exchanges had been made. This was just one week before we were due to fly and I don't have to tell you the sort of tensions in the house, and as the one most likely to get anxious how close I was to losing the plot.

A good night's sleep was something I had long forgotten about, and Jan and I were both running on adrenaline by this time, but through it all, we never had a row. In fact, we've been married over fourteen years now and I can honestly say hand on heart we have never had a row or spent days not talking to each other.

A frantic phone call to the shipping company and throwing ourselves to their mercy, they confirmed they could send a twenty-foot container on the 28th of September. Our friends who had emigrated to Australia said that when their container lorry drove off with her home in it, she collapsed on the pavement with apprehension and misgivings. And as we watched our home disappear in the container I knew exactly how she felt as my legs were buckling under me wondering what on earth we had done.

So although this was the last thing we had to do after months of planning and self-questioning, it was not something we were looking forward to. We had three strong young men lined up to help us load the container including my son Gary, who although was going to miss us terribly was determined we should follow our dream.

We had two hours to load the container included with the price, and every thirty minutes over that time would cost an extra ninety pounds. Luckily, the task was completed within the two hours and the driver was extremely helpful in packing everything so nothing would shift in transit. It is almost impossible to describe the feelings and emotions you go through when the driver clicks the security seals into place. I found it difficult to talk for a few minutes as we wandered through a now bare and empty house that now felt cold, desolate and unloved.

The next three days were spent living out of a suitcase at the Holiday Inn doing last minute shopping and seeing as much of the family as we possibly could. After the last few weeks of madness trying to sort everything out and make sure everything happened on time, it now felt like we were in the eye of the storm.

It was a sort of limbo where you know you've done as much as you possibly can, but with an uneasy feeling that there is just as much if not more to come when you reach the other side and re-enter the storm. It now felt very strange to get up in the morning and not have a list of things that need to be done before you could go to bed that night.

I know there are many reading this who have done and been through exactly the same and I think you have to experience it to appreciate how emotive it can make you, but we did, however, savour those few days because with moving to a new country and all that entailed we didn't know when we'd have the chance again.

The 2nd of October finally arrived and time to put our cat Nefi in his travel box where he would have to stay for the next ten hours until we'd arrive at our rented accommodation in Kavros western Crete. This made us both feel very guilty as we would have a bite to eat at the airport and on the plane but poor Nefi couldn't have anything until we were safely inside the apartment.

It felt very strange wheeling our cat into the airport perched on top of our luggage, but when we arrived at the animal departure area there were half a dozen cats and dogs also waiting to fly. That made us feel a bit better as up until then we felt like the only people dragging a poor animal off to a new life in a different country, and I suppose it was good he didn't know what was happening or where he was going. The staff at the animal departure centre were brilliant and said they would let Nefi out to run around for a while to stretch his legs before what would be his longest ever stay in the box.

The three hour twenty minute flight to Crete gave Jan and I time to chill out after the frantic early morning rush to make sure we didn't leave anything behind. We had shared breakfast and a much-needed coffee with the family who kindly drove us to Gatwick that gave us time for a chat before our final farewells.

We were happy when the offer to run us to the airport had been made because neither of us had slept very well and were feeling a bit frazzled when we got up. It's almost as if leaving was an anticlimax after all the weeks and months that had preceded it with all its panics and disappointments swinging us between highs and lows.

Everyone had been brilliant in the run up to us leaving, with friends wishing us well and family holding it together and supporting our dream that we knew some probably wished they could have been a part of. They all knew we had both worked hard all our lives and there had been little left for us to enjoy in personal pursuits and pleasures.

So although they would miss us terribly they also knew we had earned and deserved our adventure, and we had assured them we had not ruled out returning at some point in the future, as spirit had only shown us how to achieve our dream and not what was to come if we completed our mission and were needed elsewhere.

So here we were thirty odd thousand feet up watching the Kent coastline slip away below us as we headed towards Greece on our journey to our new life. Nefi would be curled up by now in a dark but heated compartment beneath our feet, as we had been assured the constant hum of the engines lulled animals to sleep.

We had packed some of his favourite food and his dishes so our first job would be to feed him once we were inside the apartment. We had asked our spirit friends to look after Nefi on the journey and keep him calm and peaceful as we couldn't be there to comfort him.

When we arrived at Heraklion Airport, I stayed to collect our cases while Jan went to the other end of the building to collect Nefi. We had hired a larger car this time from Mike's Rentals, so once we had negotiated the main road and filled the car up with petrol we set off on the now familiar route along the national highway.

We had arranged to meet an agent at the BP petrol station at Kavros which we were familiar with and he would show us the apartment a short drive away. It was just getting dark when we pulled up outside the apartment so after signing for the keys we got everything inside and locked the door.

It was time to let poor Nefi out of the travel box that by now must have felt like a prison and give him something to eat as his last meal was nearly twelve hours ago. To our surprise though, he was more interested in investigating his new surroundings than eating so we just let him wander to his heart's content. Jan had anticipated our time of arrival so had packed lots of goodies in our cases so we had a picnic with a hot cup of tea and would go shopping in the morning.

Although it was October we woke up to a bright warm sunny day and the picture window in the living room gave us a panoramic view of the White Mountains to our left, all the way around to the coast and the Mediterranean Sea to the far right. With fields in front of us with sheep grazing, we agreed it was a lovely spot to stay while our house was being renovated.

There was a well-stocked shop a short distance from the apartment run by Maria who spoke good English so was able to advise us on what to buy. The beach was not far from the shop and petrol station so after lunch we decided to explore the area and start to get to know our way around.

As we did on holiday, we bought fresh local bread, cheese, all the fruit and vegetables that were available because we would now be cooking our meals. Jan's cooking skills would come in very handy here because we only wanted to eat what was locally available which was not only the cheapest but very healthy. Jan made a Greek salad the same as we had eaten on previous trips and with bread made in a bakery just around the corner from Maria's, it felt like we were on holiday again.

There were lots of local hotels stretching along the beach from Kavros and walking onto the beach we were at the opposite end that we had seen from Georgioupolis. It was outside the main tourist season so it was strange to see miles of sandy beach almost deserted that gave it a lonely and strangely eerie feel.

We would, however, grow to love this time of year when winter had not fully set in and we could walk for miles on the beach, and only encounter the odd person with their dogs enjoying the freedom to run and splash in the still warm water.

What happened next I have thought about so many times and although I now know the answer, the reality was quite scary and very frustrating for Jan. We had been in Crete for about three weeks and although there was not much for me to do as we were renting I was quite content with that after all the weeks of feverish activity.

Despite having always been a positive, energetic and self-motivated person I slipped into a kind of depression and I had no mechanism to break this mood that had overtaken me. It came to a head one day as we walked along the beach and despite Jan being by my side, I felt desolate and alone as if my world had suddenly imploded around me. And worst of all, my connection to my spirit friends had disappeared to leave me feeling bereft and drifting in an alien environment where nothing made sense.

If ever I needed an angel to guide me it was now and thank goodness I had Jan to walk by my side and steer me through this haze that would be my existence for the next few weeks. It was as if she knew what I was going through and her calm words and attentiveness were total that wrapped me in a warm blanket of love and compassion.

As a child, I had an imaginary friend who talked to me, protected me and advised me on what to do, and from that time until that moment on the beach, there has always been someone guiding and advising me.

But now the quiet was deafening and oppressive to a point where I shouted out to find out where they had gone, but there was no reply and for the first time I realised how much I enjoyed and relied on whoever it was that was my constant companion.

It wouldn't be until the voices returned that I would find out this was yet another lesson for me to learn because when the depression lifted I would truly understand the devastating loneliness that it can bring. Because I was to encounter a client with just such a condition and would only be able to help her with this newly gained depth of understanding of what she was going through.

It is remembering how low and desperate I felt at that time as I waded through that mental soup that gave me the necessary tools I needed to help her through her own battles with depression.

I would learn later after I had returned to my normal self that my spirit friends had stepped back to give Jan total control over my recovery. They knew I wouldn't be able to receive their messages in my present introverted state so handed my soul over into the gentle care of an earth angel.

It is said that to truly appreciate someone's situation you must first walk in their shoes and that short but intense period that started on the beach gave me an insight into their world that led me to formulate an expedient method of treatment.

There is nothing more enriching to the soul than to have someone come through your door dull and lifeless and then leave with a sparkle in their eyes and a newfound zest for life. This was to happen more than once in the following years and I will cover a few of their stories in the appropriate chapters.

Our spirits were lifted one day when we received an email through an internet café saying our container would be delivered to the port of Heraklion on the 25th of October. Unfortunately, this was followed a little while later by a text message from the agent to say the staff at the port were on strike and therefore, we couldn't be given a release date.

We had rooms reserved above Kournas Lake where our belongings were to be stored until our house was finished. All we had to entertain ourselves in the evenings were a couple of books we had bought with us, but as soon as the container arrived we would have our television and DVDs that would give us some entertainment.

When we moved into our house we would have a satellite dish put on the roof like most of the expats to receive English stations. I don't think Jan or I had ever done so much reading before or since in those first few weeks waiting for our belongings to arrive.

I don't think any of us do things like these unless we are forced to by power cuts or other similar major breakdowns, and it certainly makes you appreciate the things we so much take for granted. Now in the age of handheld devices, there is sadly even less incentive for people to talk or socialise as our parents and grandparents did. I must admit I love my smartphone for keeping in touch with family and friends, but I hope it will never take the place of sitting and having a coffee and a chat with those we hold most dear.

On a trip to Hania, we had seen a second-hand Skoda Estate car for sale in our price range but we needed residency permits before we could buy it. So on the 29th of October, we went to the police station in Vrisses with passports, photos and they issued us permits which would last for five years.

Most official paperwork was done by hand with forms to fill in and registered in a record book but we found the policemen polite and the process efficient. With our new residency permits and all other documents we had been given, we went back to the car dealers and bought the car.

After the dealer's son took us to the government buildings in Souda to get the car transferred into our name we drove it back to the apartment. Up until then, it had been quite expensive to hire cars on the days we had to get official jobs done so it was a relief to have our own transport.

It wasn't a moment too soon either because our container was delivered to the rooms the following day, so we were able to load the car with a few home comforts for the sparsely furnished apartment. I can't tell you what a relief it was to sit down that evening after our evening meal and watch one of our favourite films.

That was a habit we adopted most evenings and it's amazing how you appreciate little comforts when you move away from the world you have grown up in. I have said to many people since then that it does a person good to move out of your comfort zone into a totally alien environment to make you appreciate what you have.

This became a prominent theme whenever I taught in a circle to push yourself in some way by stepping out of your comfort zone and immerse yourself into something you consider scary. It doesn't have to be as extreme as moving counties as in our case, but it should be something you haven't done before that gives you the potential of failure, and to do it later in life as we did certainly concentrates the mind and brings out strengths and talents you didn't know you had.

I will leave this to your imagination as only you know your situation and experiences but I think you get the idea because it's good to challenge yourself and even more important to have the ability to laugh at yourself if it all goes wrong the first time.

There are a lot of people reading this who have already done this and benefited and enriched their lives in the process and know the benefits that can be gained. I think we have all heard about Mr So and So or Mrs So and So who have done something that provokes a response from us like, "You wouldn't catch me doing that," but quite often, it's the fear of showing ourselves up in public that prevents us from trying in the first place.

But there are very few of us that are born with practical skills and talents and therefore have to learn them, and they say that necessity is the mother of invention, and we should comfort ourselves that all those people who make it look so easy, also had to learn it first and probably fell flat on their faces on their first try.

The important thing is that it should be something you have always wanted to do or some new pursuit or trend that has fired up your imagination. If attempted and succeeded at, this could give one a whole new lease of life and self-confidence, and lead to a new circle of like-minded people that could grow into friends you would otherwise never have met.

We had heard about an organisation through people we had bumped into called the CIC (Cretan International Community) that held monthly meetings in Rethymnon as a support group for expats. So on the 2nd of November, we drove to the bar from where we could see the Mediterranean Sea and introduced ourselves to the organisers. We made some good contacts that morning and the monthly newsletters gave us lots of information and people who could help with problems.

They work on the premise that whatever problem you encounter someone has already dealt with it and found a solution, failing that there is a vast network of people that cover every conceivable eventuality that may arise and can find solutions for everything from illness to boundary disputes.

We met through them people who had lived in Crete for over thirty years and so diverse and from every type of background as to make it interesting and open to all. So with this organisation to help us we felt confident that our new life in Crete was going to be enjoyable and that whatever challenges we might encounter could be easily resolved.

Chapter 16
I'll Finish It in a Month

From that first meeting with the members of the CIC until the 4th of February 2008 when work started on renovating our house we immersed ourselves in whatever activities had been organised. As a keen walker, I had signed up for a nine-kilometre walk through a deep gorge in the foothills that lie in front of the White Mountains. I was used to undertaking ten to twelve-mile charity walks in England but when I saw the goat tracks up steep hills we'd be climbing I was a bit daunted by the prospect.

Some of the rocks we climbed over were sharp and jagged so I was grateful for my sturdy boots and of course, you don't walk anywhere in hot countries without a bottle of water. I'm happy to say I completed the trek without falling over or slipping on the loose rubble and the view from the top of these lofty hills was worth the effort.

On the way down, we passed through an abandoned village which was a bit spooky and eerie with its tumbled-down walls and undergrowth where nature had reclaimed this once thriving community. Crete can seem very dry and barren but there is beauty in its weather-beaten appearance, and the diversity of flowers that bloom virtually all year round are breathtaking with their stunningly vibrant colours.

I can remember being about ninth in line walking through the gorge and all who walked before me brushed against a bed of wild thyme shrubs, so by the time I passed them the air was full of their pungent scent and the effect was quite intoxicating. This and the sight of goats peering down at us from the high rocky crags are memories that will stay with me forever and remind me of just what a jewel this island in the Mediterranean truly is.

The walk ended with a much-needed drink and a meal at a local taverna in a village at the bottom of the hills, accompanied by much good-humoured banter among the twenty or so people who took part. Unfortunately, after developing a blood condition while living there, it was one of the few walks I was able to do which is probably why it stands out so vividly in my memory.

I will never forget our first shopping trip to Champion supermarket as it was then on the 15th of November in the town of Rethymnon, and what the expats call the roundabout leading to the coastal road where the traffic lights have never been switched on for any length of time.

It's like playing dodgems but with real cars where you drive across at the first opportunity through the melee of vehicles coming from five different directions. I got used to it in the end and took it in my stride as everyone does but after that first attempt I felt kind of shaky and said I'd find another route.

We found in the end that we could get everything we needed in the local shops like Maria's in Kavros at reasonable prices and that saved on petrol. Eventually, we only went into Chania or Rethymnon if we wanted something not available locally or to pay bills and attend the CIC meetings.

Jan's mum sent a parcel out to us on the 26th of November which we picked up from Vamos post office that contained lots of goodies and Christmas presents. It was lovely to receive this as it made us feel like we hadn't totally cut our ties and there were also some items with nice memories attached to them.

This was to be the first of many parcels we would receive from our family and we also sent parcels back for children and grandchildren at Christmas and birthdays. We appreciated these boxes full of supplies and it made us feel closer when we couldn't get back to the UK for family celebrations.

Almost all the family came out to see us at various times before the 2008 recession, after which only a few could afford to do so, After this, the parcels to and from our family would become even more important in making the miles between us shrink and keep us feeling connected. Although we made a point of phoning a family member every week to keep in touch it didn't make up for having quality time with them.

Fortunately, this situation would not last and once again, our family would be able to come out to see us and enjoy the sunny weather and local cuisine. It had always been our intention for the family to spend time with us in Crete and enjoy a relaxing holiday away from the hustle and bustle of working life.

Our next adventure on the 27th of November was one that would be repeated every year around this time but this first time was indeed an experience. If you want to renew your car tax in the

UK you just go to your local post office with your documents and within twenty minutes you leave with your new tax disc.

In Crete, however, you had to take all your documents to the main tax office in the centre of Hania, and going to the second floor you stood in the first queue. After handing your documents to the clerk, he would enter your details into a computer, and in a little while he would hand you a printout and you would go and wait in the second queue.

After handing this clerk your printout and the amount of money shown on it, he would enter the details into his computer and then attach a receipt to it. You would then go and stand in a third queue where you handed the clerk your printout with the receipt attached, and in due course, you were handed back your printout with a blue sticker attached emblazoned with the year to be covered that you proudly displayed in your windscreen.

Some expats reported that this process could take them half a day so they took a packed lunch with them and a flask of tea but it never took us that long. Before leaving for this epic endurance test, we always asked our spirit friends to make it as quick as possible getting through all the queues and it worked. Asking for help was something we always did if we had to do anything that involved official paperwork or anything to do with the car.

I do believe this system has now been modified and your printout is posted to you which you can now take to your local council building and pay for car tax. The system is also now paperless which can only be a good thing as we've seen cars with so many stickers in the windscreen it must impair the drivers' vision.

Our next adventure took us on quite a long journey to a village on the peninsula of Akrotiri which is about the same distance as Hania Airport. Jan had her feet cared for by a chiropodist for many years in the UK so we needed to find someone locally who could carry on the service for her. Although this lady wasn't strictly local, she came highly recommended from quite a few of the friends we had made since we arrived in Crete.

So with the phone number we had been given, Jan made an appointment and we were to be there at eleven o'clock on the 29th of November. Despite being given directions, I found it quite hard to find as all directions look easy when you write them down, but as we all know the reality when out on the road is somewhat different.

Needless to say, we arrived ten minutes late with me flustered and harried as after so many wrong turns I was starting to think we would never find it. This inspired me when I had the computer up and running to print out detailed directions on how to find us from the Vamos and Georgioupolis directions, which proved invaluable when we started our circles.

Having eventually found her, she was completely laid back about the whole thing and sympathetic as we were not the first to lose our way and admitted the house was hard to find. Jan was however very impressed with her services which would have lasted a full hour if we hadn't been late and included nail varnish and cream massaged into her feet at the end of treatment. She became a good friend and once she found out what we did, introduced us to like-minded people who were interested in what we wanted to do. Some of the people she recommended came to us for healing treatments and some of those went on to join our development circles.

We heard through the CIC that a charity Christmas Bazaar was held every year in the old customs building in Hania Harbour and volunteers were always needed. This not only sounded like good fun but was also a very good cause as it raised much-needed funds for deserving charities in the surrounding areas.

The Bazaar was held over a weekend of the 8th and 9th of December so we volunteered for the afternoon shift on both days which was the hardest for them to fill. We helped out on the Instant Raffle and it was indeed good fun with a very upbeat atmosphere, and local groups as well as expats singing songs and carols on a makeshift stage.

We enjoyed every minute at the Bazaar immersing ourselves into all the fun activities and off the cuff stunts going on around us. A staggering amount of money was raised over the two days and we both agreed we would volunteer next year if they needed help as we hadn't laughed so much in ages.

In the run-up to Christmas, a lunch had been organised by the CIC in the Polika Café on the seafront in Rethymnon to take place on the 17th of December before the festivities started in earnest. We had been in Crete nearly three months and we chatted about how amazed we were about how much we had accomplished in such a short time especially as we knew so few people when we arrived.

Christmas for us was a quiet affair with much reflection although we did find somewhere to have Christmas dinner, and despite knowing we had come here on a mission we did miss our families. We had been given lots of encouraging messages about how busy we would become once our house was ready, but we had no idea at this stage when that would be.

And how grateful we would eventually be that we listened to our spirit friends for the incredible people we would meet and work with, and for all the people we would train and work with as we all worked for the health and wellbeing of those who came to us for treatment.

Jan and I went for a long walk along the beach from Kavros in early January and I got a real surprise as we wandered along, both daydreaming in our own thoughts. My spirit friends suddenly returned to me and told me we would eventually be going back to England when our work here was done. I was so shocked at their sudden return and at what they told me that I blurted out aloud, "Going back, I just bloody got here," at which they reprimanded me for using bad language.

We had been wandering along holding hands up until then but Jan was just as shocked by my outburst as I had been by their return, and after recovering from the shock of my outburst, she looked at me wondering what was coming next. Once I had gathered my thoughts, I told Jan our spirit friends told me they knew I was feeling trapped for some reason, so they had shown me our future that would eventually come to pass, so I could reconcile with my present situation and get on with the work I had to do unencumbered by an uncertain future.

And it certainly did the trick as I bounced back pretty quickly after the message. It was a great relief for Jan to have me feeling my old self again, as there was enough to think about and she was having to sort it all by herself which was a great strain on her. We were soon to get some more good news that would certainly lift our spirits and get us excited and breathe new life into our plans that had been put on hold.

We had a meeting with the builder towards the end of January 2008 and he told us that the permits were almost ready and he would start the work on our house soon. This gave a nice boost to our anxious mood of late, as we were paying over five hundred euros a month for rent and storage for our furniture which was draining our limited funds.

It had only been three and a half months but it seemed like much longer waiting for all the paperwork to be approved in advance of the work starting. We were walking along the promenade in Georgioupolis when we received a text message from our builder saying everything was in order and work could start in early February.

When we asked him how long the work would take, he replied confidently, "I'll finish it in a month," which seemed a bit quick, but then he was only renovating the house and not rebuilding it, as all the walls and roof were sound and just needed bringing up to modern standards along with the electrics and plumbing.

We immediately headed for the Sweet House in Georgioupolis square for a coffee and a cake to celebrate the next step in our plans being just around the corner. Jan and I had been up to see the house twice since we bought the car, and looking around the property and jungle of a garden we couldn't imagine how the builder could possibly get it done in a month. But not wanting to invite bad luck we happily accepted his prediction and asked our spirit friends to give him as much help as they could to get it finished as soon as possible.

True to his word, the builder started work on our little Greek house on the 4th of February and the driveway was awash with bricks, sand and all manner of equipment. We went up to the house three days later and were amazed that all the overgrown shrubs and saplings in front of the house had been cleared by his team of workers.

For the first time, we could see all the front of the house where previously we could only see parts of it as the rest was obscured by undergrowth. The old wooden doors that had given the bat sanctuary for so long were now gone which let in enough light to see the size and layout of the room. And now that the large bath-like structure had been removed, it was possible to see just how large this room was with its bread oven as its main feature.

With much excitement, we walked around the room with the builder discussing where the kitchen area should be and the layout of the living area. We were told if we came back in about four days when a skim of plaster had been applied to the walls we could mark where we wanted sockets for appliances, television, etc., to go.

This was good news to us as it felt like we were making real progress and kept us in a buoyant mood as we went away thinking about where we would like everything to go. After what seemed like forever, we were finally planning our new home, and there was so much more to do as this was only the kitchen/living room area.

The next time we visited the old rusty door to the middle room that we were unable to open had also been removed, so for the first time, we could look inside what would become our bedroom. This room was just as large as the kitchen, so it was decided to put an en-suite bathroom in the far right-hand corner closest to the connecting door.

All the old fittings and furniture had been cleared out of what would become a small self-contained apartment at the other end of the building that was overlooking the side garden. A lot of people we had made friends with through the Wainscott Spiritual Centre said they would like to come and stay once our healing retreat was up and running, so it was important for us to have this apartment repaired at the same time so we could keep good our promise to those good friends.

Unfortunately, within a week of starting the repairs, Crete experienced some of the worst storms and torrential rain in living memory which made it impossible for the builder to continue. Jan and I went up to the house a few days later during a break in the weather and the rain had washed some of the building materials down the road. We saw the builder in his office and although he was apologetic about not being able to meet the one-month deadline, it was clearly not his fault and nothing could be done until the weather abated.

The atrocious weather lasted for nearly two and a half weeks after which everything was sopping wet, including inside the house as there were now no doors or windows to keep it out. We felt sorry for the work crew because when the sun did finally come out they spent quite a few days drying the house out and getting more materials to replace what had been washed away. Everyone worked very hard to make up time and by the 7th of March, the first skim of plaster was on the inside walls and all the floors had been laid and finished.

At this stage, it was possible to get an idea what the inside of the house would look like, and we both agreed it would resemble an old Cornish cottage which is exactly what we both had in mind. With the inside walls painted in buttermilk, it was going to look warm and cosy and we started to plan where the furniture would go. It was all very exciting now everything was taking shape, and on our regular visits to the house, we planned every detail with the builder who happily accommodated all our quirky requests.

By the 17th of March, all the outside of the house had been plastered and painted and the bread oven in the fireplace was also finished which became the main feature that everyone who visited the house fell in love with. The progress on the house was truly impressive as they worked like Trojans, and if it had not been for the storms it most likely would have been finished within a month as promised.

Jan and I visited the house on the 30th of March and all the plumbing had been finished and the water heater and electrics were almost done. If the good weather continued it was possible for the builder to give us a date when we could move into our little stone villa, and I think we got a little squiffy that night with the celebrations.

The big day finally arrived and on the 4th of April 2008 we moved into our little Greek house, and after the months of renting, I can't tell you how good it felt to shut the door, pull the curtains and not worry about neighbours. That evening we made a nice cup of tea in our own kitchen, and then curled up on the settee giving each other a big hug at the relief that we had finally made it.

Looking back there was a funny incident on the day we moved into our house but at the time, it didn't feel that funny and was even a little scary. Two very good friends of ours who shall remain nameless helped us move our furniture from the rented apartment while the bulk of it was moved by truck from storage.

Having put our divan mattress on top of the car our friends said they would tie it on while I packed some things in a box to save time, because it was a hot day all the windows of the car were open and when I came out with the box the mattress had indeed been tied on.

Around forty feet of rope had been passed round and round through the open windows at least five times with the front and back doors now securely tied shut. I stood there gazing at the car in disbelief as apologies flew in all directions as I asked how I was going to get into the car now the doors were roped shut.

We were all hot and tired so although I was sixty years old I told them not to worry I was reasonably fit and would climb in through the window. I set off from Kavros for the third time that day and turned onto the national highway by the BP petrol station in the direction of Georgioupolis.

I had been driving for less than five minutes when the Greek traffic police pulled me into a lay-by and asked to see my documents. We didn't know until then it was an offence not to carry them with you in the car, and when I said my wife had them in her handbag the officer said, "Get out of the car."

I looked at him pleadingly and pointed to all the rope holding the doors tightly shut but he seemed unmoved by my predicament and said in an even louder voice, "Get out of the car now." I can assure you that being hot, bothered and now somewhat stressed, and with a burly policeman with a forty-five pistol strapped to his waist glaring down at me, my exit from the car was a lot less dignified than my entry a few minutes before.

Luckily, I had my mobile phone with me and rang Jan and told her what had happened and could our friends drive her to where I was and bring the documents with her. Happily for me by the time they arrived, I had managed to give the police enough information for them to give me a fixed penalty of ten-euro fine and was told to carry them with me in future.

I can only imagine the fits of laughter among the half-dozen police officers at that lay-by when I clumsily climbed back in through the car window and drove off. Over a much-needed beer that evening while licking my wounds, we presumed that my antics of that day would be the butt of every joke in every police station for miles around for months to come.

By visiting bars and tavernas in the local towns and being members of the CIC, we had made quite a few friends since we arrived in Crete. So on the 17th of May, we had a house-warming party to show off our little stone house in Kalamitsi, and for Jan and I, it was a very proud moment and a relief that we were able to make our dream come true.

Until September the previous year, we weren't even sure a property could be found for our healing retreat. But we should have known our spirit friends would find the right place for us, and here we were just over twenty months later drinking wine in the Cretan sunshine with our new found friends, and wondering what and when the next chapter of our adventure would be like and where it would take us.

But for now there was plenty to do getting the house just the way we wanted it and settling into our Greek lifestyle exploring our new village and the surrounding area, and with all the work I had to do getting the garden into shape, there would be enough to keep us both busy for months to come.

We had been given a lovely large Greek terracotta pot by one friend and a red rose for the garden by another. My first job was to find a nice sunny spot so we could see it from the kitchen door, as most of the garden was still full of weeds and undergrowth, therefore, the rose in its lovely pot would be something nice to look at until the rest was finished.

It would take us totally by surprise just how quickly our spirit friends would have us working to establish our healing retreat and the unlikely events that would lead to the right people we were destined to meet. It's always clear in hindsight how things come together, but it's a constant lesson for me to watch every event that happens because who knows which one will lead you to where you are meant to be.

Chapter 17
Can You Teach Me?

The first few weeks in our new home was chaotic as we were trying to organise the furniture to make the best use of the space while making it look homely and comfortable. Any spare time I had was spent in the garden chopping small trees down that had grown wherever seeds had landed, and digging out the roots which was hard work with a pickaxe as the ground was so dry and compacted. The side garden around the apartment was so overgrown that I found a complete forty-five-gallon oil drum hidden amongst the bushes, three feet tall weeds covering the whole area, and a grapevine that I could see where it came out of the ground but no idea where it ended.

It was in these first few weeks that a French family walked into the garden that had obviously been here before and came with the intention of buying the house. We knew nothing about the family and felt rather sorry for them as they seemed so disappointed that we had beaten them to it, so after a brief chat, they went away somewhat dejected.

Although I must admit we were pleased to have bought a property that had caught the eye of other discerning people who also had the idea of bringing it back to its former glory. It also gave us a new burst of energy knowing we had acquired a property that others thought worthy of turning into a home with its views of the majestic White Mountains. So had our spirit friends seen this coming and encouraged us to not waste any time and agree to the sale before anyone else could snap it up and deprive us of our healing retreat?

Living in rented accommodation and having our belongings in storage and waiting all that time for the renovation permit had been quite stressful. So we decided once we had settled in to take a break from our labours on the house and garden, and have a trip back to England to see our family and friends at the end of May.

In hindsight, our spirit friends must also have prompted this, because when we arrived back in the UK it was the time Miss S had been taken into a hospice near Dartford, so we made arrangements with the family to go and see her.

After catching up with family and friends, we went to see Miss S on the 8th of June and I knew this would be the last time I would see her in this world. Her family went to sit in the garden outside the ward so I could give Miss S her last healing session. Although sadly I knew it would be more like a farewell and a parting gift, that would prepare her soul for its journey to the next world so that's how I conducted the session.

My own thoughts at the time were that at best I had only postponed the inevitable for a while, but the family's heartfelt thanks for what I was able to do told a different story. And Miss S seeing my antics with the flip-flops, as with the marrow moment was the second time I had received proof that not only does the spirit world exist, but that our friends and loved ones can see and guide us when we need their help.

When we returned to Crete, Jan and I worked tirelessly on the house and garden, but as the weeks rolled past and the heat of the Cretan summer increased it saw us doing fewer hours every week. Our bodies were still conditioned to the temperate English climate and were not yet able to tolerate the extreme heat of a country which is level with the top of Africa. For me personally, it would start a process in my blood that would see me getting slower, weaker and induce chest pains that convinced me that a heart attack was imminent.

I suffered from this in silence not wanting to worry Jan until a fortuitous meeting with strangers gave me an answer to put my mind at rest. A friend of theirs had heart problems that were exacerbated by the same temperatures that were giving me trouble and slowing me down. Apparently, if you move from a cool country like England to a hot country like Crete, the only way the body can cope with it is to thin the blood down, and as I have Haemophilia A this would certainly explain my problem.

We had proof of this the following year when we became friends with a man who was on a very high dose of blood thinning drugs for his particular condition. He and his partner had a flat close to our village, and when they came out to stay for a couple of months he was able to cut his dose in half by the time they went home.

We subsequently met other people with similar conditions to his and they were all able to benefit from the warmer climate and reduce their dosage. So for me whose blood was already thin, it was a case of doing what I could, listening to my body and stopping when I'd had enough, especially when I was digging out tree roots with a pickaxe which was extremely physical work.

I had a surprise in July 2008 as a Miss H had heard about me from a friend and asked for an appointment to see me for healing. I was obviously delighted as it was what we came here to do, and although we had been told repeatedly we were going to be busy, I wasn't expecting it to happen just yet.

Miss H had problems with her lower back that was affecting her hip, and with the constant pain was feeling drained, out of salts and had been feeling fuzzy for a week before she saw me. The treatment started with a guided meditation to de-stress her and make her relaxed and calm that would create a receptive state for healing.

As I had laid her face down on the massage couch, it was easy to work on her lower back before general healing with crystals to create a sense of wellbeing. She was quite tearful during the treatment so I think there were a lot of pent-up emotions released throughout the session that left her in a lighter mood than when she arrived.

Miss H came to me for further two treatments and the first of these was in September when I used different crystals to clean and balance her chakras. This treatment was also accompanied by a guided meditation, that saw her much more relaxed than the first session as she then trusted me and knew what to expect.

The third treatment in November was a guided meditation through a rebirth that was rejuvenating and this time there were no tears. Miss H remarked afterwards that the meditation had taken her to a very nice place in her mind and she hadn't wanted to come back.

It's very uplifting to see a person enjoy and benefit from a treatment that can be tailored to their personal needs and requirements. This first client would herald the beginning of a constant flow of people coming to our healing retreat that would sometimes see me conducting three sessions a day.

At these times, I was sometimes asked if seeing this amount of people in a single day drained me, but I always replied that I get a buzz out of it. I've always said to get this sort of buzz out of healing is the spirit world's way of giving me a bonus for doing this sort of work as it puts me in a good mental place.

By the end of August, we had worked tirelessly and not ventured out much as we wanted to get the house and garden looking presentable to anyone who visited. We had gone to Georgioupolis to do some shopping and treat ourselves to a coffee in the Sweet House as we thought we deserved it.

Walking back to the car, we spotted a poster pinned to a pole announcing a country and western singer would be playing at a bar called Sinatra's that Saturday. Jan and I both like that type of music so we decided it was about time we had a night out and check out the bar as it was on our doorstep.

We were surprised to find out Sinatra's was run by an English man and was full of expats so we felt comfortable catching up with the news. When I went to the bar to order drinks, I was served by Debbie, and as we chatted, I received a familiar urge from my spirit friends to talk to her about spiritual things.

She was indeed interested in all things spiritual but after about five minutes she said, "This is very interesting but I'm not the one you should be talking to. You need to talk to Kate. I'll just finish this and I'll introduce you."

Within minutes, Jan and I were introduced to Kate who was sitting on the bar's veranda with her husband and a small group of friends. Debbie said, "You need to talk to this chap, he talks about the same stuff you do." With that, Debbie disappeared and left me standing there rather embarrassed with everyone staring at me.

Kate broke the ice by asking what I did so I told her I was a spiritual healer and a crystal healer and I had some mediumistic skills when someone needed a message. Well, that was like lighting the blue touch paper as Kate launched into a whole series of questions that luckily I was able to answer, and a few from her friends as well.

After about two hours of intense conversation about all things spiritual, Kate said to me, "Do you know of anyone who could teach me this stuff?"

To which I replied, "No," as we hadn't been in Crete that long and hadn't heard of anyone doing this sort of work.

Kate then said, "Can you teach me?" I immediately threw my hands up and said no because I didn't think I knew enough to teach anybody. To which Kate replied, "Well, you haven't stopped talking for the past two hours," for which I didn't have an answer so I said I would think about it and let her know.

We exchanged phone numbers and arranged to meet back in Sinatra's when I would give her my answer after which Jan and I headed back home. Once back indoors Jan said, "You can do this. Isn't it what you came here to do?" I had been taught by many brilliant and gifted people, but I found the prospect of teaching anyone else quite daunting because I didn't think I could measure up to them.

But I had to admit that Jan was right, because not only was it exactly the reason we went there in the first place for, but I had also been told repeatedly by the spirit that I would be very busy here. So when we went back to Sinatra's to meet Kate I said I would give it a go, but don't expect too much as I would just pass on what my teachers had taught me.

"Oh, that's good," she said, "because there are some other people who would like to come as well." I had reconciled myself to passing on what I knew to Kate but now it was getting bigger, and the panic started to kick in all over again but this time much worse.

After speaking to Kate, we spoke to some of the other people we had met who we thought might be receptive to the idea and join us. The result of those efforts was that at eleven am on the 11th of September 2008, we opened our first development circle with six people and I fully understood exactly what stage fright was.

I must admit I didn't do that much on that first circle as I was so nervous. Although the people told me later I didn't show it, but I think they were being kind. I introduced myself first and told everyone what I had done in the past and what qualifications I had, and what I wanted to achieve by running the circle. I then asked them to introduce themselves and tell us of any experiences they'd had in the past, and what they were hoping to gain from the circle meetings.

I then explained how the circles were run that Jan and I attended several in England and what we felt we had gained from the gifted people who ran them. We had amassed quite a collection of spiritual books by this time so we opened up a lending library so circle members could borrow and read them in between meetings. We also had five sets of oracle cards and each week we would spread one out and ask members to pick a card they were drawn to, and then take turns to interpret each other's cards to build-up psychic abilities.

I must admit to being surprised at how well it went and how everyone wanted to keep it going every week providing we were all free on the same day. After the following week went just as well, I thought I'd better get myself organised, so with inspiration from spirit I set about writing a development program to give some structure to learn by.

To pick the subjects for the modules, I started by going through all my teaching books like *'A Course In Miracles'* and *Betty Shine's Mind Workbook* and assembled them in order from simply learning how to relax and progressing eventually to things like astral travel. This eventually saw me over the following months writing a fifty-one module course. I also wrote a meditation compatible with each module, and the addition of things like mantic tools, psychometry and aura reading made the lessons interesting.

Kate surprised us by relaying a story to us in those first few weeks of when she was eight years old when at bedtime she would lift out of her body and float around her house. I think the rest of us all said in one voice, "You lucky, so and so, we've been trying to do that for years," and no one was more jealous than me.

I spoke to Kate recently and try as she may has not been able to replicate those experiences as an adult, as with the knowledge gained on life's journey she could have some amazing journeys. It's very sad that we lose the unquestioning belief that makes these experiences possible as we grow older, and get conditioned by society that tells us these things cannot possibly exist in a logical scientific world.

When I'm out walking, I see toddlers nattering away to supposedly imaginary friends, but are they angels or spirit friends or even elementals they can actually see and hear? Most of us lose the memory of having had these experiences as we get older, and enter a world that dictates money and possessions are the only goals worth striving for.

Kate is obviously one who has not forgotten these childhood experiences and for that, we should envy her, as I think we could all do with a little magic in our lives. But I shouldn't complain as the path of discovery spirit set me on has been quite amazing and exciting, and every time I think I'm finished discovering new things something new seems to come along and take me by surprise.

After a few weeks of running the circle, I recalled a book I had read in the mid-nineties about an old Native American woman called No-Eyes that touched my very soul in a way no other story has before or since. The old woman was blind from birth but was gifted with psychic vision, and spiritual wisdom taught to her by her shaman father that set her apart from all those around her.

No-Eyes taught many people over the years that she lived in her isolated cabin in the wilderness of the Rocky Mountains. The last one she taught before she went back to her homeland to die was Mary Summer Rain, who was charged by No-Eyes to share the incredible stories and lessons she had learnt from her with the world.

This book about No-Eyes and her life's work was the catalyst that set me on my own journey of discovery, to learn all I could about our spirit friends and how to communicate with them to find my life's mission. A journey that led me to a bar on the island of Crete, speaking to a stranger who was hanging onto my every word and with a constant stream of questions was trying to glean what I had learnt.

I found myself gushing forth a continuous flow of information and answers over a two-hour period, gained from thirty years of searching that culminated in my path crossing that of my mentor Sandra.

So was Sandra my No-Eyes so to speak, gently but firmly teaching me who I was and setting me on a journey of discovery that would reveal my purpose in life. Over the years I had worked under her tutelage, she imparted truths that made sure I would know where to find the answers I needed when she was no longer around.

So now that Kate had asked me to teach her what I'd learnt, does that mean I was now her No-Eyes and it is now my turn to pass on these truths. If this is true then the concept is mind-blowing that some unseen hand has plotted the paths of specific people to cross in an unbroken chain that could stretch back millennia, making sure the truths and the knowledge of how to find it is never lost to ensure we always have that link to the spirit world and the guidance it provides.

If this is so I couldn't even begin to express how humbled I feel that I could be a part of this lineage. And just as importantly what does that make Kate, and the others I was destined to meet and teach on this glorious island that basks in the fifth and most powerful light ray that emanates from the source.

It would mean that the number of teachers worldwide is growing experientially until it reaches a point where the light totally overwhelms the darkness, and the world will ascend to the higher spiritual plain that has been long foretold.

Chapter 18
2009
The Dream Came True

Living with one foot in this world and one foot in the next is how I feel I live my life these days. This has been a gradual process developing since the earliest days of my healing journey. To live with a foot in each world was a conscious decision I made to allow me to have the most powerful link to my angels and guides that was possible because I wanted to do the most advanced healing I was capable of with their help. This can see me get up at any hour of the night to write down ideas they give me as I'd not remember them by the morning.

It has evolved from a simple dream that involved me going to France when I retired to buy a rundown property, that I could do up around me with an easy escape route back to England if I got lonely. But then Jan came along and encouraged me to pursue a course as a healer which I had shown some aptitude for, sober as well as drunk, that led to me finding a mentor in Sandra who expanded my awareness in all things spiritual.

It evolved further still when my simple dream turned into a much more ambitious leap of faith to Crete with the encouragement of spirit, which culminated in us establishing our own healing retreat in a little Cretan village overlooking the majestic White Mountains, and developing my own psychic development course for those who wanted to find and develop their own psychic abilities.

It would not be possible to give a detailed account of all the work we did in Crete as this would fill up an entire book by itself. So I will give a concise overview year by year as it evolved, and I have changed the clients' initials for anonymity due to the personal nature of some of the treatments given, but there are some who will recognise their own stories by the dates and narrative given in the following chapters.

Our second Christmas and New Year in Crete was a bit better than the first and it started with a pre-Christmas meal for circle members on the 20th of December. This gave everyone a chance to relax and chat away from the circle meetings where we were more concerned with teaching in a workshop environment. It was good to see everyone relaxed and enjoying themselves and it was amazing listening to them and how much they had evolved spiritually in such a short time.

Jan and I had found a lot of places we liked in the year we had been living in Crete and one in Almyrida run by an English couple were serving traditional Christmas dinner. They even had sage and onion stuffing bought over from England along with Christmas pudding and custard, which made for a very festive atmosphere and with classic Xmas songs playing in the background it made us feel closer to our families.

New Year's Eve was a very noisy affair with a disco at our favourite bar in Rethymnon that was packed with people we had got to know throughout the year. With all these friendly faces and with regular healing sessions and circle meetings we were starting to feel at home in our newly adopted country.

In early January 2009, Miss B came to see me for healing with problems in the area of her right abdomen and was in constant pain. After a lengthy consultation, I gave her a full rebirth treatment to remove any negative energy that had built up in her emotional or physical being.

I then directed healing into the most painful area to target anything that might be going on using a single-point clear quartz crystal. I finished by asking the angels to take away any stress that worrying about a possible serious illness might have caused.

Despite this treatment taking away all the symptoms, Miss B had been experiencing and no longer being in pain, she took a very strong dose of natural medicine a week later and all the symptoms returned. So on the 29th of January, I repeated the entire first treatment and jokingly threatened her with all sorts of things if she took any more medicine.

I am happy to report that on the 6th of February, I received a text from Miss B that read, "Hi been to consultant 2 day and guess what? No operation needed, Thanks 4 helping me luv Miss B xx." I think that is one of the best text messages I have ever received and we have often laughed about the double treatments.

In late January, another Miss B came to see me for a free complimentary treatment because she knew lots of people, and although she was sceptical, if she experienced a rebirth treatment could recommend me to anyone who was interested. She had problems with her neck and right shoulder and the pain from this meant she hadn't slept well for a while, and in her own words she had been getting crankier the longer it went on.

As directed by my guides, I only used two crystals with Miss B where normally I would use six or seven. These were a bloodstone in her left hand and an amethyst in her right to replace the normal ones used as I was told that's all she needed.

I put targeted healing deep into her right shoulder joint to repair any damage that might have occurred, and then let it radiate out through the muscles to cover the whole area. I gave her neck area a similar treatment but put extra healing into the very top of the neck as she spent a lot of time looking down in her job.

As part of a normal rebirth for first-time clients, I gave Miss B an atonement from this and other problems she had faced in the past that could have left a negative impact. As she had never experienced anything spiritual before I also gave her a connection to the universal mind so she could understand more of the spiritual world.

Miss B had arranged to bring a bracelet for me to give a psychometric reading from and as directed had given me no information about its history or who it belonged to. Within moments of holding the bracelet, I had a picture in my mind of a young girl sitting in a meadow by a fence that ran along the side of a stream. The young girl was alone in the meadow happily picking wildflowers. I then became aware of a house at the end of the meadow with an older man standing in the doorway. I then got a very strong smell of freshly baked bread associated with the older man and I had the feeling he was connected to the young girl in some way.

Miss B was staggered by how much I was able to tell her just from holding the bracelet and told me it had belonged to her mother. The meadow and the stream were at the back of their house and she loved to be there by herself picking wildflowers and daydreaming. The smell of freshly baked bread was also correct as the house was attached to a bakery and her father was the baker. The whole scene painted an idyllic picture in my mind and brought back memories to Miss B of her mother and grandfather.

On the 19th of February, Miss P came to see me for healing who was in quite a bad place emotionally, but after treatment, she would go on to become a circle member. She described herself as having a lot of internal hate and emotional turmoil, centred around multiple personalities she had invented during childhood as self-protection.

Miss P's treatment involved a full rebirth and an atonement from the created past and she spent a lot of time crying which was good as tears cleanse the soul. A part of the rebirth can involve healing with angels and archangels, and Miss P experienced a very powerful connection to them both through the healing process.

Miss P said that after the treatment she felt free of her created childhood inventions, as they had gone to another place where she could see them but without emotional attachment. A lot of emotional baggage was removed from her throughout the treatment and whereas she was relatively quiet when she arrived, when I had finished we couldn't stop her from talking and it was wonderful to see her freely expressing herself.

Miss P's friend had bought her along for treatment and watched her throughout and saw a young girl standing by the couch as I was working. Her friend said the young girl looked like Miss P so she was convinced it was her inner child watching the healing take place.

Miss P contacted us recently to say the work she did with us set her on an amazing journey of discovery, which I look forward to hearing more about later when hopefully she will write her own account of that journey.

Every year at the beginning of March, there was a very colourful carnival in Rethymnon, so Jan and I thought we'd take a break from our toils and spend the day watching it go by. We found a spot on the main road opposite the park where we had a good view of the floats coming towards us, and as we weren't far from the main square with all its cafés we wouldn't go hungry or thirsty.

We had seen large papier-mâché figures at various spots along the national highway in previous weeks that looked like they were from earlier years. But when the carnival itself went past, the amount of effort and dedication that had gone into the floats was obvious, and everyone was wearing extraordinary costumes that had been handmade throughout the winter months.

At least half of the spectators were wearing costumes as well. There is a photo of me somewhere in a long blond wig, and a red bowler hat with a yellow daisy sticking out of the top, and Jan wore a flower garland with silver stars in her hair so we fitted right in with everyone waving and cheering. The whole thing lasted for hours from the first person to the last and the effort by the local community raised an enormous amount of money for very deserving local charities.

Kate had a healing session on the 21st of March but as she had already done so much work with us in the circle didn't really need it, but just wanted to experience what it was like for herself. I took Kate through every segment of the rebirth healing meditation and she was amazed at how much she felt and experienced, but was disappointed as there was no astral travel that she experienced as a child.

The second session Kate had that I really want to talk about was on the 15th of February 2012, as soon as I put my hands around her head she had a connection to a high priestess of Atlantis, who had long golden hair and was dressed in long flowing white robes she appeared as a vision.

As the angels touched Kate's body from head to toe, they opened up every part of her being to who she really was in this incarnation and the work she had come here to do. Halfway through the session, the Heavenly Father made Kate aware of his presence and surrounded her in a pure white light, and connected her to his loving energy to give Kate the strength and ability to complete her pre-destined mission.

When the session had finished, Kate said she was amazed at the power of the Boji stones that are a gateway to other realms of existence. She also saw the priestess a second time but this time she was dressed in white and blue with a fuller figure, but we were not told why. Through the years we worked with Kate, she became one of the most gifted psychometrists we know, and I have no doubt when the time is right she will make an incredible teacher running her own psychic development circles.

We flew back to England for a visit on the 3rd of April to see our family and friends and it had been arranged that Jan's mum would fly back with us for a month's holiday. My mother was also staying with us at this time, so being of similar age and backgrounds they would have plenty to talk about over cups of tea in the garden.

We took the two mums to as many places as possible during their stay, including a lovely lunch at Kournas Lake watching the ducks and families out in pedalos. Several visits were made to Georgioupolis and mostly to the Sweet House as they have one of the best coffee and their cakes are irresistible. Jan also has a lovely picture of her and her mum by the Seawall in Kalyves with the deep blue Mediterranean as a backdrop.

The night before Jan's mum flew home we had a last meal in Valentino's in Georgioupolis and the staff made a real fuss over our two mums. My mother stayed a little longer but after two falls had to return to England due to ill health, which is a shame but at the grand old age of ninety-two she'd had an amazing last adventure.

One of the most rewarding treatments I did was for Miss T who had five sessions with me between May 2009 and September 2011. With an Irish Celtic background, she had very similar beliefs to myself so we immediately had an immense amount to talk about and instantly bonded spiritually. Miss T went on to join us in circle spending fifteen very enjoyable and productive months with us. And towards the end of her time with us, I also trained Miss T to be a spiritual healer for which she proved extremely gifted.

That first time I saw Miss T in May she was suffering from rheumatism in her left shoulder and like most of the events in her life it had impacted negative energy into her. So in the early stages of the rebirth with Archangel Michael's help, I removed the build-up of this unwanted energy that left her more relaxed and receptive.

There appeared to be calcification in the left shoulder joint so I sent pointed healing to try and remove this, and then used the same technique to repair the ligament so the shoulder could move without pain. I also worked on Miss T's neck that was also painful, and as I sometimes do I asked our Heavenly Father for a miracle to cure these and other issues I can't mention because of client confidentiality.

Miss T said that during the treatment she saw lots of angels' hands all over her body and said she thought I had been given a special gift that people needed. I always shun this kind of praise as I don't think I'm anything special and besides there are thousands of people all over the world doing similar work as myself.

Miss M who is a gifted psychic also came to the session to see how I worked and saw an image of me watching at the start of the session as a Native American boy that gradually transformed into a grown man dressed in full medicine man costume. What Miss M saw blew me away and I found it hard to accept that it could represent me, but she is gifted to a level with many years of experience that puts it beyond any questionable doubt.

I will not bore you with all of Miss T's treatments but the fourth one on the 10th of September was special because she wanted to progress to a higher level on her spiritual journey. So I started by setting her up in a clear quartz crystal grid comprising of tumbled stones at her head and feet, with left and right single terminated points in the respective hands. I then placed an offset double terminator over her tummy which is also the energy centre and used a clear quartz pendulum in a clockwise direction to energise the crystal grid.

I then through a guided meditation had Miss T see herself on top of the highest mountain in the world on a small plateau covered in snow. A shaft of golden light then came down and she ascended through it to the higher realms, where two sentinel angels escorted her to a place where she received a special connection that would allow her to work with the higher realms and the path she wanted to follow.

Miss T went on to train as a very powerful spiritual healer and then developing into a crystal healer much the same as myself. Whenever I meet up with her now there is a transfer of energy between us that is so strong we can feel it pulsing through our bodies. It has been my privilege to work with people like Miss T, and it's like waking up a spiritual giant who has been sleeping and waiting for the spark within them to be ignited.

Miss V first came to see me in June 2009 for healing and went on to spend as much time in the circle with us as the previous Miss T. The two of them became good friends which also led to Miss V wanting to train as a spiritual healer. When I first met Miss V, she was already a fully qualified masseur with an impressive client base, but like Jan she wanted to incorporate healing into her massage to augment the service she provided.

Miss V had shoulder and neck pains due to her profession and also had something in her past troubling her although she didn't want to specify what it was. In the early stages of her rebirth, Miss V's mother connected with me from the spirit world and made me aware that her daughter was an earth angel. Miss V had also had visions in the past that connected her to the ancient Egyptians at the time the pyramids were being built.

I asked my guides and helpers to take away whatever was troubling Miss V from her past and then went on to work on her neck and shoulders. After the treatment, Miss V said that when I asked for her troubles to be taken away a shaft of golden light came down to her energy centre. Miss V told me after the treatment she felt much lighter as if something had been lifted from her, and we hoped she would no longer be burdened by the past.

Miss V's final session in August was a powerful connection to the higher realms through Archangel Michael. She wanted to discover her true spiritual path in life and what she was capable of achieving for the benefit of her clients, and the Boji stones with their powerful connection to the higher realms helped to achieve this.

Miss V said that it was the most powerful connection she had received involving lots of green light, then finally being enveloped in white light. She said words could not describe the experience. There is nothing like bringing someone to the realisation of their own potential and then watching them develop and flourish as they help and benefit humankind.

I am not giving my next client who came on the 3rd of June an initial so they can have total anonymity as my depression on Kavros beach was specifically in preparation for helping this person. You will understand why when I tell you that they arrived at my door medically diagnosed as depressed, taking two different kinds of antidepressant pills, smoking more than was good for them, drinking raki like it was going out of fashion and suicidal with dull insensate eyes.

If spirit hadn't already given me the experience of that level of depression all those months ago I don't think I would have understood how to help this person. It started off as a normal healing session as I worked my way down the body clearing negative energy, but the closer I got to the tummy area I could sense there was something wrong. This turned out to be an understatement because as I got even closer to the energy centre I could feel there was something positively nasty lurking there.

I immediately called Archangel Michael to me for his powerful protection, and also thought I might need his help if there was something suppressing this person's natural life force energy. What transpired was the worst case I would ever encounter and I think if Archangel Michael hadn't been there I might have been in real danger myself.

I'm not sure exactly what it was but I was getting a shudder down my spine, and for the first time since I had started healing, I was genuinely afraid of what I was going to encounter, and what it could possibly do to me if I didn't get this right. If I ever needed

Sandra's help it was right now but I had to be content myself with her confidence in me that I could handle whatever came my way.

With instructions from Archangel Michael, I started a process I have perfected since then of pulling white light energy in through the top of the head and all the way down to the bottom of the rib cage. I then pulled the same white light energy in through the feet and all the way up to the hips; essentially protecting the upper and lower parts of the body so whatever it was would now be trapped in the tummy area.

Archangel Michael then guided me through a technique where with his help I was able to extract whatever was lurking there. I then called for an angelic being to come and take it away as it was now trying to get into me as I had obviously deprived it of its host.

I sensed a pair of loving hands being cupped under mine so I placed it into these hands and felt it being taken far away from me at incredible speed, and I don't have to tell you how relieved I was to feel its departure.

Lorna Burns says in her books she can see Satan in people's eyes and as my encounter with this entity is indelibly etched in my memory, I think I know what she is talking about. I don't suppose I will ever get the privilege but I would like to sit down with her sometime and over a cup of tea find out what she thinks happened to me that day.

After the extraction episode, the rest of the healing session went as normal and without further incident, and I was very happy to bring the client out of the deep meditative state they had been in to a normal state of awareness. Talking at length afterwards, the client had felt something going on in the tummy area but luckily was unaware of the gravity of the situation, and when they left that day with a sparkle in their eyes I knew our little Cretan house had truly become the healing retreat we hoped it would be.

I saw the client a further three times to complete the treatment and the last time was the 21st of December and it was good to see them looking bright and happy. The anti-depressant pills were down to a bare minimum. The smoking was down to just a few a day and the raki was no longer needed. I'm happy to say there was no longer any thoughts of suicide so this was going to be a good Christmas, and especially for the client.

It is at such times as with this client that I call our Heavenly Father in to give a blessing to whoever I have on the couch. When he does come in, it is not through me as with angels and archangels as the frail human body could not cope with his intensity of unconditional love. He stands on the other side of the couch and places his hands directly on the recipient but his energy is totally overwhelming when that close. I cannot contain this amount of unconditional love and compassion when so close and it overflows from me as tears run uncontrollably down my cheeks. When this happens clients often report seeing a blindingly bright light that they can't look at which confirms to me that our Heavenly Father has indeed made a miracle happen.

The 26th of August was a very good day for us because Heather was coming to stay with us for two weeks, and we had asked all our circle members to come and see a demonstration of mediumship. I bullied poor Heather into giving this demonstration of messages from the spirit world in the second week of her stay and I still don't think she's forgiven me.

On the appointed day, so many people turned up that we had to bring the garden furniture in for them to sit on and there was so much excitement that the place was positively buzzing. After introducing everyone, I handed the meeting over to Heather and as she had never met anyone there before. The amount and accuracy of the information she brought through from family members in the spirit world was truly amazing.

After Heather had finished, there were endless questions on how to be a medium and what it felt like to be able to give people this kind of information. We took her out for a meal that evening and plied her with a copious amount of local village wine as a big thank you for showing our students what I had only been able to teach them verbally.

Heather had been a star in the eyes of our students long before she got there as we told everyone how she foretold about finding a stone arch and never looking back. She continues to be one of our best friends and spiritual advisers, and we laugh sometimes how she became an unwilling legend that our Cretan friends still talk about to this day.

We had the worst possible phone call on the 14th of October saying that Jan's mum had been rushed into the hospital and was gravely ill with a heart condition. The airline was very helpful and after hearing the situation got us an emergency flight to Gatwick at midnight on the 16th so we were in the hospital at her bedside on the 17th.

We spent as much time as we could at the hospital with other family members and Jan would make her mum's favourite sandwiches, and put them in a sandwich cool bag to take in every day that made her feel special. We also bought her all her favourite naughty cakes as the prognosis was not good, that brightened her day and it was good to see her impish grin as she tucked into them.

Unfortunately, nature took its natural course and we sadly lost her at one am on the 2nd of November at the age of eighty-one. We said our final goodbyes at her funeral on the 9th of November and were so pleased she was able to come out and stay with us earlier in the year.

It was just after the funeral that Jan bumped into a good friend who was also a gifted medium, and over a cup of tea gave Jan a message from her mum that she was finally free of pain now and back with Jan's dad. It made Jan smile as her mum said that she wouldn't need a passport now to come and see us in Crete.

I had the very greatest respect for Mummsy as I called her, as she was a talented and worldly woman who was a fountain of information and good advice, but most of all, her family was her life and top priority. She never forgot the birthday or anniversary of those she held in her heart.

Towards the end of the year, Miss B came to see me with neck and shoulder pains accompanied by dizzy spells and pains in the back of her head. I laid her face down on the couch so I could work on her upper spine just below the skull.

She was quite stressed so through a guided meditation took Miss B to a flower-covered hilltop where she would be free from the cares and worries of the physical world and left her in the care of loving angels. After clearing any negative energy from her body, I sent pinpoint healing into the top vertebra of the neck that supports the skull.

After this, I put healing into the surrounding area that might have received some damage and could be contributing to the pain. After energising the crystals I used with Miss B, I left her for a few minutes to absorb their healing energies before bringing her back to normal awareness.

Over a cup of tea, we chatted about the session and what the spirit helpers did for her. We then said our goodbyes and she went home to rest for the afternoon. I received a text message from Miss B two days later that read, "Hi you did it! No pain in the back of my head, Thanks. Miss B," which was very good news indeed.

I saw Miss B once more where she told me she was having trouble letting go of her husband who had died a few years before and couldn't move on with her life. After taking her to a sacred grotto within our earth mother through a guided meditation, I talked her through cutting her ties with her husband that might release them both.

She called me a few weeks later to say she felt much better and had started to go out with friends and have some much-needed fun. I wished her well and hoped the rest of her life would be interesting and fulfilling. Miss B said her husband would not have wanted her to be cooped up indoors when she still had so much life to live.

A very exciting and interesting year for us was drawing to a close, so on Christmas Eve, we went to a friend's bar called Oasis for a party and karaoke where we all sounded better the more we drank. I can't remember what time we left there, but it was a brilliant evening with some circle members and lots of other friends we had made since being on the island.

We had booked a table at the White Lady which was our favourite restaurant in Rethymnon for Christmas dinner with all the trimmings, including Christmas pudding and custard all imported in from the UK. We all headed home at a reasonable time as most of us were tired from the night before, which for us meant watching our favourite Christmas movie with a bottle of wine and the obligatory nibbles.

New Year's Eve saw us back at Oasis for a fancy dress party with all our friends to see in the New Year in style. Another brilliant evening and on the way home, Jan and I wondered what the new year would bring, and if it could possibly be any better than the one we were just saying goodbye to.

Chapter 19
2010
A Year of Circles

Although the healing work carried on as busy as ever, this year would be dominated by our psychic development circles, which saw me opening a second one in February and running two times a week. Also, two members of my second circle had enrolled in my spiritual healing course, that would see me guide them through a nine-month monitored program. We were told we would become very busy once we established our healing retreat, and as that prediction became a reality we were loving every minute as it unfolded.

When we started our circle meetings after Christmas, one of our group members Miss M had an old car that had broken down on the way to us for the first three weeks running, and on the fourth week's meeting it broke down on the way to us yet again. She had to call a friend to come out and fix it, and when Miss M finally arrived with profuse apologies for being late again, I knew there was a lesson we were meant to learn.

As everyone was settling down for the start of the circle, I asked my guides what I was supposed to tell them regarding the continual breakdowns. I was told to ask Miss M if she had asked for help from the angels to stop her car breaking down on the way to us, so I got everyone's attention and asked her if she had asked for help with her car, and the answer was, "No."

So I opened that week's lesson with 'asking for help from the angels, and specifically for this old car that Miss M loved and didn't want to part with.' She agreed that before she left home the following week she would ask the angels and her helpers to get her to the circle meeting on time without any breakdowns. From that day forward, her little old car never broke down again on her way to our house, so it was a good way for our spirit friends to teach us how they can help with everyday things like driving.

We had all got into the habit by then of asking for help for such things as parking places, but not for a mechanical device like a car. This was a good demonstration to us all that there is nothing our spirit friends cannot help us with if we hand the situation over into their loving care.

On the 14th of January, a Miss L came to see me for healing and reported feeling very confused and having no direction in life. She found it very difficult to relax when I started the rebirth as she had some complex decisions to make. This was made worse by her not knowing if she was making the right choices for herself or other family members.

These were decisions that no third party could or should advise on as they were intensely personal, but I think she got some clarity through the healing process. Miss L had also felt her father around her a lot, but who was not yet in the spirit world, although this is quite unusual it had given her a lot of comfort.

I told Miss L to ask for her father's help in those times when she felt distressed as it would give him permission to influence the outcome for her higher good. This I know she did quite often from then on and the situation was eventually resolved to her satisfaction. I am convinced Miss L's father had a hand in resolving the situation for his daughter, and I hope she continues to be happy wherever life takes her.

Two members of my second circle Miss T and Miss V who asked me to train them to be spiritual healers had now received their training manuals and were ready to get started. Both of them had come to me for healing before joining the development circle so had a rough idea what was involved, and both had shown an aptitude for healing as the circle meetings progressed.

So on the 19th of February, they started their Corinthian healing course which would last for the next nine months. Miss T and Miss V were my first two probationary healers since I had qualified as a trainer, so I was very keen to pass on everything I had learnt in the previous nine years. The main reason I liked the Corinthians was that they didn't keep me to a rigid regime, but allowed me to develop the way my spirit guides wanted me to.

So it was going to be interesting to see how they both developed their own individual techniques while starting with the suggested approach in the manual as I had done. I will let you know how they get on towards the end of this chapter, and how they both got on with their final exams.

On the 6th of April, a Miss N came to see me for healing who had suffered from various problems since childhood. Despite her being very nervous and anxious about the treatment, I did manage to give her a full rebirth, although I hardly touched her throughout the session. I don't think she fully relaxed but still saw lots of green light during the treatment with flashes of white light towards the end.

While talking to Miss N after the session I was surprised to hear that she had seen and spoken to spirit people for many years and considered it quite normal. And despite the problems she was experiencing, she had a strong positive approach to life, so I said we would be here if she needed us again and wished her well and hoped things would improve in her future.

A Miss I came to see me on the 9th of April with pains in her left shoulder and also problems in her neck as well as her knees. It was suspected that her neck and shoulder pains were caused by the work she had done, so I put healing deep into the two areas around her neck and shoulders to repair any damage that had developed over the years.

As Miss I was a keen walker I worked on both of her knees to remove any calcification that might have accumulated, and strengthen the joints so she could keep up with her friends who normally set a fast pace. Towards the end of the treatment, I asked Archangel Michael to cut any negative etheric ties she might have picked up from painful events in her life.

After the session, Miss I reported a pulsating energy in her back throughout the treatment and seeing a circle of blue light above her third eye. Miss I came for a second treatment on the 12th of May in which I did specific healing on the top five vertebrae of her neck. This and targeted healing to try and help straighten a curvature in her shoulders completed her treatment, and I hoped it would alleviate the pain she had been experiencing and allow Miss I to continue the walking she so enjoyed.

A Miss H came to see me on the 20th of April with lower back pains she had suffered from her early teens. She was worried she might have to undergo surgery for whatever was causing the pain and was fearful that she might have reduced mobility after the operation.

Miss H had trouble lying on her back so a number of pillows and cushions were placed under her legs and head until she was comfortable. Once relaxed, I guided her into a very deep meditative state where she felt disconnected from her physical body.

With the tension now out of her lower back, I was able to send healing deep into her lower spine to repair any damage that might be pressing against the spinal cord. Once this was completed, I sent as much energy as I could into the surrounding area to heal any other injury that might have been contributing to her condition.

Throughout the healing session Miss H saw a face she said looked very much like her great-grandfather which was a big comfort to her. After a full rebirth and back treatment, she felt very spaced out, the pain had significantly reduced and reported later that this gave her more mobility and more prolonged and restful sleep.

Miss H came for a second treatment on the 4th of April where I regressed her to a day in her childhood before the incident that caused the back problems. This enabled her to visualise her back without any pain or injury that she found very helpful. Miss H used this technique regularly afterwards as a part of her own meditations. I also sent as much healing energy as my spirit friends would give me into the lower spinal area and I sensed the spine being straightened.

I then placed my left hand over her tummy and my right hand over her third eye. As soon as I did this, I felt a powerful connection being given to her from the angelic realms. At the end of the session, Miss H said that she felt both hot and cold throughout the treatment and very relaxed and most importantly, pain free.

As with all the people I see, I wished her well for the future and encouraged her to keep up with the regression meditation. Not only would this be a pleasant experience for her but it would reinforce a belief in a pain-free, injury-free back to give a better quality of life.

My next healing session was for a gentleman who admitted he had no belief in anything outside of his own mortality and especially anything spiritual. He had bad memories attached to events in his service career that he would now rather forget. But as with so many military personnel was not able to do so as they were still quite vivid in his mind, especially as he was now retired and had more time to sit and think.

During the rebirth, I asked our Heavenly Father to give him a full atonement from his past actions and from this point he seemed to relax and follow my guided meditation. In the next part of the treatment, I asked the angels to touch the top of his head at which point there was an outpouring of emotion from him that I hoped eased his mind.

In situations such as these, I ask an archangel to join us and give a new healing energy to the recipient. In this case, it was extremely powerful. I hoped the treatment would take away the pain connected to the memories in his past so he could live in peace with those memories and enjoy the rest of his life.

As a postscript to this case, I personally don't think any serviceman who acts honourably in the defence of his country would incur karma through his actions. I relayed these thoughts to the gentleman at the time and hope they eased his mind as to any debt he thought he might have to pay in the afterlife.

My next healing session wasn't until the 16th of August for a Mr L who could only speak a few words of English. So apart from a few hand gestures, the entire treatment was done in silence, but I have heard that our spirit friends can speak any language, so they could communicate my intentions to him even if I couldn't.

When I got to his energy centre during the rebirth, it felt like it had armour plating over it so I couldn't sense if he was holding on to any emotional baggage. He gestured to his right knee and frowned so I put healing deep into the joint to heal whatever was causing him discomfort.

My spirit friends told me to place a turquoise crystal over his heart centre halfway through the healing session, which I did but I wasn't told why. It was at this point my spirit friends told me he was a priest in the days of Atlantis, which would explain the extent of his spiritual protection over his energy centre that I was not allowed to penetrate.

Because of this, my healing was limited to his physical body and I assume his spiritual welfare was protected by guardians in the higher realms. I have only encountered two other people before whose protection I couldn't penetrate, but these were both powerful teachers and healers so I was curious about his spiritual identity, but as he returned to his homeland shortly after the session I will probably never know.

A Miss R came to see me on the 24th of September with pains in the left side of her abdomen and was worried it could be something serious. She relaxed into a deep meditation very quickly, and it almost felt as if she lifted off the couch as in an out of body experience.

I sent healing deep into the left side of Miss R's abdomen to repair whatever was causing the problem and bring that part of her body back to full health. Throughout the rebirth, Miss R felt distant as if she wasn't with us, and talking to her after the session revealed that she had seen a group of elders dressed in white robes who lifted her into another realm.

Miss R was also shown a Mayan Temple in the meditation and was drawn to its energy. She told us later it was an amazing experience. Miss R said that she would like to learn more about the work I do so she could understand what her experience meant.

Miss R came for a second treatment on the 25th of January 2011, and this time through the rebirth she received a blessing from the angels that felt like she had again been lifted to a higher dimension.

Towards the end of the session, Miss R said Archangel Uriel appeared to her and took her to the Library of Knowledge where there were thousands of books. She said that it was an incredible experience, and this along with what she was shown in her first session has inspired her to want to learn about spiritual work.

Jan and I had spent months working on the house and garden and we both wanted a break to recharge our batteries. So we planned a weekend in Santorini to celebrate our wedding anniversary in September as it was just a short ferry trip from Crete. Whatever remains of the island has incredible mystical legends surrounding it, we both wanted to go there because of its possible links to the fabled land of Atlantis.

We had to be up very early on the 30th to catch the coach to Heraklion, so we could be there before the ferry's departure and the start of our three-day holiday. It had been booked through a travel agent in Georgioupolis who we had got to know quite well. We had also booked a small hotel in the capital and transfers from the harbour.

Luckily, it was a calm day so the crossing was good. As we stood on the small dock in the harbour, the view of the towering cliffs with houses clinging to them like limpets took our breath away. The taxi ride up the side of the cliff was amazing and when we reached the town at the top, it was heaving with traffic and people.

I think we expected what was left of the island to be sparsely populated with small villages here and there but this was a lively bustling place. When we had changed into more comfortable clothes, we went to explore the town, and eventually found our way to the cafés at the top of the cliffs, and we will never forget the view that greeted us.

We found somewhere to have coffee and were transfixed by the sight of donkeys making their way up the long winding path, and huge cruise liners in the bay that looked like toy boats. We went back to the same area that evening and over dinner and wine watched the legendary sunset over the Mediterranean Sea.

The following day we had arranged a coach trip that took us all over the island and were amazed at how big it was and how much there was to see. The most spectacular part for us was going to the monastery at the highest point, where you could see the entire island stretched out beneath you, but the biggest disappointment for me was the archaeological site that was closed due to an accident sometime before when a protecting roof had collapsed.

We spent three wonderful days there taking in as much of the sites as we could and were sorry to leave as it definitely had a special feel to it. We both said on the way home that we would like to go back someday and spend a week exploring the rest of the island and its treasures.

I think what fires people's imagination including ours, is that it could be the fabled land of Atlantis although no one has found any proof yet. Whatever was there before the eruption of its volcano is lost to history, but what has been left leaves tantalising glimpses that something remarkable existed there.

The 20th of October saw the start of a series of treatments for a Miss D to help with issues that she had been dealing with for a long time and had worn her down emotionally. Her rebirth included removing an accumulation of negative energy built up over many years and replacing it with positive energy.

It's remarkable how a build-up of this type of emotional baggage can manifest itself in a variety of ailments, that once removed tend to disappear of their own accord, as it was with Miss D. When the healing session was finished, she looked much brighter and reported feeling calmer and in control of her life and future. And while discussing the session afterwards, she requested a further treatment the following week to continue what we had started, as she didn't want to lose her new positive outlook.

As is usual with a second session, Miss D went quickly into a very deep meditative state as she now had confidence in me and the treatment, and said she had a much more expansive experience the second time, and felt as if she had left her body for a short while which she had done many years before.

Although she felt much better on this second week, Miss D sensed that there were still some blockages in her head and thymus areas. So this second week's session, as well as a different form of rebirth, was also to address these issues and specifically clear these areas. Talking to Miss D after the session revealed that she felt very light and positive, and requested a further treatment the following week to continue improving her outlook for the future.

The third treatment had a crystal layout for new beginnings as Miss D now felt confident in moving forward with her life and making positive changes. Healing was also directed into the bronchial tract as she reported some congestion there, and targeted healing into both hands as she had been suffering from arthritis that was causing some pain.

Towards the end of this session, I asked the angels to take Miss D to the angelic realms for special healing, and she reported seeing lots of green light throughout that part of the treatment. When she left, Miss D said she felt very much in control of her own life now and I wished her well for whatever life brought her way.

I received a phone call from Miss D requesting one last treatment on the 15th of November as she said she just wanted a booster session for grounding. I gave her a rebirth but it was designed more as a blessing than a conventional healing. When I energised the crystal layout I had given her, my guides told me to check her chakras.

When I doused them with a quartz pendulum, I found her lower three to be weak, so I changed the crystals on these chakras and energised them. When re-dousing Miss D, all her chakras made the pendulum spin robustly clockwise, so I placed my hands around her head for a final time, thanked all our spirit friends for their help and closed down the session.

Talking to Miss D after the treatment revealed that she had seen so many colours when I was working on her chakras she couldn't remember them all. When Miss D left us that final time, she said she felt very good indeed, and it was lovely to be boosted with some Attwood energy, comments like these make all the effort we put into our work worthwhile.

Miss T's final exam to qualify as a healer was on the 19th of November, and I had to laugh because she said, "He's already started writing and I haven't done anything yet!" But I was assessing her approach to her client that would set the tone for the healing session.

I was impressed with Miss T's consultation with her client as it was thorough, which gained a good perspective of what was required for the healing session. She also explained what spiritual healing was and how it worked to put her client at ease. She then lit some incense and put on gentle music to create a relaxed atmosphere, then made her client comfortable on the couch before starting.

I cannot go into detail about the session itself because it is from Miss T's private record notes and also because of client confidentiality. But I was very impressed by her technique and calm in-depth approach that made sure nothing was left out or forgotten throughout the treatment.

I always encourage trainees to not just go by the manuals and to develop their own spiritual gifts, so I was pleased to note a creative theme to Miss T's healing that showed she was listening to her guides, so discovering and covering things that might not have been apparent in the consultation.

Although Miss T's client started the session as a sceptic, she was impressed with the healing and saw blue energy throughout the treatment so would think differently from then on. To boost Miss T's confidence, I had done the same to her as Sandra had done to me. After a few weeks of training, I jumped on her couch and said, "OK, you can heal me now," and watched as the colour drained out of her and panic spread across her face.

Needless to say, I passed Miss T with flying colours and I'm confident she will develop into a great healer as her knowledge and experience grow.

Miss V had her final exam to qualify as a healer on the 24th of November and already being a qualified masseur for quite a long time her approach was very professional. Her consultation was very thorough and in-depth as she gently gained a perspective on the root causes of the problems the client was experiencing. She spent quite a while putting her client at ease by explaining what spiritual healing was and how it works before making her client comfortable on the couch.

A modesty cover was placed over the client for comfort and the music was changed to something soothing to set the tone for the session. Again I cannot go into detail about the session because of client confidentiality, but it was conducted with total professionalism and her client quickly relaxed to enjoy and benefit from the healing.

I was pleased to see Miss V spend as much time sensing and scanning her client for possible problems as well as treating those things that had been mentioned in the consultation. And although her client had experienced healing before she reported feeling hot, and her third eye became very active as the energy flowed into her body throughout the healing session.

I was also impressed with how the entire session was conducted and passed Miss V with flying colours, and I'm confident that she will develop into a very powerful healer and that her massage clients will feel the additional benefit of the incorporated healing.

A Mr K came to see me on the 30th of November and said he was feeling restless in himself and not knowing what to do with his future to overcome this. After a lengthy consultation to get him to verbalise what had led to him feeling this way, I was able to prepare him for healing as talking to a sympathetic ear is also healing in itself.

I went into quite a lot of detail about what I do and how it works during the consultation and although this helped him explain his feelings, it led to his curiosity stopping him relaxing into the guided meditation for a while. But I didn't mind as I wasn't concerned about how long it took, so long as he received what he needed from the healing session.

I could sense my spirit friends gently soothing him and he finally relaxed into the meditation, and when the angels laid their hands on him, he drifted peacefully into the experience.

I started with extensive healing on his lungs as he was smoking more than was good for him. Unfortunately, he had tried and failed to give up many times but I am happy to report that Mr K did succeed in giving up smoking a while later that improved his health as well as his mental outlook immensely.

Mr K felt pressure as I worked on his tummy area to remove a build-up of negative energies that had accumulated over the years leading to his sense of restlessness. We are all God's children and if I think someone needs it I will ask our Heavenly Father to give them his special healing, which I'm sure he did due to the amount of emotion I felt a few moments after asking for his help. Mr K said he had experienced healing before but nothing like the rebirth which I explained my guides and the angels had spent three years teaching me.

Mr K felt very light headed and spaced out when he left us so I said I would talk to him later, and warned him he might feel like this for a few days as he might be detoxing. When we went to see him a few days later, he said the effects had lasted for a couple of days, but once those effects wore off, he had lots of energy for days after the treatment, and was now forming a new perspective for what he wanted to do with the rest of his life.

We had been very busy this year with psychic development circles and the last meeting of the year was held on the 15th of December. As I said before Jan and I had been told before we came to Crete that we would be very busy with our spiritual work, but the amount of circle meetings we had fitted in amazed us when we looked back over the year.

With all we had achieved this year, we decided to have a quiet Christmas at home by ourselves to chill and watch Christmas movies. A lot of our friends were doing the same so we all agreed to save ourselves for the New Year's Eve party that had been planned.

The New Year's Eve party had been organised by our friends who ran Sinatra's Bar in Georgioupolis and whenever they organised something it was always a good night. This party was no exception with food laid out for all the guests, with beer and wine flowing freely and with appropriate music. Everyone had a good time seeing in the new year.

We all made our way home in the early hours of the morning and for Jan and me it was a lovely end to a spectacular year for us. Those of us who were free were meeting back in Sinatra's around lunchtime, as we all needed a lie in, so after a small breakfast and a large coffee, we made our way back to George as we affectionately called the village.

A few of our spiritual friends were able to make it to Sinatra's as well. So in the middle of the conversation, we wondered what the New Year would bring for us all, but in our wildest dreams, I don't think Jan or I could have conjured up a scenario that would start off a process that would alter the course of our lives yet again.

Chapter 20
2011
Something Is Changing

This was going to be a strange year for us, especially after being so busy in 2010. We were getting mixed messages from our spirit guides which didn't help. Jan and I both felt the energies change within a week or two of each other, but neither of us had any idea what was happening or what the changes meant for us or our retreat. The new year started off the way the old one had ended but it wasn't to last long, and with no obvious clues to guide us, we were drifting as if in a sailing yacht that had been becalmed.

What would make it worse two of the couples we had become good friends with were moving permanently back to the UK, and none of our family was coming out to stay with us this year as the economic downturn was pinching everyone's pockets. This combined with the change in energies that were making us feel very confused, as everything that happened to us so far had almost seemed preordained, it left us wondering just what would be in store for us as the year unfolded.

Our first circle meeting opened on the 12th of January and it was good to start generating good energies in our sanctuary again after the festivities, as at this stage nothing had changed for us and everything appeared to carry on as normal. I don't think you ever rate your own work as highly as anyone else does, and it still surprised me that people were totally absorbed in my psychic development programme.

By this time, I had them doing advanced meditations where they were clearing the clutter from their minds and were regularly astral travelling to other planets and beyond. I would watch them week by week close their eyes and blissfully drift off to other world or realms, and then come back to tell us all of the incredible experiences they'd had. It was as exciting for me as it was for them guiding them on these incredible journeys, and at the time it didn't occur to me that it could ever come to an end.

On the 18th of February, a Miss C came to see me for healing who had more than a passing interest in spiritual matters, that would eventually see her working with her own spirit guides. In her rebirth, I removed a build-up of negative energy that had accumulated since childhood, and with issues from her teens compounding this had made it more difficult for her to break this cycle.

I worked a lot on her feet to try and resolve a problem she was experiencing, and during this treatment, Miss C said her grandfather came to her along with two other people she couldn't see clearly. I had the feeling they would be guiding her onto her spiritual path that would see her developing gifts that had been waiting to be discovered.

Miss C said the Boji stones felt like heavy lumps of concrete in her hands and said she felt very sleepy after the treatment as if she could sleep for twenty-four hours. I wished her well for the future and asked her to let me know when she discovers how her spirit guides wanted her to work.

The 9th of March was the only day it snowed in our village for the whole time we lived in our little stone house in Crete. It always snowed on the mountains without fail and when it arrived, usually in October, we knew that the colder weather was on its way.

But this morning when I pulled back the curtains the garden and surrounding countryside was all white with grey leaden skies that promised more of the same. We were so surprised that we put our boots on and went outside to play in the snow, as we knew at these lower levels it wouldn't last very long as it was quite mild.

If we'd have known what was coming next we would probably have seen it as a sign that things were about to change and set our minds wondering what we could possibly do next to help our group achieve what they had originally joined us for.

On Wednesday the 23rd of March, the circle members arrived looking rather pensive and I immediately thought there had been an accident or something worse. Everyone sat in their normal places but there was none of the usual banter and laughter that always accompanied their arrival.

As I opened the meeting, I knew I had to find out and deal with whatever was worrying them before we could do anything spiritual. We had all known each other for a few years by this time and trusted each other implicitly, so we knew we could talk about anything in total confidence.

But luckily it turned out to be nothing like I had feared. Jan and I were the only members of the group to be old enough to have the luxury of a pension, so with the hardships that the 2008 economic meltdown had caused, none of them could now spare the time or the money to continue attending the circle meetings.

And some were even thinking of going back to the UK to get jobs as the money they had in savings wouldn't be enough anymore. The result of this meant today would be the last circle meeting we would ever have in Crete, which was sad because this group was only halfway through my programme and were enjoying every minute of their time with us.

This was the most sombre circle we had ever hosted and apart from the meditation which I made an extra long one I don't think their hearts were in it. We had a long chat with everyone over a cup of tea afterwards about what we would all do, and then it was a very doleful group who left us that day with endless hugs and teary eyes.

It was definitely a sad day for Jan and me as the circle meetings had become something we looked forward to each week for the joy it gave everyone, as well as a chance to spend time with the friends we had made since arriving here.

We spent the rest of the day in deep thoughts wondering where we would go from here as it had come as a complete surprise to us, and I personally wondered if this was when the prediction I was given on the beach would come true about us eventually returning to the UK to continue our work there.

An upcoming 50th birthday party with a good friend at a hotel in Georgioupolis would give us something to look forward to in the wake of our sad news. It promised to be a very good evening that would purportedly be drifting into the wee small hours, as people had come from far and wide to celebrate this special occasion.

It turned out that some of the friends and relatives were even coming from other countries, and as the host was very spiritual, as were some of the guests we would be among like-minded people. The party did not disappoint and as the hours drifted by Jan and I found ourselves answering lots of questions about what we did. It was just the tonic we needed, and having talked to so many people about what was happening in our lives we gained a perspective of what might lay in our future.

When the circle meetings closed, we planned a trip back to the UK, so we could talk to our teachers and mediums friends that had been instrumental through their insight regarding us going to Crete. So on the 10th of May, we flew to Gatwick and having already contacted these people we were now eager to pick their brains for guidance.

Sunday the 15th of May saw us going to the spiritual centre where I had my training under the watchful eye of Sandra. Although Sandra had now retired, Heather was still there who had so accurately told us that we would find an old stone arch and never look back. She did indeed have some insights for us but said nothing would happen until next year although she was not able to give us a date.

We had been away from the UK for nearly four years so had planned a six-week stay so we could see as many people as possible, so it turned into more of a fact-finding exercise than a holiday for us. We both felt a little strange walking down streets that had once been so familiar to us, and now looked and sounded slightly strange compared to what we had now come to regard as normal in our quiet Cretan village.

After talking to Heather, we hired a car and went to Hastings for the day, but not for any specific purpose as I think we were just looking for inspiration in familiar places. Although we didn't find any answers on our day out, we both felt our spirit friends were close by, which meant we would know when the time was right. We both felt that familiar presence we had when we were getting all the messages prior to moving to Crete, so we knew we would be guided in the right direction for what would be best for us.

In the following weeks, we met up with an old friend who was also a gifted medium who had so accurately relayed messages from Jan's mum. He was able to give us quite a clear indication that as we had developed significantly through our work in Crete there could be a future for us here in the UK.

We also met with my life teacher who worked in the shop where I was presented with *'A Course In Miracles',* an environment which always sent me into a blissful dream world as I walked through its doors. I was to discover later that it wasn't the shop or its contents that evoked those energies in me, but Gursel with her powerful connection with the spiritual realms. She was able to read me like a book despite me thinking that I had surrounded myself with impenetrable protection which resembled a suit of armour.

It was evident from the first time I spoke to her that she was a wise old soul who had returned to the earth plane to guide and teach people who were seeking direction. Whenever we went into the shop after that first meeting, there were always people waiting to talk with her, and it was clear that it wasn't the shop's contents that had brought them in but her loving insightful energy.

Over a cup of coffee, Gursel told us she could see us back in the UK doing our spiritual work, but not for a while as the time wasn't right. She said that we were to look for signs that would guide us and we had certainly had some practice with that, which set us all laughing as she had watched our journey unfold from the very beginning.

So we would return to Crete to continue with the work we had been sent there to do until our spirit friends gave us signs that would guide us to the next part of our exciting and very fulfilling journey. We had come back to the UK wondering what was going on and which direction we would be headed, and we were slowly building up a picture of our future through our gifted friends that was getting less and less scary.

The 3rd of July saw us at a massive car boot sale in Georgioupolis with all our friends, as we had decided to get rid of all the stuff we didn't want to take back to the UK. We had told those of our spiritual group about our possible return to the UK who we knew would keep our confidence until we knew for certain.

We were out in the open in a car park in the harbour and it was one of the hottest days we had ever experienced since moving to Crete, nearly forty degrees and there wasn't any shade apart from little beach umbrellas most of us had rigged up as best we could. It was too hot to wear anything but the skimpiest clothes we could find. There was a lot of bare flesh to try and protect, and consequently, we all got various degrees of sunburn.

Despite this, there was lots of banter and good fun and we managed to get rid of a lot of stuff we had bought over, which was mostly down to me being sentimental or what I thought would come in handy. The trouble was a lot of the things that I bought over were totally inappropriate for the lifestyle we were now living or things I had used when I was working.

But we humans are a sentimental bunch, and I had paid good money for some of the things I was now virtually giving away. But we told ourselves it was going to be another new start when we got back, and it would cost more to get most of the stuff back than it was worth, so if we wouldn't need it, it was going to have to go.

Jan and I went to one of our favourite hotels to have a drink with its owner who had become one of our like-minded spiritual friends. Among the people also having a drink, there was a lady called Clare who, it soon became clear, was also very spiritual minded, so we spent half the night talking to her about the things that interested us.

Through our conversations, we discovered that Clare had been an accomplished medium in the UK prior to moving to Crete, where she had come on a sabbatical to write a book. In fact, it is no exaggeration to say my book would never have been written without the help and encouragement of this gifted and selfless lady.

Without knowing too much about us on that first meeting, Clare gave us an impromptu reading and brought through members of our families from the spirit world. And during this reading told us that we would be moving back to the UK in about twelve months to set up a healing retreat there. She also told me I would write a book about my spiritual journey as people needed to hear my story, to be inspired as I had been inspired by earlier writers.

This last bit I found a little spooky as I've always fancied writing a book, but not one about myself that would lay my soul bare as I've always been quite a private person. But Clare explained calmly and with surprising authority, that my book would be read by those who needed the information it contained that would benefit them. And I suppose like all aspiring writers my first thought was who is going to want to know about me, as I put very little value on my own personal journey of enlightenment in terms of being of benefit to others.

But everything she said that day was so accurate that I had to take it on board although at that time I hadn't the foggiest idea how I could ever start, let alone write a whole book. So I would put it to the back of my mind for now, and like everything else wait for my spirit friends to guide and inspire me if this was truly to be a part of my future.

On the 9th of August, a Miss E came to see me for healing who was suffering from depression and needed to deal with certain issues before she could move on with her life. To achieve this, my guides advised an unusual crystal layout of double amethyst, jade, aquamarine and beryl that would generate the right energies to help her.

Through the rebirth, my guides were able to remove a build-up of negative energy that was making it difficult for Miss E to move forward in any meaningful way. I then sent healing deep into her abdomen to bring the sacral chakra back into positive motion, that should align her energies making it easier to bring about positive thoughts for the future.

Miss E was finding it difficult to commit to a relationship and was hoping the treatment would give her a clear perspective, allowing her to make a decision about the future. I think she still had other issues to deal with when she left us, but I hope she gained enough clarity through the session that would lead to a positive outcome in the future.

I am not going to give an initial to the next lady who came to see me on the 2nd of September who we met the previous evening. She was shaking from head to foot as a result of entrenched depression. The anxiety levels caused by her condition were extreme and it was difficult for her to concentrate on anything which made communication difficult.

She would not get on our couch without a thick modesty cover, and even once on the couch continued to shake uncontrollably, so I asked Archangel Michael to join us as I had a feeling I was going to need his help. It was very difficult to get her to relax enough to start the rebirth, and also due to her condition she didn't trust whatever I was about to do.

My guides instructed me to tell her to close her eyes and imagine she was surrounded by beautiful flowers, that had a wonderfully intoxicating perfume that she should breathe deep into her lungs. It was as if she could not fight this intoxicating perfume and slowly started to relax and drift off into the guided meditation I was relaying to her.

I was then able to guide her through a full rebirth and needed Archangel Michael's help to remove a lower energy attachment that was causing her to be affected in this way. Her mother had brought her along for treatment as she was not capable of driving herself, and noticed the change in her daughter as the session progressed. By the end of the treatment, the shaking had completely stopped, and the young lady was now lying peacefully on the couch absorbing all the energies around her.

Talking to the young lady afterwards, she said she felt very heavy and unable to move throughout the treatment and was now starting to return to her normal self. Her eyes were now bright and clear as they were dull and downcast when she arrived, and it was one of the most rewarding healing sessions I have ever done. She hardly spoke at all when she arrived but now was chatting as if we had been lifelong friends, and although she was going home in a few days, she promised to keep in touch to let us know how she was getting on.

A Miss D came to see me on the 29th of September for healing, and my initial feelings were that she had a large accumulation of negative energy based on her general demeanour. We had a long chat before I started any treatment as she had been interested in healing for as long as she could remember. Her father had been an accomplished healer and she had grown up accepting this sort of treatment as normal.

When I started the rebirth, I had to ask her to quiet her mind as she was tracking everything I was doing, and her inquisitiveness was stopping her slipping into the guided meditation. Once she suppressed her curiosity, however, she quickly fell into a deep and peaceful meditative state that she reported after as being the most relaxed she had been for years. The intense workload Miss D had been coping with for a few years meant she was constantly tense and suffered from aching muscles and insomnia.

I spent most of the session working on her physical as well as her emotional wellbeing, and it was good to see her finally relax and the lines of tension disappear from her face. I had the feeling Miss D's dad was with us throughout the healing session, and she confirmed afterwards she had felt his presence very strongly during the treatment.

Although Miss D had experienced healing before, she said she had never gone that deep before, and at the end felt like her body was made of lead and unable to move. She also said that her legs felt numb and I wondered if they would work when she got off the couch. So to be on the safe side, I very slowly and carefully helped her until she was standing on the floor.

After a cup of coffee and another long chat, Miss D left us to go home and said she felt very light and full of energy. That session was the start of a long friendship which I am happy to report is ongoing to this day.

The 7th of October saw a Miss I come to see me for healing with neck and shoulder pains, and a lot of tension in the muscles of her upper body. That tension stopped her from relaxing into the rebirth for quite a while, and as a mother, she worried about being able to care for her children. Once she finally relaxed into the guided meditation, I sent healing deep into the tissues of her neck and shoulders, to release the build-up of tension that could be causing the problem.

The angels did a lot of work throughout the session to bring her mind into a better place where she could cope, and I told her afterwards to ask the angels for help when she most needed it. Towards the end of the session, I asked our Heavenly Father for a miracle for Miss I, and I'm sure a blessing was given as I became extremely emotional and Miss I reported seeing a very bright light at this stage of the treatment.

Miss I said that through the treatment it felt as if she had been transported to another realm of existence that left her feeling calm, and said she would keep in touch if she had any questions about the treatment or spiritual matters.

The 18th of October to the 1st of November saw us return to the UK for a pre-Christmas visit, and to see if our spiritual friends could give us any more answers as to what the future held for us. We didn't say anything to our family at this stage because we originally thought we would be staying in Crete for a lot longer than this.

Those two weeks were very busy as we saw different people every day and spent a lot of time with family, but made sure we met up with our spiritual friends who did confirm things were going to change for us. *Here we go again*, we thought as they said that it would happen quicker than we expected, although none of them could be specific about dates.

When we returned to Crete, it almost felt like we were in limbo with no clear direction, and not knowing whether to plough our energies into staying in Crete, or possibly in returning to the UK. In the end, as usual, Jan and I handed the whole thing over to our friends in the spirit world and just got on with enjoying wherever in the world we happened to be.

As if to confuse the matter further, my development circle meetings started up again on the 9th of November, which gave the appearance of returning normality. As there hadn't been any meetings throughout the summer, it was like a joyous reunion of old friends, that certainly gave Jan and me a boost of positivity. And when the circles finished for the year on the 14th of December, it felt like all the predictions we were given about returning to the UK had started to fade.

As you can imagine, Christmas was a little subdued for us, because we felt unsettled with all the seemingly different messages we had received because no one could give us a definitive answer, but we did make up for it with the normal New Year's Eve party. That meant for a few hours at least we forgot about the future and had a brilliant time with our friends. We would face whatever came our way in the certain knowledge that whatever our spirit friends had in mind for us. It would probably be as exciting and interesting as our move to our little stone house had been, so there would be no chance of us being disappointed.

Chapter 21
2012
Vision in a Painting

Although we thought our circle meetings had finished, we heard from three women who wanted to join us if we considered starting up a new group. Of course, we were delighted to hear this as the meetings had become one of the most enjoyable aspects of our work and had always proved to be wonderfully uplifting.

So it looked like full steam ahead for now as it appeared we were going to be as busy as we had been in previous years. Having said that, we bore in mind and understood the messages we had been given from spirit, so we would make every moment count in our spiritual work if this was to be our last year running our spiritual retreat.

Our new circle meetings started on the 11th of January with four ladies, and once again our little stone house was filled with the good-natured banter that preceded every meeting. I sat in my usual place watching them excitedly chatting as they sat in what would become their regular places, and I beamed as I acknowledged they were just as happy to be there as we were to see them.

Three of these ladies were quite advanced spiritually so I was immediately able to take them on long complex journeys through meditations, and they could all see auras and interpret oracle cards. It was amazing to hear their experiences when I sent them off in meditation to the Temple of Light or to meet the guardians who looked after the Akashic Records and the Halls of Knowledge.

It was good for Jan and myself to once again be doing the work our guides had sent us there to do, and if this was to be our last year then we would go out on a high. We had no idea at that time just what a high it would turn out to be, with a vision experienced through my rebirth healing treatment that became immortalised in a painting.

On the 23rd of January, a Miss J came to see me who had constant headaches as she was spiritually sensitive and needed to regularly cut unwanted etheric ties. It took a long time for Miss J to relax into the rebirth and follow my guided meditation, but eventually, she settled down and the angels were able to start the healing process.

Just after I started relaying a new healing energy to Miss J, my guides told me to remove my left hand from her tummy, and as I did so a powerful entity stepped forward and placed a hand where mine had been. It was as if an electric shock had been delivered and Miss J physically jerked and then remained trembling for the rest of the treatment.

Talking to Miss J afterwards, she said it was as if pulses of energy entered her feet and travelled up through her entire body. She had lost a daughter to cancer some years before and said she could feel her daughter close by towards the end of the session. Miss J said the whole experience was incredibly powerful and the headaches had now gone and she felt quite calm. I explained to Miss J how to cut her ties at the end of each day to avoid another build-up that should alleviate the headaches.

On the 14th of February, a Miss A came to see me who had no physical problems, but although she had experience of working spiritually herself had never felt fully connected with her guides. As soon as I started the rebirth, Miss A was very vocal saying how beautiful it looked where I had taken her in the guided meditation.

It soon became clear to me Miss A was a very advanced soul and sobbed uncontrollably as the angels took away her accumulation of negative energy and bad memories attached to them. Miss A gasped as the last of the negative energy was taken away and alternated between laughter and tears with the relief of losing this baggage she had been carrying around for so many years.

Miss A was incredibly animated as I called in an archangel to give her a new and powerful healing energy to work with. I had to mollify her twice as it looked as if this new energy might overpower her. However, Miss A was very calm after the treatment and said it felt as if she was getting her life back on track, and promised to let me know how she felt in a few days when she had assimilated the new energy.

I told Miss A later that when the archangel was giving her the new energy I became aware that she was lying on folded wings so wondered if she was an earth angel because some gifted people have also said the same about Jan. So it was no surprise to me that an incredibly strong bond developed between Jan and Miss A after the healing session.

A Mr G came to see me on the 13th of March who I felt had never come to terms with losing his daughter and looked as if he carried the world on his shoulders. Subsequently, it took him a long time to relax, and only acquiesced when I took him into a warm cosy grotto through a guided meditation.

At this point, even a niggly cough stopped that he worried would prevent him from fully experiencing the healing and gaining any benefit from it. Mr G had an accumulation of negative energy associated with losing his daughter that was replaced with white light after its removal. This brought a new calmness to him that made the rest of the session easier and opened him up to the energies from the spirit world.

An incredible thing happened towards the end of the treatment as I became aware that his daughter was standing by his right shoulder and was asking to be connected with her father. So I placed my right hand over Mr G's heart and told his daughter to make the connection with him through me, and I would try to maintain the link for her as long as I was able.

As her loving energy flowed through me, Mr G drew in a long slow breath that made it evident he felt the connection as his daughter made the link with him. It was very moving to witness this heartwarming interaction as a daughter reached out from the spirit world to comfort her grieving father, and as she gently healed his broken heart, I could not stop tears streaming down my cheeks at being so privileged to witness this wonderful event and the peace it bestowed upon him.

The 28th of March was to be our last ever circle meeting in our healing retreat in the quiet little village on the beautiful island of Crete. If I were to be given a choice of where to establish a healing retreat I don't think I could have chosen a nicer spot with its sweeping valley of conifers and the majestic White Mountains dominating the view. And I filled this last morning with as much content as possible so it would be a lasting memory for the five of us who shared it.

I started with an exercise detailing and discussing the gifts that were bestowed on us by various ascended masters who freely shared their knowledge and wisdom with us. I then took them through a practical exercise where they drew coloured pictures by allowing their imaginations to run free and uninhibited through vivid expression.

The results can be extraordinary and I still marvel at some of the pictures I drew in these periods of mental abandonment where something inside takes over to produce hitherto untapped feelings. When we were finished, we passed the pictures around the group and each member interpreted the one they were given. Some of these readings can be very in-depth and accurate to leave you wondering how so much can be derived from quite often simple child-like drawings.

After a short break, I took them on a guided meditation that moved their consciousness into the fourth dimension to elevate their thinking and start them on a journey they could continue without me. Finally, I asked them to pick a card from our Crystal Skull oracle pack and when reseated, we did readings for each other to see what our futures held. Again it is fascinating how much detail can be derived from a, sometimes, quite simple picture that at first glance could tell you very little.

Rather than being sombre and doleful, this last meeting was surprisingly upbeat and cheerful with everyone saying how much they enjoyed it, and all saying it would inspire them to explore their own spiritual journeys and possibly one day run their own circle meetings. It was particularly rewarding for Jan and myself to know we made a difference in the short time we had spent in Crete, and that we might leave a positive legacy behind that would continue to grow when we return to the UK.

On the 21st of April, a Mr W came to see me who was very stressed through his work, which was also causing him to be depressed and worried about his future. As Mr W spoke very little English, his good friend translated for me so consequently the majority of the session was conducted without words.

Once his friend had relayed where I wanted Mr W to visualise himself for the meditation, I conducted the rest of the session between our spiritual guides. He had a very large build-up of negative energy that once removed allowed him to relax fully into the meditation.

As an archangel gave him a new healing energy, I sensed his grandmother standing beside the couch watching her grandson being healed. When I relayed this to Mr W after the treatment, he started to sob as he had been very close to her while he was growing up.

Before they left, Mr W shared with us through his friend that he very much enjoyed the experience and felt so much better, and now wanted his wife to also come for treatment and have the same experience as soon as possible.

On the 3rd of June, a very good friend of ours who lived just outside our village held a street party in honour of the Queen's diamond jubilee and kindly invited us. Around six tables were placed end to end, draped with white paper tablecloths and decorated with all sorts of things that she had brought from England for the occasion. There were bench seats and every manner of chairs from the patio to dining to deck chairs which just added to the sense of fun and organised chaos.

Jan had baked cakes for our contribution and as we could walk home we took copious amounts of local village wine, as did so many others. The party was hilarious as we all got a little squiffy with the sense of occasion, and went on all afternoon with all sorts of antics most of which luckily I can't remember. We didn't know at the time we would be returning to the UK a few months after this party, so it turned out that it would become one of the highlights for us, and a wonderful memory to come home within a year that gave us so many highs and lows.

On the 8th of June, a Miss A came to see me and although she didn't reveal any illness or condition to me. You would not have to be psychic to see something was wrong. She had lost her son in a tragic accident a few years before and had never been able to accept or come to terms with the loss. I had known the son briefly before the accident and he was not only larger than life, but one of the nicest souls I had ever met and the world is definitely a poorer place without him.

As a consequence of her sad loss, Miss I had the largest accumulation of negative energy I had ever seen, that was also hiding a more ominous problem. I had already asked Archangel Michael to join us as when I was cleaning the negative energy I became aware of an attachment, and Michael's hands were over it before I'd had a chance to ask for his help.

As the removal was taking place, I sensed a double presence had joined us, one was the son who had come to help his mum, the other presence was almost overwhelming in the most benevolent way possible. So I think a very powerful entity had come to help a soul that had lost its way and regain the serenity the treatment would give her.

Talking to Miss A after the treatment, the first thing she saw in the guided meditation was her son standing on the other side of the couch from me with his arms crossed making sure I did everything right. The second presence she saw was Jesus which explains the overwhelming benevolent energy I felt which is just as powerful as His Father's.

As Miss A slowly came out of a very deep meditative state, she felt disorientated and found it difficult to focus on anything meaningful. When I explained what happened in the treatment and what we found, she understood and relaxed on the sofa with a cup of tea to let her system return to normal in its own time.

Heather had come out to stay with us for a short while as she loved the sun, and within the quiet solitude of our healing retreat, she sensed clearly our return to the UK was imminent. So on the 20th of June with a mixture of excitement and a little regret, we flew back to the UK with Heather to start making plans for our return.

We saw as many people as we could, not only our spiritual friends but all the friends we had made over the years and garnered as much information as possible from as many sources as possible to give us positive lines of inquiry. But that couldn't have prepared us for what happened a week after we returned to Crete, that would let us know that as usual, our spirit friends were busy arranging our return for us.

The 30th of July started the way most of our days had with a mixture of work on the garden and half-heartedly sorting through what we did and didn't want to take back. But an email from a friend in the UK around eleven in the morning threw all of this out of the window and would instigate twenty-four hours of soul-searching for both of us, and in my case, a sense of apprehension that would lead to Jan making the decision for both of us.

The email was from someone we had known for quite a long while who dealt in property and told us he had found a location we hadn't considered before. But we had to make our minds up in twenty-four hours because he couldn't hold it any longer. I am not one to make instant decisions especially about something of this magnitude, but if we were going to benefit from what he had found that's exactly what we would have to do.

To say I walked around for the rest of the day in dejected confusion would be putting it mildly because I knew I was going to have to make a decision without the benefit of research and scrutiny. As a trained angel therapist and teacher, Jan had already calmly gathered the information she required from her oracle cards, while I hadn't thought of doing anything that constructive and was still struggling to commit one way or the other.

In the end, I retreated to the warm evening sunshine on our flat roof, that afforded me peace and tranquillity as the lowering sun started to turn my beautiful vista a stunning shade of orange. I had always found it easy from this unique vantage point to listen to my guides and helpers, and it was as if the answer I had been searching for came to me through the rays of the setting sun.

So in the morning we emailed our friend and asked for details of where to send the deposit to secure what would become our new home and ultimately, our new retreat. That was the start of our return journey back to our native homeland, and the slow rundown of our little stone house that had witnessed some amazing and sometimes miraculous healing that I was privileged to be involved in.

On the 26th of July, a Miss B came to see me who had been badly hurt from a negative and destructive relationship and was hoping to feel free after the treatment. As soon as I touched her head to start removing the negative energy, Miss B started to wail uncontrollably so great was the release of all the pent-up sorrow she had been carrying around as baggage.

When the removal was complete, her body became flaccid as she relaxed into a very deep meditative state. It was at this stage I became aware of a family member from the spirit world assisting me with the healing process, who had been concerned about Miss B's health and wellbeing for quite some time.

Miss B felt very light and alert once she had recovered from the deep meditation and said she knew she was meant to come and see me that day. She also said she would like to come and see us when we were settled back in the UK, and it would be lovely to catch up and see how life was treating her as we don't always get feedback once we've seen people.

The 9th of September saw us at a brilliant charity concert at the Embrosneros Amphitheatre which was one of the most eagerly anticipated of the year. It had always been well attended in previous years and this year was no exception with hot food to keep the evening chills away at the interval.

Charity events have always been well supported in Crete and this one for the Red Cross seemed even more special as we sat under the stars while listening to a variety of music. It would be events like this that we would miss the most when we were back in

England, so sitting high up in the hills with ribbons of lights twinkling below in the valleys, and the dark Mediterranean Sea with the odd boat light in the distance was a lovely memory to take back with us.

On the 19th of September, a Miss J came to see me who had been involved in a bad road accident when she was younger. This had resulted in trouble with her back and legs, especially the left knee, so after removing any negative energy associated with the accident I concentrated healing to those areas.

I was aware of a very smart-looking gentleman in old-fashioned clothes watching everything I was doing, and by my description, Miss J said it sounded like her grandfather's brother. She felt light headed and disorientated after the session and although her eyes were very moist, she hadn't cried. It's always rewarding to try and help people who have had these types of incidents impact on their lives, as it can help to resolve any residue emotions attached to them and help to pursue a more contented future.

As we had now booked our flights for our return to the UK, early October saw us take the first of our belongings to the local Nomad office in Vamos. Up until then, we had only talked about going back, but now that we had packed the first of our belongings it was starting to become real, and for the second time in five years, we were shipping our home to another country. I must admit at the age of sixty-five I didn't want to move countries ever again because it's very stressful, so I knew whatever came next this would be the end of our foreign adventures.

I had started to have ideas about this book before we left our Greek island home, but I didn't think anyone would be interested in our little adventure. And besides I couldn't apply any concentration to it with all that was going on, so I consigned it to the bin, thinking at the time it was the best place for it.

A few days later when I was resting in my usual spot, I received an unexpected message. When I asked my guides for help with whatever work I was to do when back in the UK, they said I would only be able to complete this writing project when we had moved permanently back to England.

That is why I felt it wouldn't work because we were too close to our healing retreat in Kalamitsi to look at it subjectively, and furthermore our spirit friends would reduce the amount of healing and teaching I would do for a period of time so I could concentrate on finishing the project, that's what I call forward planning. If I ever doubted my guides they were proving their existence as everything was once again slotting perfectly into place.

My last client before we left our healing retreat in Crete was a Miss K, who came to see me on the 16th of October with various muscular and joint problems. My guides suggested an unusual crystal layout to include malachite, aquamarine, jade and prehnite, and for the first time, the Boji stones were not included.

This created a very special energy they wanted me to work with, and I have learnt over the years to trust my guides implicitly. Miss K was an accomplished artist and her acceptance and understanding of the ethereal meant she readily accepted the healing and quickly relaxed into a deep restful meditation.

Miss K had a build-up of negative energy which I removed in the early stages of the rebirth before concentrating on the problems she spoke of in the consultation. I then sent healing deep into the joints and muscles that she had indicated were giving her trouble and affecting a normal range of movements. As my guides had asked for such an unusual crystal layout they knew what Miss K needed, so I was quite happy to stand back and let them control the healing process.

Miss K was going back to the UK in a few days and as her daughter lived near us in Crete, we would get updates from her if there were any improvements. As we were relocating back to the UK in six days, it was a little sad that Miss K was to be our last ever client in our little stone house that had made our dreams come true.

After the session, Miss K said she had seen angels around her during the treatment fluttering their wings, and I was to get a surprise a few days later. When we met her daughter in the village, she presented me with a beautiful painting her mother had done for me depicting a vision she had during her treatment.

The painting includes great detail of the rebirth I do, and it's difficult to express how humbling as well as gratifying it is to see your work so accurately immortalised in a painting. Across the painting Miss K had written, 'May your guardian angel protect you as you journey through life and wings enfold you to keep you safe.'

It's not often I'm stuck for words, but as I stood there looking at the painting I was choked and speechless, and as I look at it again now, it is wonderful to see the essence of my work captured so vividly. It is almost impossible for people who work in the spiritual fields to prove what they do in any meaningful way, so this painting is a precious legacy that symbolises what we, who work with our spiritual gifts, try to achieve.

Our spiritual groups, as well as our friends, had organised a leaving party for us in Sinatra's Bar on the 19th of October and a buffet had been provided by Kate. Needless to say, beer and wine flowed to the wee small hours, and after just five years in our Greek villa in Kalamitsi, it didn't seem possible we were going home in four days.

That four days flew by and on the afternoon of 23rd of October, we were on our way to Heraklion Airport filled with a mixture of excitement to be with our family again, and disappointment that our adventure was finally over. But how many people get the chance to fulfil a calling to help those in need, and to do it in a dream location like Crete just makes it all the more special.

Looking back on my journey, I think I was given a second chance to get it right. Up until then, my life had been filled with convention, by trying to do the right things within the parameters set by society. Today my life has no convention that society or religion would recognise, and if I have any parameters they are set by God's loving hand.

The most important lesson I have learnt through all this is to follow your intuition, that inner voice that nudges you in the right direction, and to make that choice even if that goes against everything you have ever been taught. And to say yes when you are being encouraged by convention to say no, to say no when you are being encouraged by convention to say yes, especially if every fibre in your being is telling you to do so.

Chapter 22
Hope

I want to end by talking about hope, because there was a time when I didn't have any, and more importantly I didn't think I deserved any. I thought good things only happened in fairytales or melancholy films.

If I had gone ahead with my plan that day I would have deprived myself of the most rewarding part of my life, that allowed me to give something back. My plan did not go ahead that day because of a mother's love, and her abiding faith that I still had a life to live even when I couldn't see it for myself.

So I want to say to anyone who might be reading this and who also thinks that they don't have a choice or future or anything to live for, having read my story, you know that I speak with some clarity and personal experience that one normally wants to give up when the prize is almost within reach. So if you are in the position I found myself in all those years ago, pour that bottle down the sink, throw those pills away, go outside and ask the angels to fill your soul with love and hope.

Start to take short walks in the morning when the air is fresh and clean, listen to the happy bird songs that lifted my soul and allowed me to see with renewed eyes, smile at people and say good morning, because ninety percent of people won't say it first but that same ninety percent will respond positively and return your greeting.

Look through your local papers, find a club or group with similar interests to yourself, make that phone call and make some new friends to socialise with. I can't guarantee you'll find an angel but I can guarantee you'll find people, male and female, who will spend time with you over coffee and lift your spirits. And from those first tentative steps, you will find a way to go forward and a reason to live and build a new rewarding life.

It's sad that all I hear nowadays is what a rotten world this has become and all you will ever find is hatred, anger and disappointment around every corner. It's a sad fact that only bad news sells, but wherever Jan and I go, we bump into nice helpful people who will pass the time of day with us, and none of these people know we are healers. They are not doing it to stand a better chance of getting into heaven. They are doing it because they are just nice people, so as the film says, 'If you look for it, love is actually all around.'

But when you are at that lowest point in your life, you start to withdraw from life itself and all it has ever meant to you. You see less of your friends and loved ones, and when asked if you're alright, use simple comments like, "Yeah, I'm fine. Just got a headache," because the last thing you want right then is to get drawn into a conversation where you have to admit that you are not fine at all, and talk about what you are really thinking about doing.

So we all have a responsibility to our friends and loved ones if we see behaviour that's out of character and should question it. We all have busy lives and it's easy to dismiss such out of character behaviour and accept he or she has just had a bad day. So if you have such suspicions about someone you know, check with other people who know them to see if they have noticed a change as well. You may just have the chance to turn someone's life around which is better than reading the obituary in the papers.

I always thought heaven was this distant place somewhere so far from us that its location was unfathomably inaccessible and out of reach to us mere mortals. But my father and my spirit helpers have proved it is just on the other side of a thin veil and our loved ones are almost close enough to touch. They have come on numerous occasions to help their loved ones during healing sessions I have conducted.

Therefore, there is no reason why they cannot be called upon to help a loved one in such despair that they are thinking of taking their own life, and you don't have to be a healer or a psychic to call for such help. But remember the law of free will means they can't intervene unless someone asks them to, and you could be just that someone. All you have to do is ask.

There is nothing special about me that gives me powers to communicate with the spirit world, in fact, the total opposite, and so much so as you have read, I'd say if I can do it anybody can do it. All I've done over the years is learn how to communicate with that next world we call heaven, and learn to trust that the people there only want the very best for us, and will help us in any way they can to fulfil our hopes and dreams.